Bunker Bean

Bunker Bean

Harry Leon Wilson

ÆGYPAN PRESS

1913

Bunker Bean
A publication of
ÆGYPAN PRESS

www.aegypan.com

To H.G. WELLS

I

*B*unker Bean was wishing he could be different. This discontent with himself was suffered in a moment of idleness as he sat at a desk on a high floor of a very high office-building in "downtown" New York. The first correction he would have made was that he should be "well over six feet" tall. He had observed that this was the accepted stature for a hero.

And the name, almost any name but "Bunker Bean!" Often he wrote good ones on casual slips of paper and fancied them his; names like Trevellyan or Montressor or Delancey, with musical prefixes; or a good, short, beautiful, but dignified name like "Gordon Dane." He liked that one. It suggested something. But Bean! And Bunker Bean, at that! True, it also suggested something, but this had never been anything desirable. Just now the people in the outside office were calling him "Boston."

"Gordon Dane," well over six feet, abundant dark hair, a bit inclined to "wave" and showing faint lines of grey "above the temples"; for Bean also wished to be thirty years old and to have learned about women; in short, to have suffered. Gordon Dane's was a face before which the eyes of women would fall in half-frightened, half-ecstatic subjection, and men would feel the inexplicable magnetism of his presence. He would be widely remarked for his taste in dress. He would don stripes or checks without a trace of timidity. He would quail before no violence of color in a cravat.

A certain insignificant Bunker Bean was not like this. With a soul aspiring to stripes and checks that should make him a man to be looked at twice in a city street, he lacked courage for any but the quietest patterns. Longing for the cravat of brilliant hue, he ate out his heart under neutral tints. Had he not, in the intoxication of his first free afternoon in New York, boldly purchased a glorious thing of silk entirely, flatly red, an article to stamp its wearer with distinction; and had he not, in the seclusion of his rented room, that night hidden the flaming thing at the bottom of a bottom drawer, knowing in his sickened soul he dared not flaunt it?

Once, truly, had he worn it, but only for a brief stroll on a rainy Sunday, with an entirely opaque raincoat buttoned closely under his chin. Even so, he fancied that people stared through and through that guaranteed fabric straight to his red secret. The rag burned on his breast. Afterward it was something to look at beyond the locked door; perhaps to try on behind drawn shades, late of a night. And how little Gordon Dane would have made of such a matter! Floated in Bean's mind the refrain of a clothing advertisement. "The more advanced dressers will seek this fashion." "Something dignified yet different!" Gordon Dane would be "an advanced dresser."

But if you have been afraid of nearly everything nearly all your life, how then? You must be "dignified" only. The brave only may be "different." It was all well enough to gaze at striking fabrics in windows; but to buy and to wear openly, and get yourself pointed at — laughed at! Again sounded the refrain of the hired bard of dress. *"It is cut to give the wearer the appearance of perfect physical development. And the effect so produced so improves his form that he unconsciously strives to attain the appearance which the garment gives him; he expands his chest, draws in his waist and stands erect."*

A rustling of papers from the opposite side of the desk promised a diversion of his thoughts. Bean was a hireling and the person who rustled the papers was his master, but the youth bestowed upon the great man a look of profound, albeit not unkindly, contempt. It could be seen, even as he sat in the desk-chair, that he was a short man; not an inch better than Bean, there. He was old. Bean, when he thought of the matter, was satisfied to guess him as something between fifty and eighty. He didn't know and didn't care how many might be the years of little Jim Breede. Breede was the most negligible person he knew.

He was nearly nothing, in Bean's view, if you came right down to it. Besides being of too few inches for a man and unspeakably old, he was unsightly. Nothing of the Gordon Dane about Breede. The little hair left him was an atrocious foggy grey; never in order, never combed, Bean thought. The brows were heavy, and still curiously dark, which made them look threatening. The eyes were the coldest of grey, a match for the hair in color, and set far back in caverns. The nose was blunt, the chin a mere knobby challenge, and between them was the unloveliest moustache Bean had ever been compelled to observe; short, ragged, faded in streaks. And wrinkles — wrinkles wheresoever there was room for them: across the forehead that lost itself in shining yellow scalp; under the eyes, down the cheeks, about the traplike mouth. He especially loathed the smaller wrinkles that made tiny squares and diamonds around the back of Breede's neck.

Sartorially, also, Bean found Breede objectionable. He forever wore the same kind of suit. The very same suit, one might have thought, only Bean knew it was renewed from time to time; it was the kind called "a decent grey," and it had emphatically not been cut "to give the wearer the appearance of perfect physical development." So far as Bean could determine the sole intention had been to give the wearer plenty of room under the arms and at the waist. Bean found it disgusting — a man who had at least enough leisure to give a little thought to such matters.

Breede's shoes offended him. Couldn't the man pick out something natty, a shapelier toe, buttons, a neat upper of tan or blue cloth — patent leather, of course? But nothing of the sort; a strange, thin, nameless leather, never either shiny or quite dull, as broad at the toe as anyplace, no buttons; not even laces; elastic at the sides! Not *shoes,* in any dressy sense. Things to be pulled on. And always the same, like the contemptible suits of clothes.

He might have done a little something with his shirts, Bean thought; a stripe or crossed lines, a bit of gay color; but no! Stiff-bosomed white shirts, cuffs that "came off," cuffs that fastened with hideous metallic devices that Bean had learned to scorn. A collar too loose, a black satin cravat, *and* no scarf-pin; not even a cluster of tiny diamonds.

From Breede and his ignoble attire Bean shifted the disfavor of his glance to Breede's luncheon tray on the desk between them. Breede's unvarying luncheon consisted of four crackers composed of a substance that was said, on the outside of the package, to be "predigested," one apple, and a glass of milk moderately inflated with seltzer. Bean himself had fared in princely fashion that day on two veal cutlets bathed in a German sauce of oily richness, a salad of purple cabbage, a profusion of vegetables, two cups of coffee and a German pancake that of itself would have disabled almost any but the young and hardy, or, presumably, a German.

Bean guessed the cost of Breede's meal to be a bit under eight cents. His own had cost sixty-five. He despised Breede for a petty economist.

Breede glanced up from his papers to encounter in Bean's eyes only a look of respectful waiting.

"Take letter G.S. Hubbell gen' traffic mag'r lines Wes' Chicago dear sir your favor twen'th instant —"

The words came from under that unacceptable moustache of Breede's like a series of exhausts from a motorcycle. Bean recorded them in his notebook. His shorthand was a marvel of condensed neatness. Breede had had trouble with stenographers; he was not easy to "take." He spoke swiftly, often indistinctly, and it maddened him to be asked to repeat. Bean had never asked him to repeat, and he inserted the a's and the's and all the minor words that Breede could not pause to utter. The letter continued:

"— mus' have report at your earl's' convenience of earnings and expenses of Grand Valley branch for las' four months with engineer's est'mate of prob'le cost of repairs and maintenance for nex' year —"

Breede halted to consult a document. Bean glanced up with his look of respectful waiting. Then he glanced down at his notes and wrote two other lines of shorthand. Breede might have supposed these to record the last sentence he had spoken, but one able to decipher the notes could have read: "That is one rotten suit of clothes. For God's sake, why not get some decent shoes next time —"

The letter was resumed. It came to its end with a phrase that almost won the difficult respect of Bean. Of a rumor that the C. & G.W. would build into certain coveted territory Breede exploded: "I can imagine nothing of less consequence!" Bean rather liked the phrase and the way Breede emitted it. That was a good thing to say to someone who might think you were afraid. He treasured the words; fondled them with the point of his pencil. He saw himself speaking them pithily to various persons with whom he might be in conflict. There was a thing now that Gordon Dane might have hurled at his enemies a dozen times in his adventurous career. Breede must have something in him — but look at his shiny white cuffs with the metal clasps, on the desk at his elbow!

Bean had lately read of Breede in a newspaper that "Conservative judges estimate his present fortune at a round hundred million." Bean's own stipend was thirty dollars a week, but he pitied Breede. Bean could learn to make millions if he should happen to want them; but poor old Breede could never learn to *look* like anybody.

There you have Bunker Bean at a familiar, prosaic moment in an afternoon of his twenty-third year. But his prosaic moments are numbered. How few they are to be! Already the door of Enchantment has swung to his scared touch. The times will show a scar or two from Bean. Bean the prodigious! The choicely perfect toy of Destiny at frolic! Bean the innocent — the monstrous!

*T*hose who long since gave Bean up as an insoluble problem were denied the advantages of an early association with him. Only an acquaintance with his innermost soul of souls could permit any sane understanding of his works, and this it is our privilege, and our necessity, to make, if we are to comprehend with any sympathy that which was later termed his "madness." The examination shall be made quickly and with all decency.

Let us regard Bean through the glass of his earliest reactions to an environment that was commonplace, unstimulating, dull — the little wooden town set among cornfields, "Wellsville" they called it, where he came from out of the Infinite to put on a casual body.

Of Bean at birth, it may be said frankly that he was not imposing. He was not chubby nor rosy; had no dimples. His face was a puckered protest at the infliction of animal life. In the white garments conventional to his age he was a distressing travesty, even when he gurgled. In the nude he was quite impossible to all but the most hardened mothers, and he was never photographed thus in a washbowl. Even his own mother, before he had survived to her one short year, began to harbor the accursed suspicion that his beauty was not flawless nor his intelligence supreme. To put it brutally, she almost admitted to herself that he was not the most remarkable child in all the world. To be sure, this is a bit less incredible when we know that Bean's mother, at his advent, thought far less highly of Bean's father than on the occasion, seven years before, when she had consented to be endowed with all his worldly goods. In the course of those years she came to believe that she had married beneath her, a fact of which she made no secret to her intimates and least of all to her mate, who, it may be added, privately agreed with her. Alonzo Bean, after that one delirious moment at the altar, had always disbelieved in himself pathetically. Who was he — to have wed a Bunker!

When little Bean's years began to permit small activities it was seen that his courage was amazing: a courage, however, that quickly overreached itself, and was sapped by small defeats. Tumbles down the slippery stairway, burns from the kitchen stove, began it. When a prized new sailor hat was blown to the center of a duck-pond he sought to recover it without any fearsome self-communing. If faith alone could uphold one, Bean would have walked upon the face of the waters that day. But the result was a bald experience of the sensations of the drowning, and a lasting fear of any considerable body of water. Ever after it was an adventure not to be lightly dared to cross even the stoutest bridge.

And flying! A belief that we can fly as the birds is surely not unreasonable at the age when he essayed it. Nor should a mere failure to rise from the ground destroy it. One must leap from high places, and Bean did so. The roof of the chicken house was the last eminence to have an experimental value. On his bed of pain he realized that we may not fly as the birds; nor ever after could he look without tremors from any high place.

Such domestic animals as he encountered taught him further fear. Even the cat became contemptuous of him, knowing itself dreaded. That splendid courage he was born with had faded to an extreme timidity. Before physical phenomena that pique most children to cunning endeavor, little Bean was aghast.

And very soon to this burden of fear was added the graver problems of human association. From being the butt of capricious physical forces he became a social unit and found this more terrifying than all that had gone before. At least in the physical world, if you kept pretty still, didn't touch things, didn't climb, stayed away from edges and windows and water and cows and looked carefully where you stepped, probably nothing would hurt you. But these new terrors of the social world lay in wait for you; clutched you in moments of the most inoffensive enjoyment.

His mother seemed to be director-general of these monsters, a ruthless deviser of exquisite tortures. There were unseasonable washings, dressings, combings and curlings — admonitions to be "a little gentleman." Loathsomely garbed, he was made to sit stiffly on a chair in the presence of falsely enthusiastic callers; or he was taken to call on those same callers and made to sit stiffly again while they, with feverish affectations of curiosity, asked him what his name was, something they already knew at least as well as he did; made to overhear their ensuing declarations that the cat had got his tongue, which he always denied bitterly until he came to see through the plot and learned to receive the accusation in stony silence.

Boys of his own age took hold of him roughly and laid him in the dust, jeeringly threw his hat to some high roof, spat on his new shoes. Even little girls, divining his abjectness, were prone to act rowdyish with him. And this especially made him suffer. He comprehended, somehow, that it was ignoble for a man child to be afraid of little girls.

Money was another source of grief. Not an exciting thing in itself, he had yet learned that people possessing desirable objects would insanely part with them for money. Then came one of the Uncle Bunkers from over Walnut Shade way, who scowled at him when leaving and gave him a dime. He voiced a wish to exchange this for sweets with a certain madman in the village who had no understanding of the value of his stock. His mother demurred; not alone because candy was unwholesome, but because the only right thing to do with money was to "save" it. And his mother prevailed, even though his father coarsely suggested that all the candy he could ever buy with Bunker money wouldn't hurt him none. The mother said that this was "low," and the father retorted with equal lowness that a rigid saving of all Bunker-given money wouldn't make no one a "Croosus," neither, if you come down to *that.*

It resulted in his being told that he could play freely with his dime one whole afternoon before the unexciting process of saving it began. Well enough, that! He had grown too fearful of life to lose that coin vulgarly out in the grass, as another would almost surely have done.

But he was beguiled in the mart of the money changers. To him, standing safely within the front gate where nothing could burn him, fall upon him, or chase him, "playing" respectfully with his new dime, came one of slightly superior years and criminal instincts demanding to inspect the treasure. The privilege was readily accorded, to arouse only contempt. The piece was too small. The critic himself had a bigger one, and showed it.

The two coins were held side by side. Bean was envious. The small coin was of silver, the larger of copper, but he was no petty metallurgist. He wanted to trade and said so. The newcomer assented with a large air of benevolence, snatched the despised smaller coin and ran hastily off — doubtless into a life of prosperous endeavor. And little Bean, presently found by his mother crooning over a large copper cent, was appalled by what followed. He had brought back "a bigger money," yet he had done something infamous. It was the first gleam of an incapacity for finance that was one day to become brilliant. He came to think money was a pretty queer thing. People cheated it from you or took it away for your own good. Anyhow, it was not a matter to bother about. You never had it long enough.

Then there was language. Language was words, and politeness. Certain phrases had to be mouthed to strangers, designed to imply a respect he was generally far from feeling. This was bad enough, but what was worse was that you couldn't use just any word you might hear, however beautiful it sounded. For example, there was the compelling utterance he got from the two merry gentlemen who passed him at the gate one day. So jolly were they with their songs and laughter that he followed them a little way to where they sat under a tree and drank turn by turn from a bottle. His ear caught the thing and his lips shaped it so cunningly that they laughed more than ever. He returned to his gate, intoning it; the fresh voice rose higher as the phrasing became more familiar. Then he was on the porch, chanting as a bard from the mere sensuous beauty of the words. Through the open door he saw three faces. The minister and his wife were calling on his mother.

The immediate happenings need not be set down. After events again became coherent he was choking back sobs and listening to the minister pray for those of unclean lips. And the minister prayed especially for one among them that he might cease to pervert the right ways of the Lord. He knew this to mean himself, for his mother glared over at him where he knelt; he was grateful for the kneeling posture at that moment; he would not have cared to sit. But all he had learned was that if you are going to use words freely it had much better be when you are alone; this, and that the minister had enormous feet, kneeling there with the toes of his boots dug into the carpet.

No sooner was this language specter laid than another confronted him; that of class distinction. Certain people were "low" and must be shunned by the high, unless the high perversely wished to be thought equally low. His mother was again the arbiter. Her rule as applied to children of his own age wrought but little hardship. She considered other children generally to be low, and her son feared them for their deeds of coarsely humorous violence. But he was never quite able to believe that his father was an undesirable associate.

In all his young life he had found no sport so good as riding on the seat beside that father while he drove the express wagon; a shiny green wagon with a seat close to the front and a tilted rest for one's feet, drawn by a grand black horse with a high-flung head, that would make nothing of eating a small boy if it ever had the chance. You drove to incoming trains, which was high adventure. But that was not all. You loaded the wagon with packages from the trains and these you proceeded to deliver in a leisurely and important manner. And some citizen of weight was sure to halt the wagon and ask if that there package of stuff from Chicago hadn't showed up yet, and it was mighty funny if it hadn't, because it was ordered special. Whereupon you said curtly that you didn't know anything about *that* — you couldn't fetch any package if it hadn't come, could you? And you drove on with pleased indignation.

Yet so fine a game as this was held by his mother to be unedifying. He would pick up a fashion of speech not genteel; he would grow to be a "rough." She, the inconsequent fair, who had herself been captivated by the driver of that very wagon, a gay blade directing his steed with a flourish! To be sure, she had found him doing this in a mist of romance, as one who must have his gallant fling at life before settling down. But the mist had cleared. Alonzo Bean, no longer the gay blade, had settled down upon the seat of his wagon. Once he had touched the guitar, sung an acceptable tenor, jested with life. Now he drove soberly, sang no more, and was concerned chiefly that his meals be served at set hours.

Small wonder, perhaps, that the mother should have feared the Bean and labored to cultivate the true Bunker strain in her offspring. Small wonder that she kept him when she could from the seat of that wagon and from the deadening influence of a father to whom Romance had broken its fine promises. Little Bean distressed her enough by playing at express-wagon in preference to all other games. He meant to drive a real one when he was big enough — that is, at first. Secretly he aspired beyond that. Some day, when he would not be afraid to climb to a higher seat, he meant to drive the great yellow 'bus that also went to trains. But that was a dream too splendid to tell.

In the summer of his seventh year, when his mother was finding it increasingly difficult to supply antidotes for this poison, she even consented to his visiting some other Beans. Unfortunately, there were no Bunkers to harbor the child of one who had made so palpable a mésalliance; but the elder Beans would gladly receive him, and they at least had never driven express wagons.

To the little boy, who had no sense of their relationship, they were persons named "Gramper" and "Grammer" whom he would do well to look down upon because they were not Bunkers. So much he understood, and that he was to ride in a stage and find them on a remote farm. It was to be the summer of his first feat of daring since he had reached years of moral discretion.

He was still so timid at the beginning of the wonderful journey that when the kind old gentleman who drove the stage stopped his horses at a point on the road where ripe red apples hung thickly on a tree, climbed the fence and returned with a capacious hat full of the fruit, he was chilled with horror at the crime. He had been freely told what was thought of people, and what was done with them, who took things not their own. Afraid to decline the two apples proffered by the robber, who resumed his seat and ate brazenly of his loot, the solitary passenger would still be no party to the outrage. He presently dropped his own two apples over the back of the stage, and later, lacking the preacher's courage, averred that he had eaten them — and couldn't eat another one, thank you. He was not a little affected by the fine bravado with which the old man ate apple after apple along miles of the road, full in the gaze of passersby, to whom he nodded in open-faced greeting, as might an honest man; but he was disappointed that there was no quick dragging to a jail, nor smiting by the hand of God, which quite as often occurred, if his mother and the minister knew anything about such matters. He decided that at least the elderly reprobate would wake up in the dark that very night and cry out in mortal agony under the realization of his sin.

And yet he, the unsullied, the fine theoretical moralist, was to return along that road a thief. A thief of parts, of depraved daring.

"Gramper" and "Grammer" proved to be an incredibly old couple, brown and withered and grey of locks, shrunken in stature, slow and feeble in action, and even rather timid themselves in their greetings. They made much of this grandchild, but they were diffident. Slowly it came to his knowledge that he was set up as a creature to adore. He enjoyed a blissful new sensation of being deferred to. Thereafter he lorded it over them, speaking in confident tones and making wild demands of entertainment. His mother had been right. They were Beans and, therefore, not much. He had brought his own silver napkin-ring and had meant to show them how wonderfully he folded and rolled his napkin after each meal. But it seemed they possessed no napkins whatever. Even his mother hadn't thought anything so repulsive as that of these people. He now boldly played the new game at table that his mother had frowned on. This was to measure off your meat and potatoes into an equal number of "bites," so that they would "come out even." If you were careful and counted right, the thing could be done every time.

And for the first time in all his years he asked for more pie. Of course this was anarchy. He knew well enough that one piece of pie is the heaven-allotted portion; that no one, even partly a Bunker, should crave beyond it; yet this fatuous old pair seemed to invite just that licentiousness, and they watched him with doting eyes while he swaggered through his second helping.

If more had been needed to show the Beanish lowness, it would have come after the first supper, for Gramper and Grammer sat out on a little vine-covered porch and smoked cob-pipes which they refilled at intervals from a sack of tobacco passed companionably back and forth. His own father was supposed to smoke but once a week, on Sunday, and then a cigar such as even a male Bunker might reputably burn. But a *pipe*, and between the lips of Grammer! She managed it with deftness and exhaled clouds of smoke into the still air of evening with a relish most painful to her amazed descendant. Yet she inspired him with an unholy ambition.

Asked the next day about the habit of smoking, Gramper said it was a bad habit; that it stunted people and shortened their days. Both he and Grammer were victims and warnings. Grammer had lumbago sometimes so you wouldn't hardly believe anyone could suffer that way and live. As for Gramper himself, he had a cough brought on by tobacco that would carry him off dead one of these days; yes, sir, just like that! And then, to point his warning, Gramper coughed falsely. Even to the unpracticed ear of his grandson the cough did not ring true. It lacked poignance.

Late that afternoon, when both the old ones slept, he abstracted a pipe, stuffed it with the rich black flakes and fled with matches to a nook of charming secrecy in the midst of the lilac clump. Thence arose presently clouds of smoke from the strongest tobacco money could buy.

At last he had dared something that didn't hurt him. He puffed valiantly, blowing out the smoke even as Grammer had done. Up to a certain moment his exaltation was intense, his scared soul expanding to greater deeds.

Then he coughed rather alarmingly. But that was to be expected. He drew in another breath of the stuff and coughed again. It was an honest cough; no doubt about that. Perhaps Gramper's cough had been honest. Perhaps the pipe he had selected was Gramper's own pipe, the one that made coughs. He became conscious of something more than throaty discomfort. Tiny beads of sweat bejeweled his brow, the lilac bush began to revolve swiftly about him. He must have taken Grammer's pipe after all — the one that led to lumbago. From revolving with a mere horizontal motion the lilacs now began also to whirl vertically. He had eaten a great deal at dinner. . . .

A pallid remnant of himself declined supper that night. Never could he sit at table again to eat of food. Gramper and Grammer were at first alarmed and there was talk of sending for a veterinary, the nearest to a professional man of medicine within miles and miles. But this talk died out after Gramper had made a cursory examination of the big yard, with especial attention to the lilac clump, where a pipe and other evidence was noticed. After that they not only became strangely reassured, but during their evening smoke on the little porch they often chuckled as if relishing in secret some rare jest. It did not occur to Bean that they laughed at him. He did not suspect that anyone could laugh at a little boy who had nearly died of lumbago. And he sat far away that night. The sight of the fuming pipes made him dizzy. His lesson had told. He was never to become an accomplished smoker.

His new spirit of adventure being thus blunted, he spent much of the next day indoors. Grammer opened the "front room" for him, no small concession, for this room was never put to vulgar use; rarely entered, indeed, save once a month for dusting. Here he found an atmosphere in keeping with his own chastened gloom, a musty air of mortality and twilight.

Such poor elegance as could be achieved by Beans alone, unaided by any Bunker, was here concentrated; a melodeon that groaned to his touch, with the startling effect of a voice from a long-closed tomb; a

center-table, luminous with varnish; gilded chairs in formal array; portraits in gilded frames; and best of all, a "whatnot," a thing to fit a
corner, having many shelves and each shelf loaded with fascinating
objects that maddened one because they must not be touched. Varnished
pine-cones, flint arrow-heads, statuettes set on worsted mats, tiny strange
boxes rarely ornamented — you mustn't even shake them to see if they
contained anything — a small stuffed alligator in the act of climbing a
pole; a frail cup and saucer; a watch-chain fashioned from Grammer's
hair probably long before she fell into evil habits; a pink china dog that
simpered; a dusty black cigar with a gay red-and-gold belt that had once
upon a time been given to Gramper by a gentleman in Chicago; a silver
cup inscribed "Baby"; a ball of clearest glass, bigger than any marble,
with a white camel at its center looking out unconcernedly; a gilded
horseshoe adorned with a bow of blue ribbon; an array of treasure, in
short, that made one suspect the Beans might have been something after
all if only they had tried.

Then on the lower shelf, when Grammer, relying on his honor, had
left the room, he made his wondrous discovery — a thing more beautiful
than ever he had dreamed of beauty; a thing that caught all the light in
the room and shot it back like a risen sun; a thing that excited,
enchained, satisfied with a satisfaction so deep that somehow it became
pain. It was a shell from the sea, polished to a dazzling brilliance of
opal and jade, amethyst and sapphire, delicately subdued, blending as
the tints in the western sky at sunset, soft, elusive, fluent. To his
rapturously shocked soul, it was a living thing. Instantly a spell was
upon him; long he gazed into its depths. It was more than deep; it was
bottomless. In some magic solution he there beheld himself and all the
world; imperiously it commanded his being. To his ear utterance came
from that lucent abyss, a murmur of voices, a confusion of tones; and
then invisible presences seemed to reach out greedy hands for him. It
was no place for a small boy, and his short legs twinkled as he fled.

Out in the friendly, familiar yard, he looked curiously about him,
basking in the sudden peace of it. A light wind stirred in the trees, the
sky was a void of blue, the scent of the lilacs came to him. That was all
reassuring; but something more came: a consciousness that he could
translate only as something vast, yet without shape or substance, that
opened to him, enfolded him, lifted him. It was a vision of boundless
magnitudes and himself among them — among them and with a power
he could put upon them. While it lasted he had a child's dim vision of
the knowledge that life would be big for him. He heard again the
confusion of voices, and his own among them, in far spacious places.

He always remembered this moment. In after years he knew it had been given him then to run an eye along the line of his destiny.

The moment passed; his mind was again vacant. He picked a green apple from the low tree under which he stood, bit into it, chewed without enthusiasm, then hurled the remnant at an immature rabbit that he saw regarding him from the edge of the lilac clump. The missile went wild, but the rabbit fled and Bean pursued it. He was not afraid of a rabbit — not of a young rabbit.

Returning from the chase, an unavailing one, he believed, only because the game used quite unfair tactics of concealment, he remembered the shell. A longing for possession seized him. It was more than that. The thing was already his; had always been his. Yet he foresaw complications. His ownership might be stupidly denied.

He went in to drag Grammer again before the whatnot, his mind sharpened to subtlety.

"Are everything there yours?" He pointed to the top shelf.

"Everything!"

He lowered the pointing finger to the second shelf.

"Are everything there yours?"

"All of 'em!"

"Everything *there?*"

"Yes, yes!"

"And this one, too?"

"For the land's sake, yes!" averred Grammer of the choice contents of the fourth shelf. She was baking pies and found herself a bit impatient of this new game.

"Well, that's all, now!" and he dismissed her, not daring to inquire as to the lower shelf. He had seen the way things were going — a sickening way. But, having shrewdly stopped at the lower shelf, having prevented Grammer from saying that those valuable objects were also hers, he had still the right to come into his own. If the shell mightn't belong to her it might belong to him; therefore it did belong to him; which, as logic, is not so lame as it sounds. At least it is a workaday average.

It occurred to him once to ask for the shell bluntly. But reason forbade this. It was not conceivable that anyone having so celestial a treasure would willingly part with it. When a thing was yours you took it, with dignity, but quietly.

During the remainder of his stay he was not conspicuously an occupant of the front room. No day passed that he did not contrive at least one look at his wonderful shell, but he craftily did not linger there, nor did he ever utter words about the thing, though these often crowded perilously to his lips.

A later day brought a letter to Grammer, and Gramper delightedly let it be known that the doctor at Wellsville had brought little Bean a fine new baby brother. Bean himself was not delighted at this. He had suffered the ministrations of that same doctor and he could imagine no visit of his to result in a situation at all pleasant to anyone concerned. If he had brought a baby it was doubtless not a baby that people would care to have around the house. He was not cheered when told that he might now go home.

He meant to stay on, and said so.

But the second day brought another letter that had a curious effect on Gramper and Grammer. Grammer cried, and Gramper told him with a strange, grave manner that now he must go. He knew that he was not told why; something, he overheard them agree, needn't be told "just yet." This was rather exciting and reconciled him to leaving.

He crept softly down the narrow stairs that night, alleging, when called to by Grammer, the need of a drink of water. When he returned his hands trembled about the shell. Swiftly it went to the bottom of his small box, his extra clothing, all his little belongings, being packed cleverly about it.

They kissed him many times the next morning, and when he looked back under the trees to where the old couple stood in front of the little weather-beaten house he saw that Grammer was crying again. His conscience hurt him a little; he wondered how they would get along without the shell. But they couldn't have it, because it was his shell.

The stage turned after a bit, and suddenly there was Gramper at the roadside, breathless after his run across a corner of the east forty. Instantly he was in the clutch of a great fear; the loss had been discovered. He sat frozen, waiting.

But Gramper only flourished the napkin-ring, and humorously taunted him with not having packed everything, after all. The stage drove on, but for the next mile his breathing was jerky.

Toward the end of the day-long ride — Gramper couldn't be running after them *that* far — he surrendered to his exultation, opened the box and drew out the shell, fondling it, fascinated anew by its varying sheen, excited by the freedom with which he now might touch it. Again he was the sole passenger and he called to the old driver, to whom nothing at all seemed to have happened because of his filching fruit.

"See my shell I found at Grammer's!"

But the old man was blind to beauty. He turned a careless eye upon the treasure, turned it off again with a formless grunt that might have been perfunctory praise, and resumed his half-muttered talk to himself, marked by little oblique nods of triumph — some endless dispute that he seemed to hold with an invisible opponent.

The owner of the shell was chilled but not daunted. There would surely be others less benighted who must acclaim the shell's charm.

Presently he was at the familiar front gate and his father, looking unusual, somehow, came to lift him down.

"See my shell I found at Grammer's!"

"Your mother is dead."

"See my shell I found at Grammer's!"

"Your mother is dead."

It was the sinister iteration by which he was stricken, rather than the news itself. The latter only stunned. His hand in his father's, he went up the walk and into the house. There were women inside, women who moved with an effect of bustling stillness, the same women who had so often asked him what his name was. They seemed to know it well enough now. He was aware that his entrance created no little sensation. One of them kissed him and told him not to cry, but he had no thought of crying. He became aware of the thing in his hands.

"See my shell I found at Grammer's!"

The invitation was a general one. They looked in silence and some of them moved about, and then through a doorway he saw in the next room an object long and dark and shining set on two chairs.

He had never seen anything like it, but its suggestion was evil. The women waited. Something seemed to be expected of someone. His father led him into that room and lifted him up to see. His mother's face was there under a glass. He could see that she wore her pretty blue dress, and on one arm beside her was something covered with white. He called softly to her.

"Mamma! Mamma!"

But she did not open her eyes.

Then he was out again where the people were, and the people seemed to forget about him. He went to his little room under the sloping roof. He had not let go of the shell and now, in the fading light from the low window, he lost himself once more in its depths. Inwardly he knew that a terror lurked near, but he had not yet felt it. Only when bedtime came did the continued silence of his mother become meaningful. When he was left alone, he cried for her, still clutching his shell.

The minister came the next day, and many people, and the minister talked to them about his mother. The two Uncle Bunkers were there, grim, hard-mouthed, glaring, for they hated each other as only brothers can hate. He wondered if they would still let him be partly a Bunker, now that his mother was gone. He wondered also at the novel consideration he saw being shown to his father. Dressed in a new suit of black, with an unaccustomed black hat, his father was plainly become a man of importance. He was one apart, and people of undoubted consequence deferred to him — to the very last. He earnestly wished his mother could see that; his nervous little mother with the flushed face and tired eyes, always terrifically concerned about one small matter or another. He thought she would have liked to see that his father was someone, after all.

II

*T*he Chicago epoch began a year later. The true nature of its causes never lay quite clearly in the mind of Bean. There was, first, an entirely new Uncle Bunker whom he had never seen, but whom he at once liked very much. He was a younger, more beautiful uncle, with a gay, light manner and expensive clothing. He wore a magnificent gold watch and chain, and jeweled rings flashed from his white fingers as he, in absent moments, daintily passed a small pocket-comb through the meshes of his lustrous brown side-whiskers. Little Bean knew that he did something on a board in Chicago; that he "operated" on the Board of Trade was the accustomed phrasing. He liked the word, and tried to picture what "operating" might mean in relation to a board.

The good people of Wellsville regarded this uncle with quite all the respect so flashing a figure deserved. Not so the two other Uncle Bunkers from over Walnut Shade way. Their first known agreement, voiced of this financier, was in saying something wise about a fool and his money.

Later, and perhaps for the last time on earth, they agreed once more. That was when the news of his marriage came to them — for what was she? Nothing but his landlady's daughter! Snip of a girl that helped her mother run a cheap Chicago boarding-house! Him that could have taken his pick, if he was going to be a fool and tie himself up! You could bet that the pair had "worked" him, that mother and the girl; landed him for his money, that was plain! Well, he'd made his bed!

Bean was not slow to liken this uncle to his mother, who had also "made her bed." He had at first a misty notion that the bride might a little resemble his father, a notion happily dispelled when he saw her. For the pair came to Wellsville. It was a sort of honeymoon combined vaguely with business. The bride was wonderfully pretty, Bean thought; dark and dainty and laughing, forever talking the most irresistible "baby-talk" to her adoring mate. Her name for him was "Boo'ful."

Bean at once fell deeply in love with this bride, a passion that was to endure beyond the life of most such affairs. She professed an infatuation equal to his own, and regretted that an immediate marriage, which he timidly advocated in the course of their first interview, was not practicable. That she was frivolous, light-minded, and would never settle down to be a good worker, was a village verdict he scorned. Who would have her otherwise? Not he, nor the adoring Boo'ful, it is certain. He determined to go to live at her house, and, strangely enough — for these sudden plans of his were most often discouraged — the thing seemed feasible. For one thing, his father was going to bring home a new mother; a lady, he gathered, who had not only settled down to be a good worker, but who, in espousing his father, would curiously not marry beneath her. Without being told so, he had absorbed from his first mother a conviction that this was possible to but few women. He felt a little glow of pride for his father in this affair.

Another matter that seemed to bear on his going away was that this brilliant and human Uncle Bunker was a "trustee." Not only a trustee, but *his* trustee; his very own, like his shell, or anything. This led to his discovery that he had money. His mother, it seemed, had left it to him; Bunker money that the two older uncles had sought and failed to divert from her on the occasion of her wedding one below her station. Money! and the capable Uncle Bunker as trustee of that money! Money one could buy things with! He was pleasantly conscious of being rather important under the glance of familiars. Even his father spoke formal words of counsel to him, as if a gulf was between them — his father now bereft of all Bunker prestige, legal or social.

And the new uncle was to "educate" him, though this was to be paid for out of that money of his very own. He was rudely shocked to learn that you had to pay money to go to school. Loathing school as he did, to pay money for your own torture — money that would buy things — seemed unutterably silly. But despite this inbecility the prospect retained its glamour.

He would have suffered punishments even worse than school for the privilege of existing near that beautiful bride, whom he was now calling, at her especial request, "Aunt Clara." She readily understood any affair that he chose to explain to her; understood about his shell and said it was the most beautiful thing in all the world. She understood, too, and was deeply sympathetic about Skipper, the dog. Skipper was one of a series of puppies that Bean had appropriated from the public highway.

Some had shamefully deserted him after a little time of pampering. Others, and these were the several that had howled untimely in the far night, had mysteriously disappeared. Bean had sometimes a hurt suspicion that his father knew more than he cared to tell about these vanishings. But Skipper had stayed and had not howled. Buffeted wastrel of a thousand casual amours, soft-haired, confiding, ungainly, he was rich in understanding if not in beauty. And yet he must be left. Even the discriminating and ever-just Aunt Clara felt that Skipper would not do well in a great city. Of course she was not clumsy enough to suggest that there were other dogs in the world, as did her less discerning husband. But she said that it would come out all right, and Bean trusted her. She knew, too, what would happen on his first night away, and came softly to his bed and solaced him as he lay crying for Skipper.

Those first Chicago days were rich in flavor. The city was a marvel of many terrors, a place of weird sounds, strange shapes and swift movements, among which — having been made timid by much adversity — you had need to be very, very careful if your hand was in no one's. The house itself was wonderful: a house of real brick and very lofty. If you started in the basement you could go "upstairs" three distinct times in it before you reached the top. He had never imagined such a house for any but kings to live in. Within were many rooms; he hardly could count them all; and regal furnishings, gay with color; and, permeating it all, a most appetizing odor of cooked food, eloquent tale of long-eaten banquets, able reminder of those to come.

Out beside the front door was a rather dingy sign that said "Boarders Wanted." His deduction after reading the sign was that the person who wanted the boarders was Aunt Clara's mother. She was like Aunt Clara in that she was dark and small, but in nothing else. She did not wear pretty dresses nor laugh nor address baby talk to "Boo'ful." She was very old and not nice to look at, Bean thought; and an uneasy woman, not knowing how to be quiet. Mostly she worked in the kitchen, after a hasty morning tour of the house to "do" the rooms. Bean was much surprised to learn that her name, too, was Clara. She did not look at all like anyone whose name would be Clara.

And presently there was to be a house even more magnificent than this, where they would all live together and where, so they jested, the old Clara wouldn't know what to do, because there would be nothing to do. The house would be ready just as soon as Boo'ful made his "next turn," and that was so near in time that there was already a fascinating picture of the lines of the house, white lines on blue paper, over which Boo'ful and Aunt Clara spent many an evening in loving dispute. It seemed that you could change the house by merely changing those lines.

Sometimes they put a curve into the main stairway or doubled the area of stained-glass window in the music-room; sometimes it was a mere detail of alteration in the butler's pantry, or the coachman's room over the stable. The old Clara displayed no interest in these details. She seemed to be content to go on wanting boarders.

This was not, as he saw it, an unlovely want. It surrounded her with gay companions at meal-time; they were "like one big family," as one of the number would frequently observe. He was the one that most often set them all to laughing by his talk like that of a German who speaks English imperfectly, which he didn't have to do at all. It was only make-believe, but very funny.

After this joyous group and his Aunt Clara, who really came first, his preference in humans was for a lady who lived two doors away. If you rang her bell she might be one of three persons. It depended on what you were looking for. She might be the manicure and chiropodist whose sign was displayed; she might be Madam Wanda, the world-renowned clairvoyant, sittings from 9 A.M. to 5 P.M., Advice on Love, Marriage and Business; sign also displayed; or she might be merely Mrs. Jackson, with a choice front room for a single gentleman, as declared by the third sign. In any case she was a smiling, plump lady with a capable blue eye and abundant dark hair that was smooth and shiny.

It was in company with his uncle that he first made her acquaintance. His uncle knew all that one need know about Love and Marriage, but it seemed that his knowledge of Business could be extended. There were times when only the gifts of a world-renowned clairvoyant could enable one to say what May wheat was going to do.

The acquaintance, lightly enough begun, ripened soon to intimacy, and so were the eyes of Bean first opened to mysteries that would later affect his life so vitally. He was soon carrying wood and coal up the back stairs of Mrs. Jackson, in return for which the lady ministered to him in her professional capacities. At their first important session on a rainy Saturday of leisure she trimmed and polished each of his ten fingernails, told his past, present and future — he was going to cross water and there was a dark gentleman he had need to beware of — and suggested that his feet might need attention.

He squirmingly demurred at this last operation, and successfully resisted it. But the bonds of their friendship were sealed over a light collation which she served. She was a vegetarian, she told him. You couldn't get on to a high spiritual plane if you ate the corpses of murdered animals. But her food seemed sufficing and she drank beer which he brought her in a neat pitcher from the cheerful store on the corner where they sold such things. Beer, she explained to him, was a strictly vegetable product, though not the thing for growing boys. The young must discriminate, even among vegetables.

They liked each other well and in a little time he had absorbed the simple tale of her activities. When you rented rooms, people sometimes left without paying you. So had gone Professor de Lavigne, the chiropodist; so had vanished the original Madam Wanda. They had left their signs, and nothing else. The rest was simple after you had been seeing how they did it — a little practice with a nail-file, a little observation of parties that came in with crêpe on, to whom you said, "Standing right there I see someone near and dear to you that has lately passed on to the spirit land"; or male parties that looked all fussed up and worried, to whom you said that the deal was coming out all right, only they were always to act on their first impulse and look out for a man with kind of brownish hair who carried a gold watch and sometimes wore gloves. She said it was strange how she could "hit it" sometimes, especially where there were initials in the hats they left outside in the hall, or a name inside the overcoat pocket. It was wonderful what she had been able to tell parties for a dollar.

Bean cared little for these details, but he was excited by the theory back of them; a world from which the unseen spirits of the dead will counsel and guide us in our daily affairs if we will listen. It was a new terror added to a world of terrors — they were all about you, striving with futile hands to touch you, whispering words of cheer or warning to your deaf ears.

Mrs. Jackson herself believed it implicitly and went each week to consult one or another of the more advanced mediums. The last one had seen the spirit of her Aunt Mary, a deceased person so remote in time that she had been clean forgotten. But it was a valuable pointer. When you come to think about it, at least seven parties out of ten, if they were any way along in years, had a dead Aunt Mary. And it was best to go to the good ones. Mrs. Jackson admitted that. You paid more, but you got more.

Uncle Bunker became of this opinion very soon. What Mrs. Jackson disclosed to him about May wheat had seemed to be hardly worth the dollar she asked. He began going to the good ones, and Bean gathered that even their superior gifts left something to be desired. The brilliant uncle began to accustom his home circle to frowns. Bean and the older Clara (she was beginning to complain about not sleeping and a pain in her side) were sensible of this change, but the younger Clara only pouted when she noticed it at all, prettily accusing her splendid consort of not caring for her as he had once professed to. She spent more time over her hair and shopped extensively for feminine trappings.

Then one day his uncle came home, a slinking wreck of beauty, and told Aunt Clara that all was lost save honor. Bean heard the interesting announcement, and gathered, after a question from his aunt, that his own patrimony had been a part of that all which was lost save honor. He heard his uncle add tearfully that one shot would end it now.

He was frightened by this, but his Aunt Clara seemed not to be. He heard her say, "There, there! Did a nassy ol' martet do adainst 'ums!" And later she was seen to take him up tea and toast and chicken.

*T*he years seemed to march more swiftly then — school and growing and little changes in the house. Boo'ful never fired the shot that would have ended all. The older Clara inconsequently died and the frivolous Clara took her place in the kitchen. She had not corrected her light manner, but slowly she changed with the years until she was almost as faded as the old Clara had been. More ambitious, however, and working to better purpose. They went to a new and finer house that would hold more boarders; and the sign, which was lettered in gold, said, "Boarders Taken," a far more dignified sign than the old with its frank appeal of "Boarders Wanted." That new sign intimated a noble condescension.

Aunt Clara had not only settled down to be a worker, but she had proved to be a manager. Boo'ful actually performed little services about the house, staying in the kitchen at meal-time to carve and help serve the food. Aunt Clara had been unexpected adamant in the matter of his taking a fine revenge on the market that had gone against him. She refused to provide the very modest sum he pleaded for to this end, and as the two old Uncle Bunkers were equally obdurate — they said they had known when he married that flutter-budget just how he would end — his leisure was never seriously menaced.

Aunt Clara was especially firm about the money because of the considerable life-insurance premium she soon began to pay. It was her whim that little Bean had not been of competent years to lose all save honor, and she had discovered a life-insurance company whose officers were mad enough to compute Boo'ful's loss to the world in dollars and cents. He was, in fact, considered an excellent risk. He did not fade after the manner of the busy Aunt Clara, that gay little wretch whose girlish graces lingered on incongruously — like jests upon a tombstone.

Bean grew to college years. Aunt Clara had been insistent about the college; it was to be the best business college in Chicago. Bean matriculated without formality and studied stenography and typewriting. Aunt Clara had been afraid that he might "get in" with a fast college set and

learn to drink and smoke and gamble. It may be admitted that he wished
to do just these things, but he had observed the effects of drink, his one
experience with tobacco remained all too vivid, and gambling required
more capital than the car fare he was usually provided with. Besides,
you came to a bad end if you gambled. It led to other things.

Nor would he, on the public street, join with any number of his class
in the college yell. He was afraid a policeman would arrest him. Even
in the more mature years of a comparatively blameless life he remained
afraid of policemen, and never passed one without a tremor. All of which
conduced to his efficiency as a student. When others fled to their
questionable pleasures he was as likely as not to remain in his chair
before a typewriter, pounding out again and again, *"The swift brown fox
jumps over the lazy dog —"* a dramatic enough situation ingeniously
worded to utilize nearly all the letters of our alphabet.

At last he was pronounced competent, received a diploma (which
Aunt Clara framed handsomely and hung in her own room beside the
pastel portrait of Boo'ful in his opulent prime) and took up a man's
work.

*T*he veil that hangs between mortal eyes and the Infinite had many
times been pierced for him by the able Mrs. Jackson. He was now to
enter another and more significant stage of his spiritual development.

His first employer was a noble-looking old man, white-bearded, and
vast of brow, who came to be a boarder at Aunt Clara's. He was a believer
in the cult of theosophy and specialized on reincarnation. Neither word
was luminous to Bean, but he learned that the old gentleman was writing
a book and would need an amanuensis. They agreed upon terms and
the work began. The book was a romance entitled, "Glimpses Through
the Veil of Time," and it was to tell of a soul's adventures through a
prolonged series of reincarnations. So much Bean grasped. The terminology of the author was more difficult. When you have chiefly learned
to write, "Your favor of the 11th inst. came duly to hand and in reply
we beg to state —" it is confusing to be switched to such words as
"anthropogenesis" and to chapter headings like "Substituting Variable
Quantities for Fixed Extraordinary Theoretic Possibilities." Even when
the author meant to be most lucid Bean found him not too easy. "In
order to simplify the theory of the Karmic cycle," dictated the white-
bearded one for his Introduction, "let us think of the subplanes of the
astral plane as horizontal divisions, and of the types of matter belonging

to the seven great planetary Logoi as perpendicular divisions crossing these others at right angles."

What Bean made of this in transcribing his notes need not be told. What is solely important is that, as the tale progressed, he became enthralled by the doctrine of reincarnation. It was of minor consequence that he became expert in shorthand.

Had he lived before, would he live again? There must be a way to know. "Alclytus," began an early chapter of the tale, "was born this time in 21976 B.C. in a male body as the son of a king, in what is now the Telugu country not far from Masulipatam. He was proficient in riding, shooting, swimming and the sports of his race. When he came of age he married Surya, the daughter of a neighboring rajah and they were very happy together in their religious studies —"

Had he, Bunker Bean, perhaps once espoused the daughter of a rajah, and been happy in religious studies with her? Had he, perchance, been even the rajah himself? Why not?

The romance was never finished. A worried son of the old gentleman appeared one day, alleged that he had run off from a good home where he was kindly treated, and by mild force carried him back. But he had performed his allotted part in Bean's life.

A few books had been left and these were read. Death was a recurring incident in an endless life. Wise men he saw had found this an answer to all problems — founders of religions and philosophies — Buddha, Pythagoras, Plato, the Christ. Wise moderns had accepted it, Max Müller and Hume and Goethe, Fichte, Schelling, Lessing. Bean could not appraise these authorities, but the names somehow sounded convincing and the men had seemed to think that reincarnation was the only doctrine of immortality a philosopher could consider.

It remained, then, to explore the Karmic past of Bunker Bean; not in any mood of lightness. A verse quoted by the old man had given him pause:

"Who toiled a slave may come anew a prince
    For gentle worthiness and merit won;
Who ruled a king may wander earth in rags
    For things done and undone."

What might he have been? For ruling once as a king, a bad king, was he now merely Bunker Bean, not precisely roaming the earth in rags, but sidling timidly through its terrors, disbelieving in himself, afraid of policemen, afraid of life?

So he confronted and considered the thing, fascinated by its vistas as once he had been by the shell. If it were true that we cast away our worn bodies and ever reclothe ourselves with new, why should not the right member of Mrs. Jackson's profession one day unfold to him his beginningless past?

III

*T*he courts havin' decided," continued Breede, in staccato explosions, "that the 'quipment is nes'ry part of road, without which road would be tot'ly crippled, you will note these first moggige 'quipment bonds take pri'rty over first-moggige bonds, an' gov'n y'sef 'cordingly your ver' truly —"

He glanced up at Bean, contracted his brows to a black menace and emitted a final detonation.

"'S all for 's aft'noon!"

He bit savagely into his unlighted cigar and began to rifle through a new sheaf of documents. Bean deftly effaced himself, with a parting glare at the unlighted cigar. It was a feature of Breede that no reporter ever neglected to mention, but Bean thought you might as well chew tobacco and be done with it. Moreover, the cigars were not such as one would have expected to find between the lips of a man whose present wealth was estimated at a round hundred million. Bulger, in the outer office, had given up trying to smoke them. He declared them to be the very worst that could be had for any money.

Before beginning the transcription of his notes, Bean had to learn the latest telephone news from the ball-ground. During the last half-hour he had inwardly raged more than usual at Breede for being kept from this information. Bulger always managed to get it on time, beginning with the third inning, even when he took dictation from Breede's confidential secretary, or from Tully, the chief clerk.

Bean looked inquiringly at Bulger now. Bulger nodded and presently strolled from his own desk to Bean's, where he left a slip of paper bearing the words, "Cubs, 3; Giants, 2; 1st 1/2 4th."

Bean had envied Bulger from the first for this man-of-the-world ease. In actual person not superior to Bean, he had a temperament of daring. In every detail he was an advanced dresser, specializing in flamboyant cravats. He would have been Bean's model if Bean had been less a coward. Bulger was nearly all that Bean wished to be. He condescended to his tasks with an air of elegant and detached leisure that raised them to the dignity of sports. He had quite the air of a wealthy amateur with a passion for typewriting.

He had once done Breede's personal work, but had been banished to the outer office after Bean's first try-out. Breede had found some mysterious objection to him. Perhaps it was because Bulger would always look up with pleased sagacity, as if he were helping to compose Breede's letters. It may have been simple envy in Breede for his advanced dressing. Bulger had felt no unkindness toward Bean for thus supplanting him in a desirable post. But he did confide to his successor that if he, Bulger, ever found Breede under his heel, Breede could expect no mercy. Bulger would grind him — just like that!

Bean dramatized this as he wrote his letters; Breede pleasantly disintegrating under the iron heel of Bulger: Breede "The Great Reorganizer," as he was said to be known "in the Street," old "steel and velvet," meeting a just fate! So nearly mechanical was his typewriting that he spoiled one sheet of paper by transcribing two lines of shorthand not meant to be a part of the letter. Only by chance did a certain traffic manager of lines west of Chicago escape reading a briefly worded opinion of the clothes he wore that would have puzzled and might have pained him, for Breede, such had come to be his confidence in Bean, always signed his letters without reading them over. Bean gasped and wisely dismissed the drama of Bulger's revenge from his mind.

At four-thirty the day's work ended and Bean was free to forget until another day the little he had been unable to avoid learning about high railroad finance; free to lead his own secret life, which was a thing apart from all that wordy foolery.

He changed from his office coat to one alleged by its maker to give him the appearance of perfect physical development, and descended to the street-level in company with Bulger. Bean would have preferred to walk down; he suffered the sensations of dying each time the elevator seemed to fall, but he could not confess this to the doggish and intrepid Bulger.

There were other weaknesses he had to cloak. Bulger proffered cigarettes from a silver case at their first meeting. Bean declined.

"Doctor's orders," said he.

"Nerves?" suggested Bulger, expertly.

"Heart — gets me something fierce."

"Come in here to Tommy's and take a bracer," now suggested the hospitable Bulger. But again the physician had been obdurate.

"Won't let me touch a thing — liver," said Bean. "Got to be careful of a breakdown."

"Tough," said Bulger. "Man needs a certain amount of it, down here in the street. Course, a guy can't *sop* it up, like you see some do. Other night, now — gang of us out, y'understand — come too fast for your Uncle Cuthbert. Say, goin' up those stairs where I live I cert'n'ly must 'a' sounded like a well-known clubman gettin' home from an Elks' banquet. Head, next A.M.? — ask me, *ask* me! Nothing of the kind! Don't I show up with a toothache and con old Tully into a day off at the dentist's to have the bridge-work tooled up. Ask me was I at the dentist's? Wow! Not! — little old William J. Turkish bath for mine!"

Bean was moved to raw envy. But he knew himself too well. The specialist he professed to have consulted had put a ban upon the simplest recreations. Otherwise how could he with any grace have declined those repeated invitations of Bulger's to come along and meet a couple of swell dames that'd like to have a good time? Bulger, considered in relation to the sex not his own, was what he himself would have termed "a smooth little piece of work." Bean was not this. Of all his terrors women, as objects of purely male attention, were the greatest. He longed for them, he looked upon such as were desirable with what he believed to be an evil eye, but he had learned not to go too close. They talked, they disconcerted him horribly. And if they didn't talk they looked dangerous, as if they knew too much. Some day, of course, he would nerve himself to it. Indeed he very determinedly meant to marry, and to have a son who should be trained from the cradle with the sole idea of making him a great left-handed pitcher; but that was far in the future. He longed tragically to go with Bulger and meet a couple of swell dames, but he knew how it would be. Right off they would find him out and laugh at him.

Bulger consumed another high-ball, filled his cigarette case, and the two stood a moment on Broadway. Breede, the last to leave his office, crossed the pavement to a waiting automobile.

"There's his foxy Rebates going to the arms of his family," said Bulger, disrespectfully applying to Breede a term that had more than once made him interesting to the Interstate Commerce Commission.

"See the three skirts in the back? That's the Missis and the two squabs. Young one's only a flapper, but the old one's a peacherine for looks. Go on, lamp her once!"

Bean turned his diffident gaze upon the occupants of the tonneau with a sudden wild dream that he would stare insolently. But his eyes unaccountably came to rest in the eyes of the young one — the flapper. He saw only the eyes, and he felt that the eyes were seeing him. The motor chugged slowly up Broadway, nosing for a path about a slowly driven truck; the flapper looked back.

"Not half bad, that!" said Bean, recovering, and speaking in what he felt was the correct Bulger tone.

"Not for mine," said Bulger firmly. "Big sister, though, not so worse. Met up with her one time out to the country place, takin' stuff for the old man the time he got kidneys in his feet. I made a hit with her, too, on the level, but say! nothin' doing there for old John W. me! I dropped the thing like it was poison ivy. Me doin' the nuptial in a family like that, and bein' under Pop's thumb the rest of my life? Ask me, that's all; *ask* me! Wake me up any time in the night and ask me."

Again Bean was thrilled, resolving then and there that no daughter of Breede's should ever wed him. Bulger was entirely right. It wouldn't do. Bulger looked at his watch.

"Well, s'long; got a date down in the next block. She's out at five. Say, I want you to get a flash at her some day. Broadway car, yesterday, me goin' uptown with Max, see? she lookin' at her gloves. 'Pipe the queen in black,' I says to Max, jes' so she could hear, y' understand. Say, did she gimme the eye. Not at all! Not at *all!* Old William H. Smoothy, I guess yes. Pretty soon a gink setting beside her beats it, and quick change for me. Had her all dated up by Fourteenth Street. Dinner and a show, if things look well. Some class to her, all right. One the manicures in that shop down there. Well, s'long!"

Looking over his shoulder with sickish envy after the invincible Bulger, Bean left the curb for a passing car and came to a jolting stop against the biggest policeman he had ever seen. He mumbled a horrified apology, but his victim did not even turn to look down upon him. He fled into the car and found a seat, still trembling from that collision. From across the aisle a pretty girl surveyed him with veiled insolence. He furtively felt of his neutral-tinted cravat and took his hat off to see if there could be a dent in it. The girl, having plumbed his insignificance, now unconcernedly read the signs above his head. There was bitterness in the stare he bestowed upon her trim lines. Some day Bulger would chance to be on that car with her — then she'd be taken down a bit — Bulger who, by Fourteenth Street, had them all dated up.

Presently he was embarrassed by a stout, aggressive man who clutched a strap with one hand and some evening papers with the other, a man who clearly considered it outrageous that he should be compelled to stand in a street car. He glared at Bean with a cold, questioning indignation, shifting from one foot to the other, and seeming to be on the point of having words about it. This was not long to be endured. Bean glanced out in feigned dismay, as if at a desired cross-street he had

Bunker Bean

carelessly passed, sprang toward the door of the car and caromed heavily against a tired workingman who still, however, was not too tired to put his sense of injury into quick, pithy words of the street. The pretty girl tittered horribly and the stout man, already in Bean's seat, rattled his papers impatiently, implying that people in that state ought to be kept off in the first place.

He had meant to leave the car and try another, but there at the step was another too-large policeman helping an uncertain old lady to the ground, so he slinkingly insinuated himself to the far corner of the platform, where, for forty city blocks, a whistling messenger boy gored his right side with the corners of an unyielding box while a dreamy-eyed man who, as Bulger would have said, had apparently been sopping it up like you see some do, leaned a friendly elbow on his shoulder, dented his new hat and from time to time stepped elaborately on his natty shoes with the blue cloth uppers. Also, the conductor demanded and received a second fare from him. What was the use of saying you had paid inside? The conductor was a desperate looking man who would probably say he knew that game, and stop the car. . . .

Something of the sort always happened to him in street cars. It was bad enough when you walked, with people jostling you and looking as if they wondered what right you had to be there.

At last came the street down which he made a daily pilgrimage and he popped from the crowd on the platform like a seed squeezed from an orange.

Reaching the curb alive — the crossing policeman graciously halted a huge motor-truck driven by a speed-enthusiast — he corrected the latest dent in his hat, straightened his cravat, readjusted the shoulder lines of the coat appertaining to America's greatest eighteen-dollar suit — "$18.00 — No More; No Less!" — and with a fear-quickened hand discovered that his watch was gone, his gold hunting-case watch and horseshoe fob set with brilliants, that Aunt Clara had given him on his twenty-first birthday for not smoking!

A moment he stood, raging, fearing. His money was safe, but they might decide to come back for that. Or the policeman might come up and make an ugly row because he had let himself be robbed in a public conveyance. He would have to prove that the watch was his; probably have to tell why Aunt Clara had given it to him.

With a philosophy peculiarly his own, a spirit of wise submission that was more than once to serve him well, he pulled his hat sharply down, braced and squared such appearance of perfect physical development as the eighteen dollars had achieved, and walked away. He had always known the watch would go. Now it was gone, no more worry.

Good enough! As he walked he rehearsed an explanation to Bulger: cleverly worded intimations that the watch had been pawned to meet a certain quick demand on his resources not morally to his credit. He made the implication as sinister as he could.

And then he stood once more before the shrine of Beauty. In the show-window of a bird-and-animal store on Sixth Avenue was a four-months-old puppy, a "Boston-bull," that was, of a certainty, the most perfect thing ever born of a mother-dog. Already the head was enormous, in contrast, yet somehow in a maddening harmony with the clean-lined slender body. The color-scheme was golden brown on a background of pure white. On the body this golden brown was distributed with that apparent carelessness which is Art. Overlaying the sides and back were three patches of it about the size and somewhat the shape of maps of Africa as such are commonly to be observed. In the coloring of the noble brow and absurdly wide jaws a more tender care was evident. There was the same golden brown, beginning well back of the ears and flowing lustrously to the edge of the overhanging upper lip, where it darkened. Midway between the ears — erectly alert those ears were — a narrow strip of white descended a little way to open to a circle of white in the midst of which was the black muzzle. At the point of each nostril was the tiniest speck of pink, Beauty's last triumphant touch.

As he came to rest before the window the creature leaped forward with joyous madness, reared two clumsy white feet against the glass (those feet that seemed to have been meant for a larger dog), barked ably — he could hear it even above the din of an elevated train — and then fell to a frantic licking of the glass where Bean had provocatively spread a hand. Perceiving this intimacy to be thwarted by some mysterious barrier to be felt but not seen, he backed away, fell forward upon his chest, the too-big paws outspread, and smiled from a vasty pink cavern. Between the stiffened ears could be seen the crooked tail, tinged with just enough of the brown, in unbelievably swift motion. Discovering this pose to bring no desired result, he ran mad in the sawdust, excavating it feverishly with his forepaws, sending it expertly to the rear with the others.

The fever passed; he surveyed his admirer for a moment, then began to revolve slowly upon all four feet until he had made in the sawdust a bed that suited him. Into this he sank and was instantly asleep, his slenderness coiled, the heavy head at rest on a paw, one ear drooping wearily, the other still erect.

For two weeks this daily visit had been almost the best of Bean's secrets. For two weeks he had known that his passion was hopeless, yet had he yearned out his heart there before the endearing thing. In the shock of his first discovery, spurred to unwonted daring, he had actually penetrated the store meaning to hear the impossible price. But an angry-looking old man (so Bean thought) had come noisily from a back room and glowered at him threateningly over big spectacles. So he had hastily priced a convenient jar of goldfish for which he felt no affection whatever, mumbled something about the party's calling, himself, next day, and escaped to the street. Anyway, it would have been no good, asking the price; it was bound to be a high price; and he couldn't keep a dog; and if he did, a policeman would shoot it for being mad when it was only playing.

But some time — yet, would it be this same animal? In all the world there could not be another so acceptable. He shivered with apprehension each day as he neared the place, lest some connoisseur had forestalled him. He quickened to a jealous distrust of any passerby who halted beside him to look into the window, and felt a great relief when these passed on.

Once he had feared the worst. A man beside him holding a candy-eating child by the hand had said, "Now, now, sir!" and, "Well, well, *was* he a nice old doggie!" Then they had gone into the store, very businesslike, and Bean had felt that he might be taking his last look at a loved one. Lawless designs throbbed in his brain — a wild plan to shadow the man to his home — to have that dog, *no matter how.* But when they came out the child carried nothing more than a wicker cage containing two pink-eyed white rabbits that were wrinkling their noses furiously.

With a last cherishing look at most of the beauty in all the world — it still slept despite the tearing clatter of a parrot with catarrhal utterance that shrieked over and over, "Oh, what a fool! Oh, what a fool!" — he turned away. What need to say that, with half the opportunity, his early infamy of the shell would have been repeated. He wondered darkly if the old man left that dog in the window nights!

He reached for his watch before he remembered its loss. Then he reminded himself bitterly that street clocks were abundant and might be looked at by simpletons who couldn't keep watches. He bought an evening paper that shrieked with hydrocephalic headlines and turned into a dingy little restaurant advertising a "Regular Dinner de luxe with Dessert, 35 cts."

There was gloom rather than gusto in his approach to the table. He expected little; everything had gone wrong; and he was not surprised to note that the cloth on the table must also have served that day for a "Business Men's Lunch, 35 cts.," as advertised on a wall placard. Several business men seemed to have eaten there — careless men, their minds perhaps on business while they ate. A moody waiter took his order, feebly affecting to efface all stains from the tablecloth by one magic sweep of an already abused napkin.

Bean read his paper. One shriek among the headlines was for a railroad accident in which twenty-eight lives had been lost. He began to go down the list of names hopefully, but there was not one that he knew. Although he wished no evil to any person, he was yet never able to suppress a strange, perverse thrill of disappointment at this result — that there should be the name of no one he knew in all those lists of the mangled. His food came and he ate, still striving — the game of childhood had become unconscious habit with him now — to make his meat and potatoes "come out even." The dinner de luxe was too palpably a soggy residue of that Business Men's Lunch. It fittingly crowned the afternoon's catastrophes. He turned from it to his paper and Destiny tied another knot on his bonds. There it was in bold print:

COUNTESS CASANOVA
Clairvoyant . . . Clairaudient
Psychometric.
Fresh from Unparalleled European Triumphs.
Answers the Unasked Question.

There was more of it. The Countess had been "prevailed upon by eminent scientists to give a brief series of tests in this city." Evening tests might be had from 8 to 10 P.M. Ring third bell.

The old query came back, the old need to know what he had been before putting on this present very casual body. Was his present state a reward or a penance? From the time of leaving the office to the last item in that sketchy dinner, he had been put upon by persons and circumstances. It was time to know what life meant by him.

And here was one who answered the unasked question!

Precisely at eight he rang the third bell, climbed two flights of narrow stairs and faced a door that opened noiselessly and without visible agency. He entered a small, dimly lighted room and stood there uncertainly. After a moment two heavy curtains parted at the rear of the room and the Countess Casanova stood before him. It could have been no other; her lustrous, heavy-lidded dark eyes swept him soothingly. Her hair was a marvelously piled storm-cloud above a full, well-rounded face. Her complexion was wonderful. One very plump, very white hand rested at the neck of the flowing scarlet robe she wore. A moment she posed thus, beyond doubt a being capable of expounding all wingy mysteries of any soul whatsoever.

Then she became alert and voluble. She took his hat and placed it in the hall, seated him before the table at the room's center and sat confronting him from the other side. She filled her chair. It could be seen that she was no slave to tight lacing.

Although foreign in appearance, the Countess spoke with a singularly pure and homelike American accent. It was the speech he was accustomed to hear in Chicago. It reassured him.

The Countess searched his face with those wonderful eyes.

"You are intensely psychic," she announced.

Bean was aware of this. Every medium he had ever consulted had told him so.

The Countess gazed dreamily above his head.

"Your spiritual aura is clouded by troubled curnts, as it were. I see you meetin' a great loss, but you mus' take heart, for a very powerful hand on the other side is guardin' you night an' day. They tell me your initials is 'B.B.' You are employed somewheres in the daytime. I see a big place with lots of other people employed there —"

The Countess paused. Bean waited in silence.

"Here" — she came out of the clouds that menaced her sitter — "take this pad an' write a question on it. Don't lemme see it, mind! When you got it all wrote out, fold it up tight an' hold it against your forehead. Never leggo of it, not once!"

Bean wrote, secretly, well below the table's edge.

"Who was I in my last incarnation?"

He tore the small sheet from the pad, folded it tightly and, with elbows on the table, pressed it to his brow. If the Countess answered that question, then indeed was she a seer.

She took up the pad from which he had torn the sheet.

"Concentrate," she admonished him. "Let the whole curnt of your magnetism flow into that question. Excuse me! I left the slate in the nex' room. My control will answer you on the slate."

She withdrew between the curtains, but reappeared very soon. Bean was concentrating.

"That'll do," said the Countess. "Here!" She presented him with a double slate and a moist sponge. "Wipe it clean."

He washed the surfaces of the slate and the seer placed it upon the table between them, enclosing within its two sections a tiny fragment of slate pencil. She placed her hands upon the slate and bade her sitter do likewise.

"You often hear skeptics say they is sometimes trickery in this," said the Countess, "but say, listen now, how could it be? I leave it to you, friend. I ain't seen your question; you held it a minute and then put it in your pocket. An' you seen the slate was clean. Now concentrate; go into the Silence!"

Bean went into the Silence without suspicion, believing the Countess would fail. She couldn't know his question and no human power could write on the inside of that slate without detection. He waited with sympathy for the woman who had overestimated her gifts.

Then he was startled by the faintest sound of scratching, as of a pencil on a slate. It seemed to issue from beneath their hands at rest there in plain sight. The medium closed her eyes. Bean waited, his breath quickening. Little nervous crinklings began at the roots of his hair and descended his spine — that scratching, faint, yet vigorous, did it come from beyond the veil?

The scratching ceased. The ensuing silence was portentous.

"Open it and look!" commanded the Countess. And Bean forthwith opened it and looked a little way into his dead and dread past. Apparently upon the very surface he had washed clean were words that seemed to have been hurriedly inscribed:

"The last time you was Napolen Bonopart."

He stared wonderingly at those marks made by no mortal hand. He thrilled with a vast elation; and yet instantly a suspicion formed that here was something to his discredit, something one wouldn't care to have known. He had read as little history as possible, yet there floated in his mind certain random phrases, "A Corsican upstart," "An assassin," "No gentleman!"

"I — I suppose — you're sure there can't be any doubt about this?"

He looked pleadingly at the Countess. But the Countess was a mere psychic instrument, it seemed, and had to be told, first of the question — he produced it with a suspicion that she might doubt his honesty — and then of the astounding answer. Thus enlightened, she protested that there could be no doubt about the truth of the answer; she was ready to stake her professional reputation on its truth. She regarded Bean with an awe which she made no attempt to conceal.

"You had your *day*," she said significantly; "pomps and powers and — and attentions!"

Bean was excitedly piecing together what fragments of data his reading had left him.

"Emperor of France —"

But someone else had rung the third bell, perhaps one of those scientists coming to be dumfounded.

"He was," the Countess replied hurriedly, "the husban' of Mary Antonett, an' they both got arrested and gilletined in the great French revolution."

He was pretty certain that this was incorrect, but the Countess, after all, was a mere instrument of higher intelligence, and she now made no pretence of speaking otherwise than humanly.

"An' my controls say they'll leave me in a body if I take a cent less 'n three dollars."

One of the controls seemed to be looking this very threat or something like it from the medium's sharpened eyes.

Bean paid hastily, thus averting what would have been a calamity to all earnest students of the occult. The advertisement, it is true, had specifically mentioned one dollar as the accustomed honorarium, but this was no time to haggle.

Napoleon!

"Don't furgit the number," urged the Countess, "an' if you got any friends, I'd appreciate —"

"Certainly! Sure thing!" said the palpitating one, and blindly felt his way into the night.

The same stars shone above the city street; the same heedless throng disregarded them; disregarded, too, the slight figure that paused a moment to survey the sky and the world beneath it through a new pair of eyes.

Napoleon!

IV

*H*e walked buoyantly home. He had a room at the top of a house in an uptown cross-street. Having locked his door and lighted a gas-jet he stood a long time before his mirror. It was a friendly young face he saw there, but troubled. The hair was pale, the eyes were pale, the nose small. The mouth was rather fine, cleanly cut and a little feminine. The chin was not a fighter's chin, yet neither chin nor mouth revealed any weakness. He scanned the features eagerly, striving to relate them with vaguely remembered portraits of Napoleon. He was about the same height as the Little Corporal, he seemed to recall, but an eagle boldness was lacking. Did he possess it latently? Could he develop it? He must have books about this possible former self of his. He had early become impatient of written history because when it says sixteen hundred and something it means the seventeenth century. If historians had but agreed to call sixteen hundred and something the sixteenth century, he would have read more of them. It was annoying to have to stop to figure.

Before retiring he went through certain exercises with an unusual vehemence. He was taking a course in jiu-jitsu from a correspondence school. Aforetime he had dreamed of a street encounter, with some blustering bully twice his size, from which, thanks to his skill, he would emerge unscarred, unruffled, perhaps flecking a bit of dust from one slight but muscular shoulder while his antagonist lay screaming with pain.

With the approach of sleep all his half-doubts were swept away. Of course he had been Napoleon. He could almost remember Marengo — or was it Austerlitz? There was a vague but not distressing uncertainty as to which of these conflicts he had directed, but he could — almost — remember.

And he had been one who commanded, and who, therefore, would make nothing of pricing a dog. He would enter that store boldly tomorrow, give its proprietor glare for glare, and demand to be told the price of the creature in the window. Napoleon would have made nothing of it.

*T*he old man came noisily from his back room and again glowered above his spectacles. But this time he faced no weakling who made a subterfuge of undesired goldfish.

Bean gulped once, it is true, before words would come.

"I — uh — what's the price of that dog in the window?"

The old man removed his spectacles, ran a hand through upstanding white hair, and regarded his questioner suspiciously.

"You vant him, hey? Vell, I tell. Fifdy dollars, you bed your life!"

The blood leaped in his veins. He had expected to hear a hundred at least. Still, fifty was a difficult enough sum. He hesitated.

"Er — what's his name?"

"Naboleon."

"*What?*" He could not believe this thing.

"Naboleon. It comes in his bedigree when I giddim. You bed your life I gif him nod such names — robber, killer, Frenchman!"

Bean felt assaulted.

"He was a fighter?"

"Yah, fider — a killer unt a sdealer. You know what?" — his face lightened a little with garrulity — "my granmutter she seen him, yah, sure she seen him, seddin' on his horse when he gone ridin' into Utrecht in eighdeen hunderd fife, with soljus. Sure she seen him; she loogs outer a winda' so she could touch him if she been glose to him, unt a soljus rides oop unt says, 'Ve gamp right here, not?' unt Naboleon he shneer awful unt say, 'Gamp here vere dey go inter dem cellus from der ganal-side unt get unter us unt blow us high wit bowder — you sheep's head! No; we gamp back in der Malibaan vere is old linden drees hunderd years old, eighd rows vun mile long, dere is vere we gamp, you gread fool!' Sure my granmutter seen him. He pull his nose mit t'um unt finger, so! Muddy boods, vun glofe off, seddin' oop sdraighd on a horse. Sure, she seen him. Robber unt big killer-sdealer! She vas olt lady, but she remember it lige it was tomorrow."

Excitement engendered by this reminiscence had well-nigh made Bean forget the dog. Once he had made people afraid. The world had trembled before him. Policemen had been as insects.

"I'll take that dog," he announced royally — then faltered — "but I haven't the money now. You keep him for me till I get it."

"Yah, you know vot? A olt man, lige me, say that same ofer lasd mont' ago, unt I nefer see him until yet!"

It was a time for extreme measures. Bean pressed seven dollars upon the dog's owner.

"And ten dollars every week; maybe more!"

The old man stowed the bills in a pocket under his apron and scratched the head of the parrot that was incisively remarking, "Oh! What a fool!" and giggling fatuously at its own jest.

"I guess you giddim. I guess mebbe you lige him, hey! He iss a awful glutton to eat!"

Napoleon!

And in the street car the first headline he saw in his morning paper was, "Young Napoleon of Finance Flutters Wall Street!"

The thing was getting uncanny.

A Napoleon of Finance!

Something, Napoleonic at least for Bunker Bean, had to be done in finance immediately. He had reached the office penniless. He first tried Bulger, who owed him ten dollars. But this was a Waterloo.

"Too bad, old top!" sympathized Bulger. "If you'd only sejested it yesterday. But you know how it is when a man's out; he's got to make a flash; got to keep up his end."

He considered the others in the office. Most of them, he decided, would, like Bulger, have been keeping their ends up. Of course, there was Breede. But Napoleon at his best would never have tried to borrow money of Breede, not even on the day of his coronation. Tully, the chief clerk, was equally impossible. Tully's thick glasses magnified his eyes so that they were terrible to look at. Tully would reach out a nerveless hand and draw forth the quivering heart of his secret. Tully would know right off that a man could have no respectable reason for borrowing five dollars on Thursday.

There remained old Metzeger who worked silently all day over a set of giant ledgers, interminably beautifying their pages with his meticulous figures. True, Bean had once heard Bulger fail interestingly to borrow five dollars of Metzeger until Saturday noon, but a flash of true Napoleonic genius now enabled him to see precisely why Bulger had not succeeded. Metzeger lived for numerals, for columned digits alone. He carried thousands of them in his head and apparently little else. He could tell to the fraction of a cent what Union Pacific had opened at on any day you chose to name. He had a passion for odd amounts. A flat million as a sum interested him far less than one like $107.69¾. He could remember it longer. It was necessary then to appeal to the poetry in the man.

A long time from across his typewriter he studied old Metzeger, tall, angular, his shoulders lovingly rounded above one of the ledgers, a green shade pulled well over his eyes, perhaps to conceal the too-flagrant love-light that shone there for his figures. Napoleon had won most of his battles in his tent.

Bean arose, moved toward the other and spoke in clear, cool tones.

"Mr. Metzeger, I want to borrow five dollars —"

The old man perceptibly stiffened and bent his head lower.

"— five dollars and eighty-seven cents until Saturday at ten minutes past twelve."

Metzeger looked up, surveying him keenly from under the green shade.

"*How* much?"

"Five eighty-seven."

There was a curious relenting in the sharpened old face. The man had been struck in a vital spot. With his fine-pointed pen he affectionately wrote the figures on a pad: "$5.87 — 12:10." They were ideal; they vanquished him. Slowly he counted out money from various pockets, but the sum was $5.90.

"Bring me the change," he said.

Bean brought it from the clerk who kept the stamp-box. Metzeger replaced three pennies in a pocket, and Bean moved off with the sum he had demanded, feeling almost as once he might have felt after Marengo.

It must be true! He couldn't have done the thing yesterday.

He omitted his visit to the dog that day and loitered for an hour in a second-hand bookshop he had often passed. He remembered it because of a colored print that hung in the window, "The Retreat from Moscow." He had glanced carelessly enough at this, hardly noting who it was that headed the gloomy procession. Now he felt the biting cold, and shivered, though the day was warm. There were pleasanter prints inside. In one, Napoleon with sternly folded arms gazed down at a sleeping sentry. In another he reviewed troops at Fontainebleau, and again, from an eminence, he overlooked a spirited battle, directing it with a masterly wave of his saber. These things were a little disconcerting to one in whom the blood-lust had diminished. He was better pleased with a steel engraving of the coronation, and this he secured for a trifle. It was a thing to nourish an ailing ego, a scene to draw sustenance from when people overwhelmed you in street cars and took your gold watch.

Then there were books about Napoleon, a whole shelf of them. A lot of authors had thought him worth writing about. He examined several volumes. One was full of dreadful caricatures that the English had delighted in. He found this most offensive and closed it quickly. Probably that explained why he had always felt an instinctive antipathy for the English.

"If you're interested in Napoleon things —" said the officious clerk, and Bean went cold. He wondered if the fellow suspected something.

"Not at all, not at all!" he protested, and refused to look at anymore books.

He took his print of the coronation, securely wrapped, and went to another store several blocks away. He could get a Napoleon book there, where they wouldn't be suspicious. He found one that looked promising, "Napoleon, Man and Lover," and still another entitled "The Hundred Days." The latter had illustrations of the tomb, which he noted was in Paris. Its architecture impressed him, and his hands trembled as he held the book open. He had been buried with pomp, even with flamboyance. Robber and killer he might have been, but the picture showed a throng of admiring spectators looking down to where the dead colossus was chested, and on the summit of the dome that rounded above that kingly sarcophagus, a discriminating nation had put the cross of Christ in gold.

Let people say what they would! With all this glory of sepulcher there must be something in the man not to be wholly ashamed of.

And yet "Napoleon, Man and Lover," which he read that night, confirmed his first impression that this strangely uncovered incident in his Karmic past was, on the whole, scandalous; not a thing he would like to have "get about." He sympathized with the poor boy driven from his Corsican home, with the charity student of Brienne, with the young artillery officer, dreaming impossible dreams. But as lover — he blushed for that ruthless dead self of his; the Polish woman, the little actress, sending for them as if they were merchandise. It seemed to him that even the not too-fastidious Bulger would have been offended by such direct brutality.

Well, he was paying dearly for it now; afraid to venture into the presence of a couple of swell dames not invincibly austere, lacking the touch-and-go gallantry of a mere Bulger who had probably never been anybody worth mentioning.

And there was the poor pathetic Louise of Prussia. Bean had already fallen in love with her face, observed in advertisements of the Queen Quality Shoe. He recalled the womanly dignity of the figure descending the shallow steps, the arch accost of the soft eyes, the dimple in the round check. She had been sent to sue him, the invader, to soften him with blandishments. He had kept her waiting like a lackey, then had sought cynically to discover how far her devotion to her country's safety would carry her. And when her pitiful little basket of tricks had been emptied, her little traps sprung, he had sent her back to her husband with a message that crushed her woman's pride and shattered the hopes of her people. He had heard the word "bounder." It seemed to him that Napoleon had shown himself to be just that — a fearful and impossible bounder. He tingled with shame. He wished he might speak to that Queen now as a gentleman would.

And yet he could not read the book without a certain evil quickening. Brutal though his method of approach had been, the man had conquered more than mere force may ever conquer. The Polish woman had come to love him; the little actress would have followed him to his lonely island. Others, too many others, had confessed his power.

He was ashamed of such a past, yet read it with a guilty relish. He recalled the flapper who had so boldly met his glance. He thought she would have been less bold if she could have known the man she looked at. He placed "Napoleon, Man and Lover" at the bottom of his trunk beside the scarlet cravat he had feared to wear. It was not a book to "leave around."

"The Hundred Days," which he read the following night, was a much less discouraging work. It told of defeat, but of how glorious a defeat! The escape from Elba, the landing in France and the march to Paris, conquering, where he passed, by the sheer magnetism of his personality! His spirit bounded as he read of this and of the frightened exit of that puny usurper before the mere rumor of his approach. Then that audacious staking of all on a throw of the dice — Waterloo and a deathless ignominy. He heard the sob-choked voices of the Old Guard as they bade their leader farewell — felt the despairing clasp of their hands!

Alone in his little room, high above the flaring night streets, the timid boy read of the Hundred Days, and thrilled to a fancied memory of them. The breath that checked on his lips, the blood that ran faster in his veins at the recital, went to nourish a body that contained the essential part of that hero — he was reading about himself! He forgot his mean surroundings — and the timidities of spirit that had brought him thus far through life almost with the feelings of a fugitive.

The Lords of Destiny had found him indeed untractable as the great Emperor, the world-figure, and, for his proudness of spirit, had decreed that he should affrightedly tread the earth again as Bunker Bean. Everything pointed to it. Even the golden bees of Napoleon! Were there not three B's in his own name? The shameful truth is that he had been christened "Bunker Bunker Bean." His fond and foolish mother had thus ingenuously sought to placate the two old Uncle Bunkers; unsuccessfully, be it added, for each had affected to believe that he took second place in the name. But the three B's were there; did they not point psychically to the golden bees of the Corsican? Indeed, an astrologist in Chicago had once told him, for a paltry half-dollar, that those B's in his name were of a profoundly mystic significance.

Again, he was of distinguished French origin. Over and over had his worried mother sought to impress this upon him. The family was an old and noble one, fleeing from France, during a Huguenot persecution, to Protestant England where the true name "de Boncoeur" had been corrupted to "Bunker." At the time of his earliest dissatisfaction with the name he had even essayed writing it in the French manner — "B. de Boncoeur Bien" — supposing "Bien" to be approximate French for "Bean."

What more natural than that the freed soul, striving for another body, should have selected one of distinguished French ancestry? The commoner would inevitably seek to become a patrician.

It was a big thing; a thing to dream and wonder and calculate about. When he was puzzled or disturbed he would resort to the shell — a thing he had clung tenaciously to through all the years — sitting before it a long time, his eyes fixed upon it with hypnotic tensity.

What should it mean to him? How was his life to be modified by it? He did not doubt that changes would now ensue. He was already bolder in the public eye. If people stared superciliously at him, he sometimes stared back. That aggressive stout man could not now have bullied him out of his seat in the car with any mere looks.

The phrase "Napoleon of Finance" had stayed in his mind. Modernly the name seemed briefly to suggest someone who made a lot of money out of nothing but audacity. Certainly it was not being applied to soldiers or statesmen. This was interesting. If he made a lot of money he could move to the country and have plenty of room for the dog. And it seemed about the only field of adventure left for this peculiar genius. He began to think about making money. He knew vaguely how this was done: you bought stocks and then waited for the melon to be cut. You got on the inside of things. You were found to have bought up securities that trebled in value over night. Those that decreased in value had been bought by people who were not Napoleons. That was the gist of it. A Napoleonic mind would divine the way. "Napoleon knew human nature like a book," said one of the inspired historians. That was all you needed to know. He resolved to study human nature.

At precisely ten minutes past twelve on the following Saturday he laid upon old Metzeger's desk the exact sum of five dollars and eighty-seven cents. One less gifted as to human nature would have said, "Thank you!" and laid down five dollars and ninety cents. Bean fell into neither trap. Metzeger looked quickly at the clock and silently took the money. He had become the prey of a man who surmised him accurately.

Then occurred one of those familiar tragedies of the wage slave. The whole week long he had looked forward to the ball game. In the box that afternoon would be the Greatest Pitcher the World Had Ever Known. This figure had loomed in his mind that week bigger at times than all his past incarnations. He was going to forego a sight of his dog in order to be early on the ground. He would see the practice and thrill to the first line-up. He had lived over and over that supreme moment when the umpire sweeps the plate with a stubby broom and adjusts his mask.

The correct coat was buttoned and the hat was being adjusted when the door of the inner office opened with a sharp rattle.

"Wantcha!" said Breede.

There was a fateful, trembling moment in which Breede was like to have been blasted; it was as if the magnate had wantonly affronted him who had once been the recipient of a second funeral in Paris. Keeping Bean from a ball game aroused that one-time self of his as perhaps nothing else would have done. But Breede was Breede, after all, and Bean swallowed the hot words that rose to his lips. His perturbation was such, however, that Breede caught something of it.

"Hadjer lunch?"

"No!" said Bean, murderously.

"Gitcha some quick. Hurry!"

He knew the worst now. The afternoon was gone.

"Don't want any!" It was a miniature explosion after the Breede manner.

"C'mon, then!"

He was at the desk and Breede dictated interminably. When pauses came he wrote scathing comments on Breede's attire, his parsimony in the matter of food, his facial defects, and some objectionable characteristics as a human being, now perceived for the first time. He grew careless of concealing his attitude. Once he stared at Breede's detached cuffs with a scorn so malevolent that Breede turned them about on the desk to examine them himself. Bean went white, feeling "ready for anything!" but Breede merely continued his babble about "Federal Express" stock, and "first mortgage refunding 4 percent gold bonds," and multifarious other imbecilities that now filled a darkened world.

He jealously watched the letters Breede answered and laid aside, and the sheaf of reports that he juggled from hand to hand. His hope had been that the session might be brief. There was no clock in the room and he several times felt for the absent watch. Then he tried to estimate the time. When he believed it to be one o'clock he diversified his notes with a swift summary of Breede's character which only the man's bitterest enemies would have approved. At what he thought was two o'clock he stripped him of the last shreds of moral decency. When three o'clock seemed to arrive he did not dare put down, even in secretive shorthand, what he felt could justly be said of Breede. After that it was no good hoping. He relaxed into the dullness of a big despair, merely reflecting that Bulger's picture of Breede under his heel had been too mushily humane. What Bean wished at the moment was to have Breede tied to a stake, and to be carving choice morsels from him with a dull knife. He made the picture vivacious.

At what he judged to be four-thirty a spirited rap sounded on the door.

"C'min," yelled Breede.

Entered the flapper. Breede looked up.

"Seddown! View of efforts bein' made b' cert'n parties t' s'cure 'trol of comp'ny by promise of creatin' stock script on div'dend basis, it is proper f'r d'rectors t' state policy has been —"

The flapper had sat down and was looking intently at Bean. There was no coquetry in the look. It was a look of interest and one wholly in earnest. Bean became aware of it at Breede's first pause. At any other time he would have lowered his eyes before an assault so direct and continuous. Now in his hot rage he included the flapper in the glare he put upon her unconscious father.

He saw that she was truly enough a flapper; not a day over eighteen, he was sure. Not tall; almost "pudgy," with a plump, browned face and grey eyes like old Breede's, that looked through you. He noted these details without enthusiasm. Then he relented a little because of her dress. The shoes — he always looked first at a woman's shoes and lost interest in her if those were not acceptable — were of tan leather and low, with decently high heels. (He loathed common-sense shoes on women.) The hose were of tan silk. So far he approved. She wore a tailored suit of blue and had removed the jacket. The shirtwaist — he knew they were called "lingerie waists" in the windows — was of creamy softness and had the lines of the thing called "style." Her hat was a straw that drooped becomingly. "Some dresser, all right!" he thought, and then, "Why don't she take a look at old Cufflets there, and get him in right?"

Again and again he hardened his gaze upon her. Her eyes always met his, not with any recognition of him as a human being, but with some curious interest that seemed remote yet not impersonal. He indignantly tried to out-stare her, but the thing was simply not to be done. Even looking down at her feet steadily didn't dash her brazenness. She didn't seem to care where *he* looked. After a very few minutes of this he kept his eyes upon his notebook with dignified absorption. But he could feel her glance.

"— to c'nserve investment rep'sented by this stock upon sound basis rather than th' spec'lative policy of larger an' fluc'chating div'dends yours ver' truly what time's 'at game called?"

Thus concluded Breede, with a sudden noisy putting away of papers in an open drawer at his side.

Bean looked up at him, in open-mouthed fear for his sanity.

"Hello, Pops!" said the flapper.

"'Lo, Sis! What time's 'at game called?"

"Three," said Bean, still alarmed.

Breede looked at his watch.

"Jus' got time to make it."

He arose from the desk. Bean arose. The flapper arose.

"Take y' up in car," said Breede, most amazingly.

Bean pulled his collar from about his suddenly constricted throat.

"Letters!" He pointed to the notebook.

"Have 'em ready Monday noon. C'mon! Two-thirty now."

The early hour was as incredible as this social phenomenon.

"Daughter!" said Breede, with half a glance at the flapper, and deeming that he had performed a familiar social rite.

"Pleased to meet you!" said Bean, dazedly. The flapper jerked her head in a double nod.

Of the interval that must have elapsed before he found himself seated in the grandstand between Breede and the flapper he was able to recall but little. It was as if a dense fog shut him in. Once it lifted and he suffered a vision of himself in a swiftly propelled motorcar, beside an absorbed mechanician. He half turned in his seat and met the cool, steady gaze of the flapper; she smiled, but quickly checked herself to resume the stare; he was aware that Breede was at her side. And the fog closed in again. It was too unbelievable.

A bell clanged twice and his brain cleared. He saw the scurry of uniformed figures to the field, the catcher adjusted his mask. The Greatest Pitcher the World Has Ever Known stood nonchalantly in the box, stooped for a handful of earth and with it polluted the fair surface of a new ball. A second later the ball shot over the plate. The batter fanned, the crowd yelled.

All at once Bean was coldly himself. He knew that Breede sat at his right; that on his left was a peculiar young woman. He promptly forgot their identities, and his own as well, and recalled them but seldom during the ensuing game.

It is a phenomenon familiar to most of us. The sons of men, under the magic of that living diamond, are no longer little units of souls jealously on guard. Heart speaks to heart naked and unashamed; they fraternize across deeps that are commonly impassable, thrilling as one man to the genius of the double-play, or with one voice hurling merited insults at a remote and contemptuous umpire. It is only there, on earth, that they love their neighbor. There they are fused, and welded into that perfect whole which is perhaps the only colorable imitation ever to be had on earth of the democracy said to prevail in Heaven.

There was no longer a Bean, a Breede, a flapper. Instead were three merged souls in three volatile bodies, three voices that blended in cheers or execration. At any crisis they instinctively laid gripping hands upon each other and, half-rising, with distended eyes and tense half-voices, besought some panting runner to "Come on! Come *on*, you! Oh, come *on!*" There were other moments of supreme joy when they were blown to their feet and backs were impartially pounded. More than once they might have been observed, with brandishing fists, shouting, "Robber! Robber! *Robber!!!*" at the unperturbed man behind the plate who merely looked at an indicator in his hand and resumed his professional crouch quite as if nothing had happened.

And there were moments of snappy, broken talk, comments on individual players, a raking over the records. It was not Breede who talked to Bean then. It was one freed soul communicating with another. He none too gently put Breede right in the matter of Wagner's batting average for the previous year and the price that had been paid for the new infielder. And Breede in spirit sat meekly at his feet, grateful for his lore.

Of an absent player, Breede said he was too old — all of thirty-five. He'd never come back.

"They come back when they learn to play ball above the ears," retorted Bean with crisp sapience. "How about old Cy Young? How about old Callahan of the Sox? How about Wagner out there — think he's only nineteen — hey? Tell me *that!*"

He looked pityingly at the man of millions thus silenced.

Two men scored from third and second, thanks to a wild throw.

"Inside play, there?" said Breede.

"Inside, nothing!" retorted Bean arrogantly. "Matty couldn't get back to second and they *had* to run. If that Silas up there hadn't gone foamy in the fighting-top and tried to hit that policeman over by the fence with the ball, where'd your inside play been? D'you think the Pirates are trying to help 'em play inside ball? Inside, nothing!"

Again Breede looked respectful, and the flapper listened, lustrous-eyed.

The finish was close. With two men out in the last half of the ninth and two strikes called on the batter, a none too certain single brought in the winning run. The clinging trio shrieked — then dazedly fell apart. Life had gone from the magic. The vast crowd also fell apart to units, flooding to the narrow gates.

Outside Breede looked at Bean as if, faintly puzzled, he was trying to recall the fellow's face. One could fancy him saying, "Prob'ly some chap works in m' office."

Father and daughter entered the car. Bean raised his dented hat. Breede was oblivious; the flapper permitted herself a severe double nod. The motor chugged violently. Bean, moving on a few steps, turned. The flapper was looking back. She stared an instant then most astonishingly smiled, a smile that seemed almost vocal with many glad words. Bean felt himself smile weakly in response.

He walked a long way before he took a car, his eyes on the pavement, his mind filled with a vision. When the flapper smiled it did something to him, but what it was he couldn't tell. She had a different face when she smiled; her parting lips made a new beauty in the world. He thought the golden brown of her hair rather wonderful. It was like the golden brown of the new dog. He recalled little details of her face, the short upper lip, the forward chin, the breadth of the brow. There was something disconcerting about that brow and the eyes like her father's — probably have her own way! Then he remembered that he must have noticed a badge pinned to the left lapel of a jacket that had been fashioned — with no great difficulty, he thought — to give its wearer the appearance of perfect physical development. He couldn't remember when he had precisely noted this badge, perhaps in some frenzied moment in the game's delirium, but it was vividly before him now — "VOTES FOR WOMEN!" What did that signify in her character? Perhaps something not too pleasant.

Still — he lived again through the smile that had seemed to speak.

*T*hree days later, at the close of an afternoon's grinding work, the grim old man at the desk looked up as Bean was leaving the room.

"S'good game!"

"Fine!" said Bean, as he closed the door.

But for this reference and one other circumstance Bean might have supposed that Breede had forgotten the day. The other circumstance was an area of rich yellowish purple on the arm which Breede had madly gripped in moments of ecstasy, together with painful spots on his right side where the elbow of Breede had almost continuously jabbed him.

V

*T*he latest Napoleonic dynasty was tottering. The more Bean read of that possible former self, the less he admired its manifestations. A Corsican upstart, an assassin, no gentleman! It was all too true. Very well, for that vaunted force of will, but to what base ends had it been applied! He was merciless to himself, an egotist and a vulgarian. How it would shock that woman, as yet unidentified, who was one day to be the mother of the world's greatest left-handed pitcher. Take the flapper — impossible, of course, but just as an example — suppose she ever came to know about the Polish woman and the actress, and the others! How she would loathe him! And you couldn't tell what minute it might become known. People were taking an interest in such matters. He wished he had cautioned the Countess Casanova to keep the thing quiet. Probably she had talked.

He must go further into that past of his. Doubtless there were lessons to be drawn from the Napoleonic episode, but just now, when he was all confused, the thing — he put it bluntly — was "pretty raw."

"With Napoleon, to think was to act." So he had read in one chronicle. Very well, he would act. Again he would stand, with fearless eyes, at the portal of the vaulted past.

At eight o'clock that night he once more rang the third bell. He had feared that the Countess Casanova might have returned to European triumphs, but the solicitations of the scientific world were still prevailing.

He stood in the little parlor and again the Countess appeared from behind the heavy curtains, a plump white hand at the throat of her scarlet gown.

He was obliged to recall himself to her, for the Countess began to tell him that his aura was clouded with evil curnts.

"You told me what I was — last time, don't you remember? You know, you said, it was written on the slate what I was —" He could not bring himself to utter the name. But the Countess remembered.

"Sure; perfectly! And what was you wishing to know now?"

She surveyed him with heavy-lidded eyes, a figure of mystery, of secret knowledge.

"I want you to tell me who I was before that — before *him.*"

The Countess blinked her eyes rapidly, as if it hurried calculation.

"And I don't mean *just* before. I want to go 'way back, thousands of years — what I was *first.*" He looked helplessly around the room, then glanced appealingly at the Countess. The flushed and friendly face was troubled.

"Well, I dunno." She pondered, eying her sitter closely. "Of course all things is possible to us, but sometimes the conditions ain't jest right and y'r c'ntrol can't git into rapport with them that has been gone more'n a few years. Now this thing you're after — I don't say it can't be done — f'r money."

"If I learned something good, I wouldn't care anything about the money," he ventured.

The Countess glanced up interestedly.

"That's the way to look at it, friend, but how much you got on you?"

"Twenty-two dollars," confessed Bean succinctly.

"Would you part from twenty, if you was told what you want to know?"

"Yes; I can't stand that other thing any longer."

The Countess narrowed her eyes briefly, then became animated.

"Say, listen here, friend! That's a little more delikit work than I been doin', but they's a party near here — lemme see —" She passed one of the plump white hands over her brow in the throes of recollection. "I think his name is Professor Balthasar. I ain't ever met him, understand what I mean? but they say he's a genuine wonder an' no mistake; tell you anything right off the reel. You set right there and lemme go see if I can't call him up by telephone."

She withdrew between the curtains, behind which she carefully pulled sliding doors. Bean heard the murmur of her voice.

He waited anxiously. His Napoleon self was already fading. If only they would tell him something "good." Little he cared for the twenty dollars. He could get along by borrowing seventeen-seventy-nine from Metzeger. The voice still murmured. Only the well-fitting doors prevented Bean from hearing something that would have been of interest to him.

"That you, Ed?" the Countess was saying. "Listen here. 'Member th' one I told you about, thinks he's the original N.B. — you know who — well he's a repeater; here now wantin' t' know who he was before then, who he was *first* y'understand. An' say, I ain't got the right dope for that an' I want you to get over here quick's you can an' give him about a ten-minute spiel. Wha's that? Well, they's twenty, an' I split with you. But listen here, Ed, I get the idee this party's worth nursin' along. I dunno, something *about* him. That's why I'm tellin' you. I want it done right. Course, I could do enough stallin' muself t' cop the twenty; tell him Julius Caesar or the King of China or somebody, but I ain't got the follow-up, an' you can't tell *how* much he might be good for later. Take my tip: he's a natural born believer. Sure, twenty! All right!"

The doors slid back and the Countess reappeared between the curtains.

"I'm 'fraid I'll have to disappoint you," she began. "The Professer was called out t' give some advice to one the Vandabilts. But I got his private secatary on the wire an' he's gone out to chase him up. We'll haf to wait an' see."

Bean was sorry to be causing this trouble.

"Perhaps I better come another night."

"No, you don't! You set right there!" She seemed to listen to unspoken words, looking far off. "There! My control says he's comin'; he's on the way."

Bean was aghast before this power.

"'Nother thing," pursued the Countess in her normal manner, "keep perfec'ly still when he comes. Don't tip him off what you want. Let him do the talkin'. If he's the real thing he'll know what you want. They say he's a wonder, but what do *we* know about it? Let him prove it!"

Bean felt that he and the Countess were a pair of shrewd skeptics.

The third bell rang and a heavy tread was heard on the stairs. The mere sound of its mounting was impressive. The Countess laid a reminding finger on her lips, as she moved toward the door.

There appeared an elderly man, in a black frockcoat, loose-fitting and not too garishly new, a student's coat rather than a fop's.

"Is this Perfesser Balthasar?" inquired the Countess in her best manner.

"At your service, Madam!" He permitted himself a courtly inclination, conferred upon the Countess a glistening tall hat, and then covered his expansive baldness with a skullcap of silk which he drew from an inner pocket.

"I feared we was discommoding you," ventured the Countess, elegantly apologetic; "your secatary said you was out advisin' one the Vandabilts —"

"A mere trifle in the day's work, Madam!" He brushed it aside with an eloquent hand. "My mission is to serve. You wished to consult me?"

"Not me; but this young gentaman here —"

"Ah!" He turned to face Bean, who had risen, regarding him with serious eyes and twirling a curled moustache meditatively.

"I see, I see! An imprisoned soul seeking the light!" He came nearer to Bean, staring intently, then started with dramatic suddenness as if at an electric shock from concealed wires.

"What is this — what is this — what *is* this?"

Bean backed away defensively. The professor seemed with difficulty to withdraw his fascinated gaze, and turned apologetically to the Countess.

"You will pardon me, Madam, but I must ask you to leave us. My control warns me that I am in the presence of an individuality stronger than my own. His powerful mind is projecting the most vital queries. I shall be compelled to disclose to him matters he would perhaps not wish a third person to overhear. I see a line of mighty rulers, ruthless, red-handed — the past of his soul."

The Countess murmurously withdrew. The two males faced each other.

The professor was a mere sketch of a man, random, rakish, with head aslant and shifty eyes forever dropping away from a questioner's face. He abounded in inhuman angles and impossible lines. It seemed that he must have been rather dashingly done in the first place, then half obliterated and badly mended with fumbling, indecisive touches. His restless hands unceasingly wrung each other as if he had that moment made his own acquaintance and was trying to infuse a false geniality into the meeting.

When he spoke he had a trick of opening his mouth for a word and holding it so, a not overclean forefinger poised above an outheld palm. It seemed to the listener that the word when it came would mean much. His white moustache alone had a well-finished look, curving jauntily upward.

"Sit there!" An authoritative finger pointed Bean to the chair he had lately occupied.

He sat nervously, suffering that peculiar apprehension which physicians and dentists had always inspired.

"Most amazing! Most astounding!" muttered the professor as if to his own ear alone. He sat in a chair facing Bean and regarded him long and intently. At brief intervals his face twitched, his body stiffened, he seemed to writhe in some malign grasp.

Bean gripped the arms of his chair. His tingling nerves were accurately defining his spine. He waited, breathless.

"I see it all," breathed the professor in low, solemn tones, his eyes fixed above Bean's head. "First the pomp and glitter of a throne. You wrench it from a people whose weakness you play upon with a devilish cunning, you ascend to it over the bodies of countless men slain in battle. Power through blood! You are cruel, insatiable, a predatory monster. But retribution comes. You are hurled from your throne. Again you ascend it, but only for a brief time. You fight your last battle; you *lose!* You are captured and taken to a lonely island somewhere far to the south, there to be imprisoned until your death. Afterward I see your body returned to the city that was once your capital. It now lies in a heavy stone coffin. It is in a European city. I can almost hear the name, but not plainly. I cannot get the name under which you ruled. I look into the abyss and the cries of your victims drown it. Horror piles upon horror!"

Bean was leaning forward, tense with excitement, his mouth open. "Yes, that's just the way I felt about it," he murmured.

"But this was only a few paltry years ago, perhaps a hundred. It passes from my view. I am led back, away from it — far back — the cries of those you slaughtered echo but faintly — the scene changes —"

The professor paused. Bean had cowered in his chair, wincing under each blow. He wiped his face and crumpled the moist handkerchief tightly in one hand.

"Perhaps the name may come to me now," continued the professor. "But your superior personality overwhelmed me at first; you are so self-willed, so dominant, so ruthless. The name, the name!" He cried the last words commandingly and snapped his fingers at the delinquent control. "There! I seem to hear —"

"Never mind that name," broke in Bean hastily. "Let it go! I — I don't want to know it. Go on back farther!"

Again the professor's look became trancelike.

"Ah! What a relief to be free from that blood-lust!" He breathed deeply and his eyes rolled far up under their lids.

"What is this? A statesman, still crafty, still the lines of cunning cruelty about the mouth. The city is Venice in the fourteenth century. He is dressed in a richly bejeweled robe and toys with an inlaid dagger. He is plotting the assassination of a Doge —"

"Please get still farther back, can't you?" pleaded Bean.

The seer struggled once more with his control.

"I next see you at the head of a Roman legion, going forth to battle. You are a tyrant, ruling by fear alone, and with your own sword I see you cut off the heads of —"

"Farther back," beseeched the sitter. "I — I've had enough of all that battle and killing. I — I don't *like* it. Go on back to the very first."

Patiently the adept redirected his forces.

"I see a poet. He sings his deathless lay by a roadside in ancient Greece. He is an old man, feeble, blind —"

"Something else," broke in the persistent sitter, resolving not to pay twenty dollars for having been a blind poet.

The professor glanced sharply at him. Perhaps his control did not relish these interruptions. He seemed to suppress words of impatience and began anew.

"Ah! Now I see your very first appearance on this planet. You were born from another as yet unknown to our astronomers. You are now" — he lowered his eyes to the sitter's face — "an Egyptian king."

Detecting no sign of displeasure at this, he continued with refreshed enthusiasm.

"It is thousands of years ago. You are the last king of the pre-dynastic era —"

"What kind of a king — one of those fighters?"

"You are a wise and good king. I see a peaceful realm peopled by contented subjects."

"*That's* what I want to know. Go on; tell me more. Married?"

"Your wife is a princess of rare beauty from — from Mesopotamia. You have three lovely children, two boys and a girl, and your palace on the banks of the Nile is one of the most beautiful and grand palaces ever erected by the hand of man. You are ministered to by slaves, and your councilors of state come to you with their reports. You are tall, handsome and of a most kingly presence. Your personal bravery is unquestioned, you are an adept in all manly sports, but you will not go to war as you very properly detest all violence. For this reason there is little to relate of your reign. It was uneventful and distinguished only by your wise and humane statesmanship —"

"What name?" asked Bean, in low, reverent tones.

"The name — er — the name is — oh, yes, I get it — the name is Ram-tah."

"Can I find him in the histories?"

"You cannot," answered the seer emphatically. "I am probably the only living man that can tell you very much about him."

"When did he — pass on?"

"At the age of eighty-two years. He was deeply mourned by all his people. He had been a king of great strength of character, stern at moments, but ever just. His remains received the treatment customary in those times, and the mummy was interred in the royal sepulcher which is now covered by the sands of the centuries. Anything else?"

Bean was leaning forward in his chair, his eyes lost in that far, glorious past.

"Nothing else, now, I think. If I could see you again some time, I'd like to ask —"

"My mission is to serve," answered the other, caressing the moustache with a deft hand. "Anything I can do for you, anytime, command me."

The Countess appeared from between the curtains.

"Was the conditions right?" she asked.

"They have been, at least *so* far," replied the professor crisply, with a side-glance at Bean who seemed on the point of leaving.

"Say, friend, I guess you're forgetting something, ain't you?" demanded the Countess archly.

And Bean perceived that he had indeed forgotten something. He rectified the oversight with blushing apologies, while the professor inspected the mantel ornaments with an absent air. What was twenty dollars to a king and a sire of kings? He bowed himself from the room.

They listened until the hall door closed.

"There's yours, Ed. You earned it all right, I'll say that. My! don't I wish I was up on that dope."

"You were the wise lady to send for me, Lizzie. You'd have killed him off right here. As it is, he'll come back. He's a clerk somewhere, drawing twenty-five a week or so. He ought to give up at least five of it every week; cigarette money, anyway. Anything loose in the house?"

"They's a couple bottles beer in the icebox. Gee! ain't he good, though! If he only had the roll some has!"

*I*n his little room far up under the hunched shoulders of the house, Bunker Bean sat reviewing his Karmic past. Over parts of it he shuddered. That crafty Venetian plotting to kill, trifling wickedly with the inlaid dagger; the brutal Roman, ruling by fear, cutting off heads! And the blind poet! He would rather be Napoleon than a blind poet, if you came down to that. But the king, wise, humane, handsome, masterly, with a princess of rare beauty from Mesopotamia to be the mother of his three lovely children. That was a dazzling vision to behold, a life sane and proper, abounding in majesty both moral and material.

He sought to live over his long and peaceful but brilliant reign. Then he dwelt on his death and burial. They had made a mummy of him, of course. Somewhere that very night, at that very instant, his lifeless form reposed beneath the desert sands. Perhaps the face had changed but little during the centuries. He, Bunker Bean, lay there in royal robes, hands folded upon his breast, as lamenting subjects had left him.

And what did it mean to him now? He thought he saw. As King Ram-tah he had been *too* peaceful. For all his stern and kingly bearing might he not have been a little timid — afraid of people now and then? And the Karmic law had swept him on and on into lives that demanded violence, the Roman warrior, the Venetian plotter, the Corsican usurper!

He saw that he must have completed one of those vast Karmic cycles. What he had supposed to be timidity was a natural reaction from Napoleonic bravado. Now he had finished the circle and was ready to become again his kingly self, his Ram-tah self — able, reliant, fearless.

He expanded his chest, erected his shoulders and studied himself in the glass: there was undoubted majesty in the glance. He vibrated with some fresh, strange power.

Yes; but what about tomorrow — out in the world? in daylight, passing the policeman on the corner, down at the office? Would he remain a king in the presence of Breede, even in the lesser presence of Bulger, or of old Metzeger from whom he purposed to borrow seventeen dollars and seventy-nine cents? All right about being a king, but how were other people to know it? Well, he would have to make them feel it. He must know it himself, first; then impress it upon them.

But a sense of unreality was creeping back. It was almost better to remember the Napoleon past. There were books about that. He pictured again the dead Ram-tah in trappings of royalty. If he could only *see* himself, and be sure. But that was out of the question. It was no good wishing. After all, he was Bunker Bean, a poor thing who had to fly when Breede growled "Wantcha." He sat at his table, staring moodily into vacancy. He idly speculated about Breede's ragged moustache; he thought it had been blasted and killed by the words Breede spoke. A moment later he was conscious that he stared at an unopened letter on the table before him.

He took it up without interest, perceiving that it came from his Aunt Clara in Chicago. She would ask if he had yet joined the Y.M.C.A., and warn him to be careful about changing his flannels.

"Dear Bunker" [it began],

"My own dear husband passed to his final rest last Thursday at 5 p.m. He was cheerful to the last and did not seem to suffer much. The funeral was on Saturday and was very beautiful and impressive. I did not notify you at the time as I was afraid the shock would affect you injuriously and that you might be tempted to make the long trip here to be with me. Now that you know it is all over, you can take it peacefully, as I am already doing. The life-insurance people were very nice about it and paid the claim promptly. I enclose the money which wipes out all but —"

He opened the double sheet. There were many more of the closely written lines, but he read no farther, for a check was folded there. His trembling fingers pulled the ends apart and his astounded eyes rested on its ornate face.

It was for ten thousand dollars.

*A*t six minutes after eight the following evening the Countess Casanova, moved from her professional calm, hurriedly closed the sliding doors between the two rooms of her apartment and sprang to the telephone where she frantically demanded a number. The delay seemed interminable to her, but at last she began to speak.

"That you, Ed? F'r God's sake, beat it over here quick. That boob las' night is back here an' *he's got it.* I dunno — but something *big,* I tell you. He's actin' like a crazy man. Listen here! He wants t' know can you *locate* it — see it lyin' there underground. Why, the mummy; yes. M-u-m-m-i-e. Yes, sure! He's afraid mebbe they already dug him up an' got him in a musée somewheres, but if it's still there he wants it. Yes, sure thing, dontchu un'stand? *Wants* it! How in — how can I tell? That's up to you. Git here! Sure — fifty-fifty!"

Bean glanced up feverishly as the Countess reappeared. She was smoothing her hair and readjusting the set of the scarlet wrapper. Her own excitement was apparent.

"It's all right. I think he'll come, but it was a close call. He was jes' packin' his grip f'r Wash'n'ton. Got a telegraph from the Pres'dent today t' come at once. Of course he'll miss a big fee. The Pres'dent don't care f'r money when it's a question of gittin' th' right advice —"

"Oh, money!" murmured Bean, and waved a contemptuous hand.

His manner was not lost upon his hearer.

"Lots of money made in a hurry, these days," she suggested, "or got hold of some way — gits left to parties — thousand dollars, mebbe — two, three, four thousand?"

Again he performed the pushing gesture, as if he were discommoded by money. He scarcely heard her voice.

The Countess did not venture another effort to appraise his wealth. She fell silent, watching him. Bean gazed at a clean square on the wall-paper where a picture had once hung. Then the authoritative tread was again heard on the stairway, and again the Countess Casanova welcomed Professor Balthasar to her apartment. She expressed a polite regret for having annoyed him.

Professor Balthasar bestowed his shiny hat upon her, enveloped his equally shiny skull with the silken cap and assured her that his mission was to serve. Bean had not risen. He still stared at the wall.

"I'll jes' leave you alone with our friend here," said the Countess charmingly. The professor questioned her with a glance and she shook her head in response, yet her gesture as she vanished through the curtains was one of large encouragement.

The professor faced Bean and coughed slightly. Bean diverted his stare to the professor and seemed about to speak, but the other silenced him with a commanding forefinger.

"Not a word! I see it all. You impose your tremendous will upon me."

He took the chair facing Bean and began swiftly:

"I see the path over the desert. I stop beside a temple. Sand is all about. Beneath that temple is a stone sarcophagus. Within it lies the body of King Tam-rah —"

"Ram-tah!" corrected Bean gently.

"Did I not say Ram-tah?" pursued the seer. "There it has lain sealed for centuries, while all about it the tombs of other kings have been despoiled by curiosity hunters looking for objects of interest to place in their cabinets. But Ram-tah, last king of the pre-dynastic period, though others will tell you differently, but that's because he never got into history much, by reason of his uniformly gentlemanly conduct. He rests there today precisely as he was put. I see it all; I penetrate the heaped sands. At this moment the moon shines upon the spot, and a night bird is calling to its mate in the mulberry tree near the northeast corner of the temple. I see it all. I am there! What is this? What is this I get from you, my young friend?"

The professor seemed to cock a psychic ear toward Bean.

"You want — ah, yes, I see what you want, but that, of course, humanly, would be impossible. Oh, quite impossible, quite, quite!"

"*Why*, if you're sure it's there?"

"My dear sir, you descend to the material world. I will talk to you now as one practical man to another. Simply because it would take more money than you can afford. The thing is practicable but too expensive."

"How do you know?"

"It is true, I do not know. My control warned me when I came here that your circumstances had been suddenly bettered. I withdraw the words. I do not know, but — you will pardon the bluntness — *can* you afford it?"

"What'd it cost? That's what I want to know."

"Hum!" said the professor. He was unable to achieve more for a little time. He hum'd again.

"There's the labor and the risk," he ventured at last. "Of course my agents at Cairo — I have secret agents in every city on the globe — could proceed to the spot from my carefully worded directions. They could do the work of excavating. So far, so good! But they would have to work quietly and would be punished if discovered. Of course here and there they could bribe. Naturally, they would have to bribe, and that, as you are doubtless aware, requires money. Again, entering this port the custom-house officials would have to be bribed, and they've gone up in price the last few years. My control tells me that this mummy is one they've been looking hard for. It's about the only one they haven't found. The loss will be discovered and my men might be traced. It requires an enormous sum. Now, for instance, a thousand dollars" — he regarded Bean closely and was reassured — "a thousand dollars wouldn't anymore than start the work. Two thousand" — his eyes were steadily upon Bean now — "would further it some. Three thousand might see it pretty well advanced. Four thousand, of course, would help still farther and five thousand" — he had seen the shadow of dismay creep over the face of his sitter — "five thousand, I *think*, might put the thing through."

Bean drew a long breath. The professor had correctly read the change in his face at "five thousand," but it had been a sudden fear that his whole ten thousand was not going to suffice for this prodigious operation.

"I can afford that," said Bean shortly. He hardly dared trust himself to say more. His emotion threatened to overcome him.

The professor suffered from the same danger. He, too, dared trust himself to say no more than the few necessary words.

"There must be a payment down," he said with forced coldness.

"How much?"

"A thousand wouldn't be any too much."

"Enough?"

"Well, perhaps not enough," the professor nerved himself to admit.

"I'll give you two, now. Give you the rest when you get — when you get It here."

"You move me, I confess," conceded the professor. "I will undertake it."

"How long will it be, do you think?"

"I shall give orders by cable. A month, possibly, if all goes well."

"I'll give you check." He gulped at that. It was the first time he had ever used the words.

The Countess parted the curtains. Curiously enough she carried a pen and ink, though no one remarked upon the circumstance.

Bean had that morning left a carefully written signature at the bank where his draft had been deposited. He later wondered how the scrawl he achieved now could ever be identified as by the same hand.

And he was conscious, even as he wrote, that the Countess Casanova and Professor Balthasar were laboring under an excitement equal to his own. It *was* a big feat to attempt.

As before, they waited until he had closed the lower door.

"Oh, Ed!" breathed the Countess emotionally.

"Anything loose in the house?" asked the professor.

"They's a couple bottles beer in the icebox, but *Oh, Ed!*"

VI

*A*gain we chant pregnant phrases from the Bard of Dress: "It is cut to give the wearer the appearance of perfect physical development. And the effect produced so improves his form that he unconsciously strives to attain the appearance which the garment gives him; he expands his chest, draws in his waist, and stands erect."

A psychologist, that Bard! acutely divining a basic law of this absurd human nature. In a beggar's rags few men could be more than beggars. In kingly robes, most men could be kings; could achieve the finished and fearless behavior that is said to distinguish royalty.

Bunker Bean, the divinely credulous, now daily arrayed himself in royal vestures, set a well-fashioned crown upon the brow of him and strode forth, scepter in hand. Invisible were these trappings, to be sure; he was still no marked man in a city street. But at least they were there to his own truth-lit eyes, and he most truly did "expand his chest, draw in his waist, and stand erect." Yea, in the full gaze of inhumanly large policemen would he do these things.

This, indeed, was one of the first prerogatives his royalty claimed. He discovered that it was not necessary for any but criminals to fear policemen. It might still be true that an honest man of moderate physique and tender sensibilities could not pass one without slight tremors of self-consciousness; but by such they were — a most prodigious thought — to be regarded as one's paid employees; within the law one might even greet them pleasantly in passing, and be answered civilly. Bean was now equal to approaching one and saying, "Good evening, Officer!" He would sometimes cross a street merely to perform this apparently barren rite. It stiffened his spine. It helped him to realize that he had indeed been a king and the sire of kings; that kingly stuff was in him.

So marked an advance in his spirit was not made in a day, however. It came only after long dwelling in thought upon his splendid past. And, too, after he had envisioned the circumstance that he was now a man of means. The latter was not less difficult of realization than his kingship. He had thought little about money, save at destitute moments; had dreamed of riches as a vague, rather pleasant and not important possibility. But kings were rich; no sooner had his kingship been proclaimed than money was in his hand. And, of course, more money would come to him, as it had once come on the banks of the Nile. He did not question how nor whence. He only knew.

It was three days before he bethought himself to finish the reading of Aunt Clara's letter, suspended at sight of the astounding enclosure. He had begun that letter a harried and trivial unit of the toiling masses. He came to finish it a complacent and lordly figure!

"— I enclose the check which wipes out all but $7,000 of that money from your dear mother with which dearest Edward so rashly speculated years ago, in the hope of making you a wealthy man. I am happy to say that $5,000 of this I can pay at once out of the money I have saved. I have been investing for years, as I could spare it, in the stock of the Federal Express Company, and now have fifty shares, which I will transfer to you at par, though they are quoted a little above that, if you are willing to accept them. The balance I will pay when I have sold the house and furnishings, as with my dearest husband gone I no longer have any incentive to keep on working. I am tired. It is a good safe stock paying 4½ percent and I would advise you to keep it and also put the Ins. money into the same stock. A very nice man in the Life Ins. office said it ought to pay more if the business was better managed. If you turned your talents to the express business you might learn to manage it yourself because you always had a fine head for such things, and by owning a lot of their stock you could get the other stockholders to elect you to be one of their directors, which would be a fine occupation for you, not too hard work and plenty of time to read good books which I hope you find same now of evenings in place of frittering away your time with associations of a questionable character, and ruining your health by late hours and other dissipation though I know you were always of good habits.

> "Affectionately,
> "Aunt Clara.

"P.S. — It has rained hard for two days."

There it was! Money *came* to you. Federal Express was only a name to him; he had written it sometimes at Breede's dictation. But his Aunt Clara was old enough to know about such things, and he would follow her advice, though being a director of an express company seemed as unexciting as it was doubtless respectable: what he had at times been wild enough to dream was that he should be the principal owner of a major-league baseball club, and travel with the club — see every game! If he should, temporarily, become the director of an express company, he would have it plainly understood that he might resign at any moment.

Night and morning he surveyed himself in the glass. Not in the way of ordinary human conceit; he was clear sighted enough as to the pulchritude of his present encasement; but with the eyes of the young who see visions. Raptly scrutinizing his meager form he chanted a line of verse that seemed apposite:

"Build thou more stately mansions, O my soul!"

He was already persuaded that his next incarnation would enrich the world with something far more stately than the mansion that he at present occupied; something on the Gordon Dane order, he suspected. And it was not too soon to begin laying those unseen foundations — to think the thought that must come before the thing. He was veritably a king, yet for a time must he masquerade as a wage-slave, a serf to Breede, and an inferior of Bulger's, considered as a mere spectacle.

He began to word long conversations with these two; noiseless conversations, be it understood, in which the snappy dialogue went unuttered. His sarcasm to Bulger in the matter of that ten-dollar loan was biting, ruthless, witty, invariably leaving the debtor in direst confusion with nothing to retort. Bean always had the last word, both with Bulger and Breede, turning from them with easy contempt.

He was less hard on Breede than on Bulger, because of the ball game. A man who could behave like that in the presence of baseball must have good in him. Nevertheless, in this silent way, he curtly apprised Breede of his intentions about working beyond stipulated hours, and when Breede was rash enough to adopt a tone of bluster, Bean silenced him with a magnificent "I can imagine nothing of less consequence!"

He carried this silent warfare into public conveyances and when stout aggressive men glared at him because he had a seat he quickly and wittily reduced them to such absurdity in the public eye that they had to flee in impotent rage. The once modest street row with a bully twice his size was enlarged in cast. There were now, as befitted a king, two bullies, who writhed in pain, each with a broken arm, while the slight but muscular youth with a knowledge of jiu-jitsu walked coolly off, flecking dust from one of his capable shoulders. Sometimes he paused long enough to explain the affair, in a few dignified words, to an admiring policeman who found it difficult to believe that this stripling had vanquished two such powerful brutes. Sometimes another act was staged in which he conferred his card upon the amazed policeman and later explained the finesse of his science to him, thereby winning his deathless gratitude. He became quite chummy with this officer and was never to be afraid of anything anymore.

He glowed from this new exercise. He became more witty, more masterful, while the repartee of his adversaries sank to wretched piffle. He met disaster only once. That was when his conscience began to hurt him after a particularly bitter assault on Bulger in which the latter had been more than usually contemptible in the matter of the overdue debt. He felt that he had really been too hard on the fellow. And Bulger, who must have been psychically gifted himself, came over from his typewriter at that moment and borrowed an additional five without difficulty. In later justification, Bean reflected that he would almost certainly have refused this second loan had it not been for his softened mood of the moment. Still he was glad that, with his instinctive secrecy he had kept from Bulger any knowledge of his new fortune. With Bulger aware that he had thousands of dollars in the bank, something told him that distressing complications would have ensued.

He debated several days about this money. He resolved, at length, that a thousand dollars should be devoted to the worthy purpose of living up to his new condition. A thousand dollars would, for the present, give him an adequate sensation of wealth. Three thousand more must be paid to Professor Balthasar when his secret agents brought It from Its long-hidden resting-place. Suppose the professor pleaded unexpected outlays, officials not too easily bribed or something, and demanded a further sum? At once, in a crowded street, he brought about a heated interview with the professor, in which the seer was told that a bargain was a bargain, and that if he had thought Bean was a man to stand nonsense of any sort he was indeed wildly mistaken. Bean was going to hold him to the exact sum, and his parting sting was that the professor had better get a new lot of controls if his old ones hadn't been able to tell him this. After he had cooled a little he reflected that if there were really any small sums the professor would be out of pocket, he would of course not be mean.

This left him four thousand dollars with which to buy his way into the directorate of that express company, as suggested by Aunt Clara. He had learned a great deal about buying stocks. He knew there was a method called "buying on a margin" which was greatly superior to buying the shares outright: you received a great many more shares for a given sum. Therefore he would buy thus, and the sooner be a director. He liked to think of that position in his moments of lesser exaltation. He recalled his child-self sitting beside his father on the seat of an express wagon. It was queer how life turned out — sometimes you couldn't get away from a thing. Maybe he would always be a director; still he could go into baseball, too.

He did his business with the broker without a twinge of his old timidity. Indeed, he was rather bored by the affair. The broker took his money and later in the day he learned that he controlled a very large number of the shares of the Federal Express Company. He forgot how many, but he knew it was a number befitting his new dignity. Having done this much he thought the directorship could wait. Let them come to him if they wanted him. He had other affairs on.

There was the new dog.

It was not the least of many great days in Bean's life, that golden afternoon when he sped to the bird-and-animal store and paid the last installment of Napoleon's ransom. The creature greeted him joyously as of yore through the wall of glass, frantically essaying to lick the hand that was so close and yet so unaccountably withheld.

The money passed, and one dream, at least, had been made to come true. For the first time he was in actual contact with the wonderful animal.

"He knows me," said Bean, as the dog hurled itself delightedly upon him. "We've been friends a long time. I think he got so he expected me every afternoon."

Napoleon barked emphatically in confirmation of this. He seemed to be saying: "Hurry! Let's get out of here before he puts me back in that window!"

The old man confessed that he would miss the little fellow. He advised Bean to call him "Nap." "Napoleon" was no right name for a dog of any character.

"You know what that fellow been if he been here now," he volunteered at parting. "I dell you, you bed your life! He been a gompanion unt partner in full with that great American train-robber, Chessie Chames. Sure he would. My grantmutter she seen him like she could maybe reach out a finger unt touch him!"

"I'll call him Nap," promised Bean. He had ceased to feel blamable for the shortcomings of Napoleon I, but it was just as well not to have the name used too freely.

When he issued to the street, the excited dog on a leash, he was prouder than most kings have ever had occasion to be.

Now, he went to inspect flats. He would at last have "apartments," and in a neighborhood suitable for a growing dog. He bestowed little attention on the premises submitted to his view, occupying himself chiefly with observing the effect of his dog on the various janitors. Some were frankly hostile; some covertly so. Some didn't mind dogs — but there was rules. And some defeated themselves by a display of overenthusiasm that manifestly veiled indifference, or perhaps downright dislike.

But a janitor was finally encountered who met the test. In ten seconds Bean knew that Cassidy would be a friend to any dog. He did not fawn upon the animal nor explode with praise. He merely bestowed a glance or two upon the distinguished head, and later rubbed the head expertly just back of the erect ears; this, while he exposed to Bean the circumstances under which one steam-heated apartment, suitable for light housekeeping, chanced to be vacant. The parties, it appeared, was givin' a Dutch lunch to a gang of their friends at 5 A.M. of a morning, and that was bad enough in a place that was well kep' up; but in the sicin' place they got scrappin', which had swiftly resulted in an ambulance call for the host and lessee, and the patrol wagon for his friends that were not in much better shape themselves, praise Gawd. But the place was all cleaned up again and would be a jool f'r anny young man that could take a drink, or maybe two, and then stop.

Bean knew Cassidy by that time, and his inspection of the apartment was perfunctory. Cassidy would be a buckler and shield to the dog, in his absence. Cassidy would love him. The dog, on his spread forefeet, touched his chest to the ground and with ears erect, eyes agleam, and inciting soprano gurgles invited the world to a mad, mad, game.

Cassidy only said, "Aw, g'wan! *Would* you, now!" But each word was a caress. And Cassidy became Bean's janitor.

He moved the next day, bringing his effects in a cab. The cabman professed never to have seen a dog as "classy" as Nap, and voiced the cheerful prophecy that in any bench show he would make them all look like mutts. He received a gratuity of fifty cents in addition to the outrageous fee he demanded for coming so far north, although he had the appearance of one who uses liquor to excess, and could probably not have qualified as a judge of dogs.

Bean's installation, under the guidance of Cassidy, was effected without delay. The apartment proved to be entirely suitable for a king in abeyance. There was a bedroom, a parlor, an alcove off the latter that Cassidy said was the libr'y an' a good place f'r a dawg t' sleep, and beyond this was a feminine diminutive of a kitchen, prettily called a "kitchen-ette."

Bean felt like an insect in such a labyrinth of a place. He forgot where he put things, and then, overcome by the vastness and number of rooms, forgot what he was looking for, losing himself in an abstracted and fruitless survey of the walls. He must buy things to hang on the walls, especially over certain stains on the wall of the parlor, or throne-room, to which in the heat of battle, doubtless, certain items of the late Dutch lunch had been misdirected.

But he knew what to buy. Etchings. In the magazine stories he read, aside from the very rich characters who had galleries of old masters, there were two classes: one without taste that littered its rooms with expensive but ill-advised bric-à-brac; and one that wisely contented itself with "a few good etchings." He bought a few good etchings at a department store for $1.97 each, and felt irreproachable. And when he had arranged his books — about Napoleon I and ancient Egypt — he was ready to play the game of living. Mrs. Cassidy "did" his rooms, and

Cassidy already showed the devotion of an old and tried retainer. The Cassidys made him feel feudal.

At night, while Nap fought a never-decided battle with a sofa-pillow, or curled asleep on the couch with a half-inch of silly pink tongue projecting from between his teeth, he read of Egypt, the black land, where had been the first great people of the ancient world. He devoured the fruit of the lotus, the tamarisk, the pomegranate, and held cats to be sacred. (Funny, that feeling he had always had about cats — afraid of them even in childhood — it had survived in his being!) There he had lived and reigned in that flat valley of the Nile, between borders of low mountains, until his name had been put down in the book of the dead, and he had gone for a time to the hall of Osiris.

Or, perhaps, he read reports of psychical societies, signed by men with any number of capital letters after their names: cool-headed scientists, university professors, psychologists, grave students all, who were constantly finding new and wonderful mediums, and achieving communication with the disembodied. He could tell them a few things; only, of course, he wouldn't make a fool of himself. He could *show* them something, too, when the secret agents of Professor Balthasar came bringing It.

Or he looked into the opal depths of his shell, and saw visions of his greatness to come, while Nap, unregarded, wrenched away one of his slippers and pretended to find it something alive and formidable, to be growled at and shaken and savagely macerated.

*T*here came, on a certain fair morning, a summons from Breede, who was detained at his country place by the same malady that Bulger had once so crudely diagnosed. Bean was to bring out the mail and do his work there. The car waited below.

At another time the expedition might have attracted him. He had studied pictures of that country place in the Sunday papers. Now it meant a separation from his dog, who was already betraying for the Cassidys a greater fondness than the circumstances justified; and it meant an absence from town at the very time when the secret agents might happen along with It. Of course he could refuse to go, but that would cost him his job, and he was not yet even the director of an express company. Dejectedly he prepared for the journey.

"Better take some things along," suggested Tully, who had conveyed the order to him. "He may keep you three or four days."

Bulger followed him to the hall.

"Look out for Grandma, the Demon!" warned Bulger. "'F I was the old man I'd slip something in her tea."

"Who — who is she?" demanded Bean.

"Just his dear, sweet old mother, that's all! Talk you to death — suffergette! Oh! say!"

Reaching the street, his gloom was not at all lightened by the discovery of the flapper in the waiting car. She gave him the little double-nod and regarded him with that peculiar steely kindness he so well remembered. It was undoubtedly kind, that look, yet there was an implacable something in its quality that dismayed him. He wondered what she exactly meant by it.

"Get in," commanded the flapper, and Bean got in.

"Tell him where to go for your things."

Bean told him.

"I'm glad it's on our way. Pops is in an awful state. He swore right out at his own mother this morning, and he wants you there in a hurry. Maybe we'll be arrested for speeding."

Bean earnestly hoped they would. Pops in health was ordeal enough. But he remained silent, trusting to the vigilance of an excellent constabulary. The car reached the steam-heated apartment without adventure, however, and he quickly secured his suit-case and consigned the dog for an uncertain period to a Cassidy, who was brazenly taking more than a friendly interest in him. Cassidy talked bluntly of how "we" ought to feed him, as if he were already a part owner of the animal.

The car flew on, increasing a speed that had been unlawful almost from the start. He wondered what the police were about. He might write a sharp letter to the newspapers, signed, "Indignant Pedestrian," only it would be too late. He was being volleyed at the rate of thirty-five miles an hour into the presence of a man who had that morning sworn at his mother. He wished he could, say for one day, have Breede back there on the banks of the Nile — set him to work building a pyramid, or weeding the lotus patch, foot or *no* foot! He'd show him!

He switched this resentment to the young female at his side. He wanted her to quit looking at him that way. It made him nervous. But a muffled glance or two at her disarmed this feeling. She was all right to look at, he thought, had pretty hands and "all that" — she had stripped off her gloves when they reached the open country — and she didn't talk, which was what he most feared in her sex. He recalled that she had said hardly a word since the start. He might have supposed himself forgotten had it not been for that look of veiled determination which he encountered as often as he dared.

A young dog dashed from a gateway ahead of them and threatened the car furiously. They both applied imaginary brakes to the car with feet and hands and taut nerves. The puppy escaping death by an inch, trotted back to his saved home with an air that comes from duty well performed. They looked from the dog to each other.

"I'd make them against the law," said Bean.

"How could you? The idea!"

"I mean motors, not dogs."

"Oh! Of course!"

They had been brought a little together.

"You go in for dogs?" asked the flapper.

He hesitated. "Going in" for dogs seemed to mean more. "I've got only one just now," he confessed.

Wooded hills flew by them, the white road flickered forward to their wheels.

"You interested in the movement?" demanded the flapper again.

"Yes," he said.

"Granny will be delighted to know that. So many young men aren't."

"What make is it?" he inquired, preparing to look enlightened when told the name of the vehicle in which they rode.

"Oh, I mean the Movement — *the* movement!"

"Oh, yes," he faltered. "Greatly interested!" He remembered the badge on her jacket, and Bulger's warning about Grandma, the Demon.

"Granny and I marched in the parade this year, clear down to Washington Square. If she wasn't so old we'd both run over to London and get arrested in the Strand for breaking windows."

Bean shuddered.

"We're making our flag now for the next parade — big blue cloth with a gold star for every state that has raised woman from her degradation by giving her a vote."

He shuddered again. Although of legal years for the franchise, he had never voted. If you tried to vote some ward-heeler would challenge you and you'd like as not be hauled off to the lock-up. And what was the good of it! The politicians got what they wanted. But this he kept to himself.

"Granny'll put a badge on you," promised the flapper. "We have to take advantage of every little means."

He was still puzzling over this when they turned through a gateway, imposing with its tangle of wrought iron and gilt, and at a decorously reduced speed crinkled up a wide drive to the vast pile of grey stone that housed the un-filial Breede.

A taller and, Bean thought, a prettier girl than the flapper stepped aside for them, looking at Bean as they passed. One could read her look as one could not read the flapper's. It was outrageously languishing.

"Flirts with everyone, makes no difference *who!*" explained the flapper with a venomous sniff.

Bean laughed uneasily.

"She's my own dear sister, and I love her, but she's a perfect cat!"

Bean made deprecating sounds with his lips.

"I suppose people have been wondering where I was," confessed the flapper as they descended upon the granite steps. "I forgot to tell them I was going. Better hurry to Pops or he'll be murdering someone."

A man took his bag and preceded him into the big hall.

"Engaged, too!" called the flapper bitterly.

He found Breede imprisoned in a large, light room that looked to the west. Below the windows a green hill fell sheerly away to the bank of a lordly river, and beyond rose other hills that shimmered in the haze. A light breeze fluttered the gaily striped awnings. Breede, at a desk, turned his back upon the fair scene and fumed.

"Take letter G.M. Watkins, Pres'den I 'n' N.C. Rai'way," began Breede as Bean entered the room. "Dear sir repline yours of 23d instan' would say Ouch! damn that foot don't take that regardin' traffic 'greement now'n 'fect that 'casion may rise 'n near future to 'mend same in 'cordance with stip'lations inform'ly made at conf'rence held las' Janwary will not'fy you 'n due time 'f change is made yours very truly have some lunch brought here 'n a minute may haf' t' stay three four days t'll this Whoo! damn foot gets well take letter H.J. Hobbs secon' 'sistant vice Pres'den' D. 'n' L.S. Rai'way New York, New York, dear Hobbs mark it pers'nal repline yours even date stock purchases goin' forward as rapidly's thought wise under circumstances it is held mos'ly 'n small lots an' too active a market might give rise t' silly notions about it —"

The day's work was on, familiar enough, with the exception of Breede's interjections; he spoke words many times that were not to be "taken down." And yet Bean forebore to record his wonted criticisms of his employer's dress. There was ground for them. Breede had never looked less the advanced dresser. But Bean's mind was busy with that older sister, she of the marvelously drooping eyes. He had recognized her at once as the ideal person with whom to be wrecked on a desert island. A flirt, and engaged, too, was she? No matter. He wrecked himself with her, and they lived on mussels and edible roots and berries, and some canned stuff from the ship, and he built a hut of "native thatch," and found a deposit of rubies, gathering bushels of them, and he became her affianced the very day the smoke of the rescuing steamer blackened the horizon. And throughout an idyllic union they always thought rather regretfully of that island; they had had such a beautiful time there. And his oldest son, who was left-handed, pitched a ball that was the despair of every batter in both leagues!

Such had been the devastation of that one drooping glance. This vision, enjoyed while he ate of the luncheon brought to him, might have been prolonged. He hadn't remembered a quarter of the delightful contingencies that arise when the right man and woman are wrecked on an island, but he looked up from his plate to find Breede regarding him and his abundant food with a look of such stony malignance that he could eat no more — Breede with his glass of diluted milk and one intensely hygienic cracker!

But during pauses in the afternoon's work the island vision became blurred by the singular energies of the flapper. What did she mean by looking at him that way? There was something ominous about it. He had to admit that in some occult way she benumbed his will power. He did not believe he would dare be wrecked on a desert island with the other one, if the flapper knew about it.

At last there was surcease of Breede.

"Have 'em ready in the morning," he directed, referring to the letters he had dictated. "G'wout 'n' 'muse yourself when you get time," he added hospitably. "Now I got to hobble to my room. If you see any women outside, tell 'em g'wan downstairs if they don't want to hear me."

He stood balanced on one foot, a stout cane in either hand. Bean opened the door, but the hall was vacant. Breede grunted and began his progress. It was, perhaps, not more than reasonably vocal considering his provocation.

Bean uncovered a typewriter and sat to it, his notebook before him. For a moment he reverted to the island vision. They could be attacked by savages from another island, and he would fight them off with the rifles he had salvaged from the ship. *She* would reload the weapons for him, and bind up his head when he was wounded. He fought the last half of the desperate battle with a stained bandage over his brow.

There was a sharp rap at the door and it opened before he could call. The flapper entered.

"Don't let me disturb you," she said, and walked to the window, as if she found the place only scenically interesting.

Bean murmured politely and began upon his letters. The flapper was relentless. She sat in her father's chair and fastened the old look of implacable kindness upon him. He beat the keys of the machine. The flapper was disturbing him atrociously.

A few moments later another rap sounded on the door, and again it opened before he could call. A shrewd-looking, rather trim old lady with carefully coiffed hair stood in the doorway.

"Don't let me disturb you," she said, and again Bean murmured.

"Mr. Bean, my grandmother," said the flapper.

"Keep right on with your work, young man," said the old lady in commanding tones, when Bean had acknowledged the presentation. "I like to watch it."

She sat in another chair, very straight in her lavender dress, and joined with the flapper in her survey of the wage-slave. This was undoubtedly Grandma, the Demon.

Bean continued his work, thinking as best he could above the words of Breede, that she must be a pretty raw old party, going around, voting, smashing windows, leading her innocent young grandchild into the same reckless life. Nice thing, that! He was not surprised when he heard a match lighted a moment later, and knew that Grandma was smoking a cigarette. Expect anything of *that* sort!

He had wished they would go before he finished the last letter, but they sat on, and Grandma filled the room with smoke.

"Now he's through!" proclaimed the flapper.

"How old are you?" asked Grandma, as Bean arose nervously from the machine.

He tried jauntily to make it appear that he must "count up."

"Let me see. I'm — twenty-three last Tuesday."

The old lady nodded approvingly, as if this were something to his credit.

"Got any vicious habits?"

Bean weakly began an answer intended to be facetious, and yet leave much to be inferred regarding his habits. But the Demon would have none of this.

"Smoke?"

"No!"

"Drink?"

"No!" He desperately wondered if she would know where to stop.

"How's your health? Ever been sick much?"

"I can't remember. I had lumbago when I was seven."

"Humph! Gamble, play cards, bet on races, go around raising cain with a lot of young devils at night?"

"No, I don't," said Bean, with a hint of sullen defiance. He wanted to add: "And I don't go round voting and breaking windows, either," but he was not equal to this.

"Well, I don't know —" She deliberated, adjusting one of her many puffs of grey hair, and gazing dreamily at a thread of smoke that ascended from her cigarette. She seemed to be wondering whether or not she ought to let him off this time. "Well, I don't know. It looks to me as if you were too good to be true."

She rose and tossed her cigarette out of the window. He thought he was freed, but at the door she turned suddenly upon him once more.

"What in time *have* you done? Haven't you ever had any fun?"

But she waited for no answer.

"I knew she'd admire you," said the flapper. "Isn't she a perfectly old dear?"

"Oh, yes!" gasped Bean. "Yes, yes, yes, indeed! She is *that!*"

VII

*B*ean had once attended a magician's entertainment and there suffered vicariously the agony endured by one of his volunteer assistants. Suavely the entertainer begged the help of "some kind gentleman from the audience." He was insistent, exerting upon the reluctant ones the pressure of his best platform manner.

When the pause had grown embarrassing, a shamed looking man slouched forward from an aisle seat amid hearty cheers. He ascended the carpeted runway from aisle to stage, stumbled over footlights and dropped his hat. Then the magician harried him to the malicious glee of the audience. He removed playing-cards, white rabbits and articles of feminine apparel from beneath the coat of his victim. He seated him in a chair that collapsed. He gave him a box to hold and shocked him electrically. He missed his watch and discovered it in the abused man's pocket. And when the ordeal was over the recovered hat was found to contain guinea-pigs. The kind gentleman from the audience had been shown to be transcendently awkward, brainless, and to have a mania for petty thievery. With burning face and falling glance, he had stumbled back to his seat, where a lady who had before exhibited the public manner of wife to husband toward him, now pretended that he was an utter and offensive stranger.

Bean, I say, had once suffered vicariously with this altruistic dolt. His suffering now was not vicarious. For three days he endured on the raw of his own soul tortures even more ingeniously harrowing.

To be shut up for three hours a day with Breede was bad enough, but custom had a little dulled his sensitiveness to this. And he could look Breede over and write down in beautiful shorthand what he thought of him.

But the other Breedes!

Mrs. Breede, a member of one of the very oldest families in Omaha, he learned, terrified him exceedingly. She was an advanced dresser — he had to admit that — but she was no longer beautiful. She was a plucked rose that had been too long kept; the petals were rusting, crumpling at the edges. He wondered if Breede had ever wished to be wrecked on a desert island with her. She surveyed Bean through a glass-and-gold weapon with a long handle, and on the two subsequent occasions when she addressed him called him Mr. Brown. Once meeting him in the hall, she seemed to believe that he had been sent to fix the telephone.

And the flapper's taller sister of the languishing glance — how quickly had she awakened him from that golden dream of the low-lying atoll and the wrecked ship in a far sea. She *did* flirt with "anyone," no doubt about that. She adroitly revealed to Bean an unshakable conviction that he was desperately enamored of her, and that it served him right for a presumptuous nobody. She talked to him, preened herself in his gaze, and maddened him with a manner of deadly roguishness. Then she flew to exert the same charm upon anyone of the resplendent young men who were constantly riding over or tooting over in big black motorcars. They were young men who apparently had nothing to do but "go in" for things — riding, tennis, polo, golf. To all of them she was the self-confident charmer; just the kind of a girl to make a fool of you and tell about it.

Twenty-four hours after her first assault upon him he was still wrecking the ship at the entrance to that lagoon, but now he watched the big sister go down for the third time while he placidly rescued a stoker to share his romantic isolation.

The flapper and Grandma, the Demon, were even more objectionable, and, what was worse, they alarmed him. Puzzled as to their purpose, he knew not what defense to make. He was swept on some secret and sinister current to an end he could not divine.

The flapper lay in wait for him at all hours when he might appear. Did he open a door, she lurked in the corridor; did he seek refuge in the gloom of the library, she arose to confront him from its dimmest nook; did he plan a masterly escape by a rear stairway, she burst upon him from the ambush of some exotic shrub to demand which way he had thought of going. He had never thought of a way that did not prove to have been her own. The creature was a leech! If she had only talked, he believed that he could have thrown her off. But she would not talk. She merely walked beside him insatiably. Sometimes he thought he could detect a faint anxiety in the look she kept upon him, but, mostly, it was the look of something calm, secure, ruthless. Something! It unnerved him.

It was usually probable that Grandma, the Demon, would join them, the silver cigarette case dangling at her girdle. Then was he sorely beset. They would perhaps talk about him over his head, discuss his points as if he were some new beast from the stables.

"I tell you, he's over an inch taller than I am," announced the flapper.

"U-u-mm!" replied Grandma, measuring Bean's stature with narrowed eye. "U-u-mm!"

"You show her!" commanded flapper, in a louder voice, as if she believed him deaf. She grasped his arm and whirled him about to stand with his back to hers.

"There!" said the flapper tensely, her eyes staring ahead. "There!"

"You're scrooching!" accused the Demon.

"Not a bit! — and see how square his shoulders are!" She turned to point out this grace of the animal.

"Ever take any drugs? Ever get any habits like that?" queried the Demon. Plainly Bean's confession to an unusual virtue had aroused her suspicion. He might be a drug fiend!

He faltered wretchedly, wishing Breede would send for him.

"I — well, I used to be made to take sulfur and molasses every spring . . . but I never kept it up after I left home."

"Hum!" said the old lady, looking as if he could tell a lot more if he chose.

She gripped one of his biceps. He was not ashamed of these. The night and morning drill with that home exerciser had told, even though he was not yet so impressive as the machine's inventor, who, in magazine advertisements, looked down so fondly upon his own flexed arm.

"For goodness' sake!" exclaimed the Demon respectfully.

Bean thrilled at this, feeling like a primitive brute of the cave times, accustomed to subduing women by force.

After that they seemed tacitly to agree that they would pretend to show him over the "grounds." Bean hated the grounds, which were worried to the last square inch into a chilling formality, and the big glass conservatory was stifling, like an overcrowded, overheated audito-

rium. And he knew they were "drawing him out." They looked meaningly at each other whenever he spoke.

They questioned him about his early life, but learned only that his
father had been "engaged in the express business." He was ably reticent.

Did he believe that women ought to be classed legally with drunkards,
imbeciles and criminals? He did not, if you came down to that. Let
them vote if they wanted to. He had other things to think about, more
important. He didn't care much, either way. Voting didn't do any good.

He had taken the ideal attitude to enrage the woman suffragist. She
will respect opposition. Careless indifference she cannot brook.
Grandma opened upon him and battered him to a pulpy mass. Within
the half hour he was supinely promising to remind her to give him a
badge before he left; and there was further talk of his marching at the
next parade as a member of the Men's League for Woman's Suffrage,
or, at the very least, in the column of Men Sympathizers.

He wondered, wondered! Were they trying to assure themselves that
he was a fit man to be in the employ of old Breede? He could imagine
it of them; as soon as they thought about voting they began to interfere
in a man's business. Yet this suspicion slept when he was with the flapper
alone. Sometimes he was conscious of liking very much to be with her.
He decided that this was because she didn't talk.

The evening of his last day came. Breede, in a burst of garrulity, had
said: "Had enough this; go town tomorrow!" The flapper, and even the
Demon, had seemed to be stirred by the announcement. He resolved to
be more than ever on his guard. But they caught him fairly in the open.

"How do you like his hair parted that way in the middle?" demanded
the flapper, with the calculating eye of one who ponders changes in a
dwelling-house.

"U-u-mm!" considered the Demon gravely. "Not bad. Still, perhaps — !"

"Exactly what I was thinking!" said the flapper cordially. Then, to
Bean, her tone slightly raised:

"Which way?"

"Got to get off a bunch of telegrams," lied Bean.

"Oh, all right! We'll wait for you," said the flapper. "Right there," she
added, pointing to the most expensive pergola on the place.

In the dusk of an hour later he slunk stealthily down a rear stairway
and made a cautious detour into the grounds. He earnestly meant to
keep far from that pergola. Wait for him, would they? Well, he'd show
them! Always spying on a man; *hounding* him! What business was it of
theirs whether he had habits or not . . . any kind of habits?

But he was to find himself under a spell such as is said to bring the weak-willed bird to the serpent's maw. His traitorous feet dragged him toward the trap. The odor of a cigarette drew his revolted nostrils. He could hear the murmurous duet.

Talking about him! Of course! He would like to break in on them and for a little while be a certain Corsican upstart in one of his most objectionable moods. That would take them down a bit. But, instead, he became something entirely different. With the stealth of the red Indian he effaced himself against a background of well-groomed shrubbery and crept toward the murmur. At last he could hear words above the beating of his heart.

"How can you *know?*" the Demon was saying. "A child of your age?"

The flapper's tone was calm and confident as one who relates a phenomenon that has become a commonplace.

"I knew it the very first second I ever saw him — something went over me just like that — I can't tell how, but I knew."

"Well, how can you know about him?"

"Oh, him!" The words implied that the flapper had waved a deprecating hand. "Why, I know about him in just the same way; you can't tell how. It comes over you!"

The Demon: (A long-drawn) "U-u-mm!"

The flapper: "And he makes me perfectly furious sometimes, too!"

There was a stir as if they were leaving. Bean retreated a dozen feet before he breathed again. So that was their game, was it? He'd see about that!

He waited for them to emerge, but they had apparently settled to more of this high-handed talk. Then, like an icy wave to engulf him, came a name — "Tommy Hollins." It came in the Demon's voice, indistinguishable words preceding it. And in the flapper's voice came "Tommy Hollins!" gently, caressingly, it seemed. In truth, the flapper had sniffed before uttering it, and the sniff had meant good-natured contempt but Bean had lost the sniff.

Now he had it! Tommy Hollins! He identified the youth, a yellow-headed, pink-faced lout in flannels who was always riding over, and who seemed to "go in" for nearly everything. He had detected a romping intimacy between the two. So it was Tommy Hollins. At once he felt a great relief; he need worry no longer over the singular attentions of this young woman. Let Tommy Hollins worry! He could admit, now, how grave had been his alarm. And there was nothing in it. He could meet her without being afraid. He was almost ready to approach them genially and pass an hour in light conversation. He advanced a few steps with this intention, but again came the voice of the flapper replying, apparently, to some unheard admonition. It came, cold and terrible.

"I don't care. I've got the right to choose the father of my own children!"

He blushed for this language, a blush he could feel mantling his very toes. He fled from there. He saw that the moment was not for light conversation. And even as he fled he caught the Demon's prolonged "U-u-mmm!"

Yet when he left in the morning the flapper lurked for him as ever, materializing from an apparently vacant corridor. He greeted her for the first time without ulterior questioning. He thought he liked her pretty well now. And she was undeniably good to look at in the white of her tennis costume; the hair, like Nap's spots in its golden brown, was filleted with a scarlet ribbon, and her eyes shone from her freshened face with an unwonted sparkle – decision, certitude – what was it? He deemed that he knew.

"Tommy Hollins coming to play," she vouchsafed in explanation of the racquet she carried. "Are you glad to go?"

"Glad to see my dog again." He smiled as a man of the world. He was on the verge of coquetry, now that he knew it to be safe.

"We'll bring him along too, next time."

"Oh, the next time!" He put it carelessly aside.

"You'll be out again, soon enough. I simply know Pops is going to have another bad spell – in a week or so."

He could have sworn that the eyes of Breede's daughter gleamed with cold anticipatory malice. He shuddered for Breede. And he wished Tommy Hollins well of his bargain. Flirt, indeed! All alike!

"Chubbins!" called the unconscious father from afar.

"Yes, Pops!" She gripped his hand with a well-muscled fervor. "Oh, he'll have another in a little while, don't you worry!" And she was off, with this evil in her heart, to a father but now convalescent.

Marveling, he walked on to the Demon's ambuscade. She pounced upon him from behind a half-opened door.

"I want to say one word, young man. Oh, you needn't think I don't see the way things are going. I'm not blind if I am seventy-six! If you're the tender and innocent thing you say you are, you look out for yourself. I know you all! If you don't break out one time you do another. I'd a good deal rather you'd had it over before now and put it all behind you – don't interrupt – but you're sound and clean as far as I can see, and you've got a good situation. I don't say it couldn't be worse. But if you are – well, you see that you *stay* that way. Don't try to tell me. I've seen enough of men in my time –"

He broke away from her at Breede's call. The flapper jerked her head twice at him, very neatly, as the car passed the tennis court. She was beginning a practice volley with Tommy Hollins, who was disporting himself like a young colt.

"Chubbins!" he thought. Not a bad name for her, though it had come queerly from Breede. For the first time he was pricked with the needle of suspicion that Hollins might not be the right man for the flapper. Hearing her called "Chubbins" somehow made it seem different. Maybe Hollins, who seemed all of twenty, wouldn't "make her happy." He thought it was something that the family ought to consider very seriously. He was conscious of a willingness to consider it himself, as a friend of the family and a well-wisher of Chubbins.

*H*e was back in the apartment and in the presence of a document that swept his mind of all Breedes. Never had he in fancy ceased to be king Ram-tah, cheated of historic mention because of his wisdom and goodness. He had looked commiseratingly upon Breede's country-house, thinking of his own palace on the banks of the slow-moving Nile. "— probably made this place look like a shack!" he had exultantly thought. And the benign monarch had ended his reign in peace, to be laid magnificently away, to repose undisturbed while the sands drifted over him — until —

The hour had come. "My men have succeeded, after incredible hardships," wrote Professor Balthasar. "The *goods* will be delivered to you Thursday night, the tenth. I trust the final payment will be ready, as, relying on your honor, I have advanced —"

The rest did not matter. His honor was surely to be relied upon. The money had been richly earned. An able man, this Balthasar! He had achieved the thing with admirable secrecy. Bean had feared the hounds of the daily press. They might discover who It was, to whom It was going; discover the true identity of Bunker Bean. The whole thing might come out in the papers! But Balthasar had known how. He approved the caution that had led him to speak of "the *goods*"; there was something almost witty about it.

He leaned far out a window, listening, straining his eyes up and down the lighted avenue. There was confusion in his mind as to how It could most fittingly be brought to him. The sable vision of a hearse drawn by four lordly black horses at first possessed his mind. But this was dismissed; there was no death! And the spectacle would excite comment. The idea of an ambulance, which he next considered, seemed equally impracticable. It would have to be done quietly; Balthasar would know. Trust Balthasar!

He heard the rhythmic clump-clump of a horse's hoofs on the asphalt pavement. This was presently accompanied by the sounds of wheels. An express wagon came under the street-lights. Balthasar rode beside the driver, his frock coat and glossy tall hat having been relinquished for the garb of an ordinary citizen. Back of them in the wagon he could distinguish the lines of an Object. It had come to him in a common express wagon, in a common crate, and the driver did not even wear a black mask. Balthasar had cunningly eluded detection by pretending there was nothing to conceal.

He drew back from the window and with fast beating heart went to open the door. They were already on the stairway. Balthasar was coming first. With sublime effrontery he had impressed Cassidy to help carry It, and Cassidy was warning the expressman to look out for that turn an' not tear inta th' plashter.

It was lowered to the floor in the throne-room. Cassidy and the expressman puffed freely and looked at the thing as if wondering how two men had ever been equal to it.

"'Twould be brickybac," said Cassidy genially.

"That there hall's choked with dust," said the expressman with seeming irrelevance.

"I noticed it meself," said Cassidy.

"Clogged me throat up fur fair," continued the expressman huskily.

"Pay the men liberally and let them be on their way," said Balthasar. Bean pressed money upon both and they departed.

"You couldn't get me to do it again for twice the money," said Balthasar; "the nervous strain I've been under. A custom-house detective was on our trail, but one of my men took care of him — at a dark corner."

Bean shuddered.

"They didn't —"

"Oh, nothing serious. He'll be as well as ever in a few days. Got a hatchet." He gestured significantly toward the crate.

But this was too precipitate for Bean. He could not disinter himself — it seemed like that — under the eyes of Balthasar.

"Not now! Not now! You've done your part — here!" He passed Balthasar the check he had written earlier in the evening.

"I'll leave you, then," said the professor. "But one thing, don't handle it much. It might disintegrate. I bid you farewell, my young friend."

Bean, at the door, listened to his descending steps. The professor was whistling. He recognized the air, "Call Me Up Some Rainy Afternoon." It was a lively air and the professor rendered it ably but quite softly.

The door locked, he was back staring at the crate that concealed his dead self. He was helpless before it. The fleshly tenement of a great king who had later flashed upon the world as Napoleon I, and was now Bunker Bean! Could he bear to look? He trembled and knew himself weak. Yet it would be done, some time.

There was a vigorous knock at the door. All was discovered!

The crime of assault at the dark corner had been traced to his door. Balthasar had betrayed him. The Egyptian authorities had discovered their loss. The thing was there. He was caught red-handed.

He reached the door and cautiously opened it an inch. Cassidy stood there, armed with a hatchet. They would use violence!

"Hatchet!" said Cassidy, genially extending the weapon. He wiped his mouth with the back of his hand. The aroma of beer stole into the room.

"F'r brox brickybac!" insinuated Cassidy.

"Thanks!" said Bean, accepting the tool.

"We kem frum th' sem county, Mayo, him an' me," volunteered Cassidy. "G'night!"

Once more Bean faced the crate. It must be done at once. Discovery was too probable. Gingerly he forced the blade under one of the boards and pried. The nails screeched horribly as they were withdrawn. The task was simple enough; the crate was a flimsy affair to have withstood so difficult a journey. But after each board was removed he peered to the street from behind the closed blind, half expecting to find policemen drawn to the spot.

A smoothly packed layer of excelsior greeted his eyes. It was rather reassuring. He felt that he might be unpacking any casual object. Exposed at last was the wooden case that enveloped him!

Awestruck, he looked down at it for a long time. He recognized the workmanship, having seen a dozen such in the museum in the park. He knelt by it and ran a reverent hand over its painted surface. In many colors were birds and beasts, and men in profile, and queer marks that he knew to be picture-writing; processions of slaves and oxen, reapers and water-bearers. The tints were fresh under their overlaying lacquer. There was even a smell of varnish. He wondered if the contents — if It — were in the same remarkable state of preservation. He rapped on the thin wood — it was cedar, he thought, or perhaps sycamore. The sound was musical, resonant; the same note that had vibrated how many thousands of years before.

Nap came up to smell, seeming to suspect that the box might contain food. He stretched his forepaws to the top of the case and betrayed eagerness.

"Napoleon!" cried Bean sternly, putting the dog's complete name upon him for the first time. He was banished to his couch and made to know that leaving it would entail unpleasantness.

The thought of the Corsican came back with a new significance. In that embodiment he had felt, perhaps dimly recalled, his Egyptian life. Had he not been drawn irresistibly to Egypt? "In the shadow of the pyramids," he had read in a history, "the conqueror of Italy dreamed of the pomp and power of a crown and scepter, and upon his return to France from the Egyptian expedition, with characteristic energy he set himself to work to bring the dream to pass —" It was plain enough. He knew now the inner meaning of that engraving he had bought, in which Napoleon stood in rapt meditation before the Sphinx. They had all — King, Emperor, Bean — been dreamers that brought their dreams to pass. He mused long, staring down at the case; a queerly shaped thing, fashioned to follow the lines of the human form. From the neck the shoulders rounded gracefully. They might have been cut to give the wearer the appearance of perfect physical development; at least they seemed to fit him neatly.

It occurred to Bean that the case should not lie prone. It suggested death where death was not. He pulled out more excelsior until he could raise the case. It was surprisingly light and he leaned it upright against the wall. He now tried to pretend that everything was over. He gathered boards, excelsior and the crate and piled them in the kitchenette, which they approximately filled.

But inevitably he was brought back. He stood with hands upon the cover of the upreared case, drew a long shivering breath and gently lifted it off. His eyes were upon the swathed figure within, then slowly they crept up the yellowed linen and came to rest upon the bared face.

He had tried feebly to prefigure this face, but never had his visioning approached the actual in its majestic, still beauty. The brow was nobly broad, the nose straight and purposeful, the chin bold yet delicate. The grimness of the mouth was relieved by a faint lift of the upper lip, perhaps an echo of the smile with which he greeted death. There was a gleam of teeth from under the lip. The eyes had closed peacefully; the lids lay light upon their secrets as if they might flutter and open again. On cheek and chin was a discernible growth of dark beard; the hair above the brow was black and abundant. It was a kingly face, a face of command, though benign. It was all too easy to believe that a crown had become it well. And there had been no weakening at the end, no sunken cheeks nor hollowed temples. The lines were full. The general color was of rich red mahogany.

He ran a tremulous hand over the face, smoothed the thick hair, fingered the firm lips that almost smiled. Under the swathing of linen he could see where the hands were folded on the breast. Low down on the right jaw was unmistakably a mole, a thing that had strangely survived on Bean's own face. Again he ran a hand over the features, then a corroborating hand over his own. Intently and long he studied each detail, nostrils, eyebrows, ears, hair, the tips of the just-revealed teeth.

"God!" he breathed. It was hardly more than a whisper and was uttered in all reverence.

Then —

"God! how I've changed!"

VIII

On the following afternoon, among the Sunday throng in the Metropolitan Museum of Art, a slender young man of inconsiderable stature, alert as to movement, but with an expression of absent dreaming, might have been observed giving special attention to the articles in those rooms devoted to ancient Egypt. Doubtless, however, no one did observe him more than casually, for, though of singularly erect carriage, he was garbed inconspicuously in neutral tints, and his behavior was never such as to divert attention from the surrounding spoils of the archaeologist.

Had his mind been as an open book, he would surely have become a figure of interest. His mental attitude was that of a professional beau of acknowledged preeminence; he was comparing the self at home in the mummy case with the remnants of defunct Pharaohs here exposed under glass, and he was sniffing, in spirit, at their lack of kingly dignity and their inferior state of preservation. Their wooden cases were often marred, faded, and broken. Their shrouding linen was frayed and stained. Their features were unimpressive and, in too many instances, shockingly incomplete. They looked very little like kings, and the laudatory recitals of their one-time greatness, translated for the contemporary eye, seemed to be only the vaporings of third-class pugilists.

Sneering openly at a damaged Pharaoh of the fourth dynasty, he reflected that some day he would confer upon that museum a relic transcending all others. He saw it enshrined in a room by itself; it should never be demeaned by association with those rusty cadavers he saw about him. This would be when he had passed on to another body, in accordance with the law of Karma. He would leave a sum to the museum authorities, specifically to build this room, and to it would come thousands, for a glimpse of the superior Ram-tah, last king of the pre-dynastic period, surviving in a state calculated to impress every beholder with his singular merits. Ram-tah, cheated of his place in history's pantheon, should here at last come into his own; serene, beauteous, majestic, looking every inch a king, where mere Pharaohs looked like — like the coffee-stained, untidy fragments they were.

He left the place in a tolerant mood. He had weighed himself with the other great dead of the world.

That night he sat again before this old king, staring until he lost himself, staring as he had before stared into the depths of his shell. The shell, when he had looked steadily at it for a long time, had always seemed to put him in close touch with unknown forces. He had once tried to explain this to his Aunt Clara, who understood nearly everything, but his effort had been clumsy enough and had brought her no enlightenment. "You look into it — and it makes you *feel!*" was all he had been able to tell her.

But the shell was now discarded for the puissant person of Ram-tah. The message was more pointed. He drew power from the old dead face that yet seemed so living. He was himself a wise and good king. No longer could he play the coward before trivial adversities. He would direct large affairs; he would live big. Never again would he be afraid of death or Breede or policemen or the mockery of his fellows — or women! He might still avoid the latter, but not in terror; only in a dignified dread lest they talk and spoil it all.

He would choose, in due time, a worthy consort, and a certain Crown Prince would, in further due time, startle the world with his left-handed pitching. It was a prospect all golden to dream upon. His spirit grew tall and its fiber toughened.

To be sure, he did not achieve a kingly disregard for public opinion all in one day. There was the matter of that scarlet cravat. Monday morning he excavated it from the bottom of the trunk, where it lay beside "Napoleon, Man and Lover." He even adjusted it, carelessly pretending that it was just any cravat, the first that had come to hand. But its color was still too alarming. *It* — so he usually thought of the great Ram-tah — would have worn the cravat without a tremor, but It had been born a king. One glance at the thing about his neck had vividly recalled the awkward circumstance that, to the world at large, he was still Bunker Bean, a youth incapable of flaunt or flourish.

Let it not be thought, however, that his new growth showed no result above ground. He purchased and wore that very morning a cravat not entirely red, it is true, but one distinguished by a narrow red stripe on a backing of bronze, which the clerk who maneuvered the sale assured him was "tasty." Also he commanded a suit of clothes of a certain light check in which the Bean of uninspired days would never have braved public scrutiny. Such were the immediate and actual fruits of Ram-tah's influence.

There were other effects, perhaps more subtle. Performing his accustomed work for Breede that day, he began to study his employer from the kingly, or Ram-tah, point of view. He conceived that Breede in the time of Ram-tah would have been a steward, a keeper of the royal granaries, a dependable accountant; a good enough man in his lowly station, but one who could never rise. His laxness in the manner of dress was seen to be ingrained, an incurable defect of soul. In the time of Ram-tah he had doubtless worn the Egyptian equivalent for detached cuffs, and he would be doing the like for a thousand incarnations to come. All too plainly Breede's Karmic future promised little of interest. His degree of ascent in the human scale was hardly perceptible.

Bean was pleased at this thought. It left him in a fine glow of superiority and sharpened his relish for the mad jest of their present attitudes — a jest demanding that he seem to be Breede's subordinate.

Naturally, this was a situation that would not long endure. It was too preposterous. Money came not only to kings but to the kingly. He troubled as little about details as would have any other king. Were there not steel kings, and iron kings, railway kings, oil kings — money kings? He thought it was not unlikely that he would first engage the world's notice as an express king. He had received those fifty shares of stock from Aunt Clara and regarded them as a presage of his coming directorship. But he took no pride in this thought. Baseball was to be his life work. He would own one major-league team, at least; perhaps three or four. He would be known as the baseball king, and the world would forget his petty triumphs as a director of express.

He deemed it significant that the present directors of that same Federal Express Company one day held a meeting in Breede's office. It showed, he thought, how life "worked around." The thing was coming to his very door. With considerable interest he studied the directors as they came and went. Most of them, like Breede, were men whose wealth the daily press had a habit of estimating in rotund millions. He regarded them knowingly, thinking he could tell them something that might surprise them. But they passed him, all unheeding, moneyed-looking men of good round girth, who seemed to have found the dollar-game worth while.

The most of them, he was glad to note, were in dress slightly more advanced than Breede. One of them, a small but important-looking old gentleman with a purple face and a white parted beard, became on the instant Bean's ideal for correctness. From his grey spats to his top-hat, he was "dignified yet different," although dressing, for example, in a more subdued key than Bulger. Yet he was a constantly indignant looking old gentleman, and Bean guessed that he would be a trouble-maker on any board of directors. It seemed to him that he would like to take this person's place on the board; oust him in spite of his compelling garments.

And Breede would know then that he was something more than a machine. On the whole, he felt sorry for Breede at times. Perhaps he would let him have a little of the baseball stock.

So he sat and dreamed of his great past and of his brilliant future. Perhaps, after all, Bean as the blind poet had been not the least authentic of Balthasar's visions.

And inevitably he encountered the flapper in this dreaming; "Chub-bins," he liked to call her. More and more he was suspecting that Tommy Hollins was not the man for Chubbins. He would prefer to see her the bride of an older man, two or three, or even four, years older, who was settled in life. A young girl — a young girl's parents — couldn't be too careful!

He was not for many days at a time deprived of the sight of the young girl in question. She had formed a habit of calling for her father at the close of his day's hard work. And she did not wait for him in the big car; she sat in his office, where, after she had inquired solicitously about his poor foot, she settled her gaze upon Bean. And Bean no longer evaded this gaze. She was a clever, attractive little thing and he liked her well. He thought of things he would tell her for her own good at the first opportunity.

He wondered guiltily when Breede's next attack might be expected, and he had a lively impression that the flapper, too, was more curious than alarmed about this. He seemed to feel that she was actually wishing to be told things by him for her own good.

However that may be, his next summons to the country place came without undue delay, and it is not at all improbable that Breede fell a victim to what the terminology of one of our most popular cults identifies as "malicious animal magnetism."

On this occasion he was not oppressed by those attentions which the flapper and Grandma, the Demon, still bestowed upon him. Where he had once fled, he now put himself in the way of them. He listened with admirably simulated interest to Grandma's account of the suffrage play for which she was rehearsing. She was to appear in the mob scene. He was certain she would lend vivacity to any mob. But he was glad that the flapper was not to appear. Voting and smashing windows were bad enough.

He tried at first to talk to the flapper about Tommy Hollins, whom he airily designated as "that Hollins boy." It seemed to be especially needed, because the Hollins boy arrived after breakfast every day and left only in the late afternoon. But the flapper declined nevertheless to consider him as meat for serious converse.

Bean considered that this was sheer flirting, whereupon he flung principle to the winds and flirted himself.

"You show signs of life," declared Grandma, who was quick to note this changed demeanor. And Bean smirked like a man of the world.

"She never set her mind on anything yet that she didn't get it," added Grandma, naming no one. "She's like her father there."

And Bean strolled off to enjoy a vision of himself defeating her purpose to ensnare the Hollins youth. Once he would have considered it crass presumption, but that was before a certain sarcophagus on the left bank of the Nile had been looted of its imperial occupant. Now he merely recalled a story about a King Cophetua and a beggar maid. It was a comparison that would have intensely interested the flapper's mother, who was this time regarding Bean through her glazed weapon as if he were some queer growth the head gardener had brought from the conservatory.

Grandma deftly probed his past for affairs of the heart. She pointedly had him alone, and her intimation was that he might talk freely, as to a woman of understanding and broad sympathy. But Bean made a wretched mess of it.

Certainly there had been "affairs." There was the girl in Chicago, two doors down the street, whom he had once taken to walk in the park, but only once, because she talked; the girl in the business college who had pretty hair and always smiled when she looked at him; and another who, he was almost sure, had sent him an outspoken valentine; yes, there had been plenty of girls, but he hadn't bothered much about them.

And Grandma, plainly incredulous, averred that he was too deep for her. Bean was on the point of inventing a close acquaintance with an actress, which he considered would be scandalous enough to compel a certain respect he seemed to find lacking in the old lady, but he saw quickly that she would confuse and trip him with a few questions. He was obliged to content himself with looking the least bit smug when she said:

"You're a deep one — too deep for me!"

He tried hard to look deep and at least as depraved as the conventions of good society seemed to demand.

He was beginning to enjoy the sinful thing. The girl was of course plighted to the Hollins boy, and yet she was putting herself in his way. Very well! He would teach her the danger of playing with fire. He would bring all of his arts and wiles to bear. True, in behaving thus he was conscious of falling below the moral standards of a wise and good king who had never stooped to baseness of any sort. But he was now living in a different age, and somehow —

"I'm a dual nature," he thought. And he applied to himself another phrase he seemed to recall from his reading of magazine stories.

"I've got the artistic temper!" This, he gathered, was held to explain, if not to justify, many departures from the conventional in affairs of the heart. It was a kind of licensed madness. Endowed with the "artistic temper," you were not held accountable when you did things that made plain people gasp. That was it! That was why he was carrying on with Tommy Hollins' girl, and not caring *what* happened.

In his times of leisure they walked through the shaded aisles of those too well-kept grounds, or they sat in seats of twisted iron and honored the setting sun with their notice. They did not talk much, yet they were acutely aware of each other. Sometimes the silence was prolonged to awkwardness, and one of them would jestingly offer a penny for the other's thoughts. This made a little talk, but not much, and sometimes increased the awkwardness; it was so plain that what they were thinking of could not be told for money.

They did tell their wonderful ages and their full names and held their hands side by side to note the astonishing differences between the "lines." A palmist had revealed something quite amazing to the flapper, but she refused to tell what it was, with a significance that left Bean in a tumultuous and pleasurable whirl of cowardice. Their hands flew apart rather self-consciously. Bean felt himself a scoundrel — "leading on" a young thing like that who was engaged to another. It was flirting of the most reprehensible sort. But there was his dual nature; a strain of the errant Corsican had survived to debauch him.

And if she didn't want to be "led on," he thought indignantly, why did she so persistently put herself in the way of it? She was always there! Serve her right, then! Serve the Hollins boy right, too!

Grandma eyed them shrewdly with her Demon's glance of questioning, but did nothing to keep them apart. On the contrary, she would
often brazenly leave them together after conducting them to remote
nooks. She made no flimsy excuses. She seemed indifferent to the fate
of this tender bud left at the mercy of one whom she affected to regard
as a seasoned roué.

There were four days of this regrettable philandering. On the fifth
Breede manifested alarming symptoms of recovery. He ceased to be the
meek man he was under actual suffering, and was several times guilty
of short-worded explosions that should never have reached the ears of
good women.

Said the flapper in tones of genuine dismay that evening:

"I'm afraid Pops is going to be well enough to go to town tomorrow!"

Even Grandma, pacing a bit of choice turf near at hand, rehearsing
her lines in the mob scene, was shocked at this.

"You are a selfish little pig!" she called.

"But *he* will have to go away, if Pops goes," said the flapper, in
magnificent extenuation.

The words told. Grandma seemed to see things in a new light.

"You come with me," she commanded; "both of you."

Ahead of them she led the way to that pergola where Bean had once
overheard their talk.

"Sit down," said Grandma, and herself sat between them.

"You are a couple of children," she began accusingly. "Why, when I
was your age —" She broke off suddenly, and for some moments stared
into the tracery of vines.

"When I was your age," she began once more, but in a curiously
altered voice — "Lord! What a time of years!" She spoke slowly, softly,
as one who would evoke phantoms. "Why, at your age," she turned
slightly to the flapper, "I'd been married two years, and your father was
crawling about under my feet as I did the housework."

She was still looking intently ahead to make her vision alive.

"What a time of years, and how different! Sixty years ago — why, it
seems farther back than Noah's ark. The log cabins in the little clearings,
and people marrying when they wanted to — always early, and working
hard and raising big families. I was the only girl, but I had nine brothers.
And Jim, your father's father, my dear, I remember the very moment he
began to take notice of me, coming out of the log church one Sabbath.
He only looked at me, that was all, and I had to pretend I didn't know.
Then he came nights and sat in front of the big open fire, with all of
us, at first. But after a little, the others would climb up the ladder to
the loft and leave us, and we'd maybe eat a mince pie that I'd made —

I was a good cook at sixteen — and there would be a pitcher of cider, and outside, the wind would be driving the snow against the tiny windowpanes — I can hear that sound now, and the sputtering of the backlog, and Jim — oh, well!" She waved the scene back.

"When we were married, Jim had his eighty acres all cleared, a yoke of nice fat steers, a cow, two pigs, and a couple of sheep; not much, but it seemed enough then. The furniture was home-made, the tableware was tin plates and pewter spoons and horn-handled knives, and a set of real china that Pa and Ma gave us — that was for company — and a feather-bed and patch-work quilts I'd made, and a long-barreled rifle, and the best coon-dog, Jim said, in the whole of York State. Oh, well!"

Bean became aware that the old lady had grasped his hand, and he divined that she was also holding a hand of the flapper.

"And my! such excitement you never did see when little Jim came! We began to save right off to send him to a good seminary. We were going to make a preacher out of him; and see the way he's turned out! Lord, what would his father make of this place and our little Jim, if he was to come back?

"I lost him before he got to see many changes in the world. I remember we did go to a party in Fredonia one time, where a woman from Buffalo wore a low-necked gown, and Jim never got over it. He swore to the day of his death that any woman who'd wear 'a dug-out dress' was a hussy. He didn't know what the world could be coming to, when they allowed such goings-on. Poor Jim! I was still young when he went, and of course — but I couldn't. I'd had my man and I'd had my baby, and somehow I was through. I wanted to learn more about the world, and little Jim was growing up and had a nice situation in the store at Fredonia, working early and late, sleeping under the counter, and saving his fifty dollars clear every year. I knew he'd always provide for me — Dear me! how I run on! Where was I?"

Bean's hand was released, and Grandma rose to her feet, turning to look down upon them.

"I forgot what I started to say, but maybe it was this, that the world hasn't changed so much as folks often think. I get to watching young people sometimes — it seems as if they were like the young people in my day, and I think any young man that's steady and decent and has a good situation — what I mean is this, that he — well, it depends on the girl, as it always did."

She turned and walked to the end of the pergola, fifty feet away. There she threw up a clenched fist and began to emit groans, cries of hoarse rage and ragged phrases of abuse. She was again rehearsing her lines in the mob scene of the equal-suffrage play. At the head of her fellow mobs-women, she hurled harsh epithets at the Prime Minister of the oldest English-speaking nation on earth. There seemed to be no escape for the Prime Minister. They had him.

"We've broken windows, we'll break heads!" shouted the Demon, and a gardener crossing the grounds might have been seen to quicken his pace after one backward look.

The pair on the bench were inattentive. They had instinctively drawn together, but they were silent. In Bean's mind was a confusion of many matters: Breede sleeping under a counter — people in log-cabins getting married — the best coon-dog in York State — a yoke of nice fat steers —

But beneath this was a sharpened consciousness of the girl breathing at his side. She seemed curiously to be waiting — waiting! The silence and their stillness became unbearable. Something must break . . . their breaths were too long drawn. He got to his feet and the flapper was unaccountably standing beside him. It was too dark to see her face, but he knew that for once she was not looking at him; for once that head was bent. And then, preposterously, without volition, without fore-knowledge, he was holding her tightly in his arms; holding her tightly and kissing her with a simple directness that "Napoleon, Man and Lover," could never have bettered.

There is no record of Napoleon having studied jiu-jitsu.

For one frenzied moment he was out of himself, a mere conquering male, unthinking, ruthless, exigent. Then the sweet strange touch of her cheek brought him back to the awful thing he had done. His reason worked with a lightning quickness. Terrified by his violence she would wrench herself free and run screaming to the house. And then — it was too horrible!

He waited, breathless, for retribution. The flapper did not wrench herself away. Slowly he relaxed the embrace that had made a brute of him. The flapper had not screamed. She was facing him now, breathless herself. He put her a little way from him; he wanted her to see it as he did.

The flapper drew a long and rather catchy breath, then she adjusted a strand of hair misplaced by his violence.

"I *knew* it!" she began, in tones surprisingly cool. "I knew it ever so long ago, from the very first moment!"

He tried to speak, but had no words. His utterance was formless. "When did *you* first know?" she persisted. She was patting her hair into place with both hands.

He didn't know; he didn't know that he knew now; but recalling her speech he had overheard, he had the presence of mind to commit a soulful perjury.

"From the very first," he lied glibly. "Something went over me — just like *that*. I can't tell you how, but I knew!"

"You made me so afraid of you," confessed the flapper.

"I never meant to, couldn't help it."

"I'm horribly shy, but I knew it had to be. I felt powerless."

"I *know*," he sympathized.

"Our day has come!" roared Grandma from out of the gloom. "We know our rights! We've broken glass! We break heads!" This was followed by "Ar! Ar! Ar!" meant for sinister growls of rage. It seemed to be the united voice of the mob.

They drew apart, once more self-conscious. They walked slowly out, passed the mob scene, which ignored them, and went with awkward little hesitations up the wide walk to the Breede portal. To Bean's suddenly cooled eye, the vast grey house towered above him as a menace. He had a fear that it might fall upon him.

At the entrance they stood discreetly apart. Bean wondered what he ought to say. His sense of guilt was overwhelming. But the flapper seemed clear-headed enough.

"You leave it to me," she said, as if he had confided his perplexity to her. "Leave it all to me. *I've* always managed."

"Yes," said Bean, meaning nothing whatever.

She made little movements that suggested departure. She was regarding him now with the old curious look that had puzzled him.

"You're just as perfectly nice as I knew you were," she announced, with an obvious pride in this bit of proved wisdom.

"Good-night!"

From a distance of five feet she bestowed the little double-nod upon him and fled.

"Good-night!" he managed to call after her. Then he was aware that he had wanted to call her "Chubbins!" He liked that name for her. If he could only have said "Good-night, Chubbins —"

For that matter he basely wanted again to — but he thought with shame that he had done enough for once. A pretty night's work, indeed! If Breede ever found it out —

When he left with Breede in the morning, she was on the tennis-court. Brazenly she engaged in light conversation across the net with no other than Thomas Hollins, Junior. She did not look up as the car passed the court, though he knew that she knew. Something in the poise of her head told him that.

He didn't wonder she couldn't face him in the light of day. He smiled bitterly, in scorn for the betrayed Tommy.

IX

*B*ack in the lofty office that Saturday morning he sat under the eye of Breede, in outward seeming a neat and efficient amanuensis. In truth he was pluming himself as a libertine of rare endowments. He openly and shamelessly wished he had kissed the creature again. When the next opportunity came she wouldn't get off so lightly, he could tell her that. It was base, but it was thrilling. He would abandon himself. He would take her hand and hold it the very first time they were alone together. Well might she be afraid of him, as she had confessed herself to be. She little knew!

It was, though, pretty light conduct on her part. It was possible that he would not see her again. Perhaps a baggage like that would already have forgotten him; would have treated the thing as trivial, an incident to laugh about, even to regale her intimates with. Probably he had done nothing more than make a fool of himself as usual. Votes for women, indeed! He thought they should first learn how to behave properly with young men who weren't expecting things of that sort.

"— this 'mount'll then become 'vailable f'r purpose shortenin' line an' reducin' heavy grades," dictated the unconscious father of the baggage.

"I kissed that smug-faced little brat of yours last night," wrote Bean immediately thereafter. He didn't care. He would put the thing down plainly, right under Breede's nose.

"With 'creased freight earnin's these 'provements may be 'spected t' pay f'r 'emselves," continued Breede.

"And I don't say I wouldn't do the same thing over again," Bean slipped in skillfully.

He winced to think he might some day have a daughter of his own that would "carry on" just so with young men who would be all right if they were only let alone. He found new comfort in the reflection that his first-born would be a boy — to grow up and be the idol of a nation.

But a little later he was again thinking of her as "Chubbins," wishing he had called her that, wishing she had stayed longer out in the scented night — the wonderful smoothness of her yielding cheek! Her little tricks of voice and manner came back to him, her quick little patting of Grandma's back at unexpected moments, the tilting of her head like a listening bird, that inexplicable look as her eyes enveloped him, a tiny scar at her temple, mark of an early fall from her pony.

He became sentimental to a maudlin degree. She would go on in her shallow way of life, smashing windows, voting, leading perfectly decent young men to do things they never meant to do; but he, the tender, the true, the ever-earnest, he would not recover from the wound that frail one had so carelessly inflicted. He would be a changed man, with hair prematurely greying at the temples, like Gordon Dane's, hiding his hurt under a mask of light cynicism to all but persons of superior insight. The heartless quip, the mad jest on his lips! And years afterward, a deeply serious and very beautiful woman would divine his sorrow and win him back to his true self.

The wedding! The drive from the church! The carriage is halted by a street crowd. A stalwart policeman appears. He has just arrested two women, confirmed window-smashers — Grandma, the Demon, and the flapper. The flapper gives him one long look, then bows her head. She sees all the nobility she has missed. Serve her right, too!

Noon came and he was about to leave the office. He was still the changed man of quip and jest. Desperately he jested with old Metzeger, who was regretfully, it seemed, relinquishing his adored ledgers from Saturday noon until Monday morning.

"Say, I want to borrow nineteen thousand eleven hundred and eighty-nine dollars and thirty-seven cents until the sixteenth at seven minutes to eleven."

Old Metzeger repeated the numbers accurately. He looked wistful, but he knew it was a jest.

"Telephone for Boston Bean!" cried an office boy, dryly affecting to be unconscious of his wit.

He rushed nervously for the booth. No one in the great city had ever before found occasion to telephone him. He thought of Professor Balthasar. Balthasar would warn him to fly at once; that all was discovered.

He held the receiver to his ear and managed a husky "Hello!"

At first there were many voices, mostly indignant: "I want the manager!" "Get off the line!" "A hundred and nine and three quarters!" "That you, Howard? Say, this is —" "Get — off — that — line!" "Or I'll know the reason why before tomorrow night!" And then from Bedlam pealed the voice of the flapper, silencing these evil spirits.

"Hello! Hello! This line makes me perfectly furious. Tomorrow about three o'clock — you're to give us tea and things, some nice place — Granny and me. Be along in the car. I remember the number. Be there. Good-bye!"

There was the rattle of a receiver being hung up. But he stood there not believing it — tea and car and be there — The receiver rattled again.

"You knew who I was, *didn't* you?"

"Yes, right away," muttered Bean. Then he brightened. "I knew your voice the moment I heard it." The madness was upon him and he soared. "You're Chubbins!" He waited.

"Cut out the Chubbins stuff, Bill, and get off there!" directed a coarse masculine voice from the unseen wire-world.

He got off there with all possible quickness. His first thought was that she probably had not heard the magnificent piece of daring. It was too bad. Probably he never could do it again. Then he turned and discovered that he had left the door of the telephone booth ajar. Chubbins might not have heard him, but Bulger assuredly had.

"Well, well, well!" declaimed Bulger in his best manner. "Look whom we have with us here tonight! Old Mr. George W. Fox Bean, keeping it all under his hat. Chubbins, eh? Some name, that! Don't tell me you thought it up all by yourself, you word-painter! Miss Chubbsy Chubbins! Where's she work?"

Bean saw release.

"Little manicure party," he confessed; "certain shop not far from here. Think I'm going to put *you* wise?"

Bulger was pleased at the implication.

"Ain't got a friend, has she?"

"No," said Bean. "Never did have one. Some class, too," he added with a leer that won Bulger's complete respect. He breathed freely again and was humming, "Love Me and the World Is Mine," as they separated.

But when he was alone the song died. The thing was getting serious. And she was so assured. Telling him to be there as if she were Breede himself. How did she know he had time for all that tea and Grandma nonsense? Suppose he had had another engagement. She hadn't given him time to say. Hadn't asked him; just *told* him. Well, it showed one thing. It showed that Bunker Bean could bring women to his feet.

His afternoon recreation, there being no baseball, was to lead Nap triumphantly through Central Park to be seen of an envious throng. He affected a lordly unconsciousness of the homage Nap received. He left adoring women in his wake and covetous men; and children demanded bluntly if he would sell that dog; or if he wouldn't sell him would he give him away, because they wanted him.

Surfeited with this easily won attention, he sat by the driveway to watch the endless parade of carriage folk. His eye was for the women in those shining equipages. Young or old, they were to him newly exciting. His attitude was the rather scornful one of a conqueror whose victories have cost him too little. They had been mysteries to him, but now, all in a day, he understood women. They were vulnerable things, and men were their masters. Votes, indeed!

His own power over them was abundantly proved. Any of them passing heedlessly there would, under the right conditions, confess it. Let him be called to their notice and they'd be following him around, forgetting plighted vows, getting him into places screened with vines and letting themselves be led on; telephoning him to give them and Grandma tea and things of a Sunday in some nice place — hanging on his words. Of course it had always been that way, only he had never known it. Looking back over his barren past he surveyed minor incidents with new eyes. There was that girl with the pretty hair in the business college, who always smiled in the quick, confidential way at him. Maybe she wouldn't have been a talker!

And how far was this present affair going? Pretty far already: clandestine meetings and that sort of thing. Still, he couldn't help being a man, could he? And Tommy Hollins, poor dupe!

In the steam-heated apartment It had been locked in a closet, which in an upright position It fitted nicely. He did not open the door that night. He felt that he was venturing into ways that the wise and good king would not approve. He could not face the thing while guilt was in his heart. A woman had come between them.

*A*t three o'clock the next afternoon he lounged carelessly against the basement railing of the steam-heated apartment. With Nap on a leash he was keenly aware that he was "some class." He was arrayed in the new suit of a quiet check. The cravat with the red stripe shimmered in the sunlight. He had a new straw hat with a colored band, bought the day before at a shop advertising "Snappy Togs for Dressy Men." He lightly twirled a yellow stick and carried yellow gloves in one hand. He was almost the advanced dresser, dignified but unquestionably a bit different. He seemed to be one who has tamed the world to his ends; but, though he stood erect, expanded his chest and drew in his waist, as instinctively do all those who wear America's greatest eighteen-dollar suit, he was nevertheless wondering with a lively apprehension just what was going to be done with him. This life of "affairs" was making him uncomfortable.

Taking Nap along, he somehow felt, was a wise precaution. He didn't know what mad thing you might expect of Grandma, the Demon, but surely nothing very discreditable could occur in the presence of that innocent dog. And he would play the waiting game; make 'em show their hands.

At twenty minutes after three he wondered if he mightn't reasonably disappear. He would walk in the park and say afterward — if there should be an afterward — that he had given them up. An easy way out. He would do it. Twenty minutes more passed and he still meant to do it, knowing he wouldn't.

Then came the blare of a motor horn and Breede's biggest and blackest car descended upon him, stopping neatly at the curb.

He retained his calm, nonchalantly doffing the new straw hat.

"Just strolling off," he said; "given you up."

"Pops wanted to come," explained the flapper. "I had a perfectly annoying time not letting him. What a darling child of a dog! *Does* he want to — well, he *shall!*"

And Nap did at once. He seemed in the flapper to be greeting an old friend. He interrogated his lawful owner from the flapper's embrace, then reached up to implant a moist salute upon the ear of Grandma, who at once removed herself from his immediate presence.

"Sit there yourself," she commanded Bean. And Bean sat there beside the flapper, with Nap between them. The car moved gently on under the gaze of the impressed Cassidy, who had clattered up the iron stairway. Cassidy's gaze seemed to say, "All right, me lad, but you want t' look out f'r that sort. I know th' kind well!"

The car was moving swiftly now, heading for the north and the open.

"They cut us off yesterday," said the flapper. "I know I shall simply make a lot of trouble for that operator some day."

He wondered if she had heard that mad "Chubbins!" But now the flapper smiled upon him with a wondrous content, and he could say nothing. Instead of talking he stroked the head of Nap, who was panting with the excitement of this celestial adventure.

"I like you in that," confided the flapper with an approving glance. He wondered if she meant the hat, the cravat or America's very best suit for the money.

"I like *you* in that," he retorted with equal vagueness, at last stung to speech.

"Oh, this!" explained the flapper in pleased deprecation. "It's just a little old rag. What's his darling name?"

"Eh? Name? Napoleon, Man and — I mean Napoleon. I call him Nap," he said shortly, feeling himself in chameleonlike sympathy with the cravat.

Grandma, on the seat in front of them, stared silently ahead, but there was something ominous in her rigidity. She had the air of a captor.

Once when his hand was on Nap the flapper brazenly patted it. He pretended not to notice.

"Everything's all right," she said.

"Of course," he answered, believing nevertheless that everything was all wrong.

They had come swiftly to the country and now swept along a wide highway that narrowed in perspective far and straight ahead of them. He watched the road, grateful for the slight hypnotic effect of its lines running toward him. He must play the waiting game.

"Here's the inn," said the flapper. They turned into a big green yard and drew up at the steps of a rambling old house begirt with wide piazzas on which tables were set. This would be the nice place where he was to give them tea and things. They descended from the car, and he was aware that they pleasantly drew the attention of many people who were already there having tea and things: the big car and Grandma and the flapper in her little old rag and Nap still panting ecstatically, and, not least, himself in dignified and a little bit different apparel, lightly grasping the yellow stick and the quite as yellow gloves. It was horribly open and conspicuous, he felt; still, getting out of a car like that – and the flapper's little old rag was something that had to be looked at – he was drunk with it. Following a waiter to a table he felt that the floor was not meeting his feet.

They were seated! The shocking affair was on. The waiter inclined a deferential ear to the gentleman from the large and costly car.

"Tea and things," said the gentleman with a very bored manner indeed, and turned to rebuke the rare and costly dog with harsh words for his excessive emotion at the prospect of food.

The waiter manifested delight at the command; one could not help seeing that he considered it precisely the right one. He moved importantly off. The three regarded each other a moment.

Bean played the waiting game. The flapper played her ancient game of looking at him in that curious way. Grandma looked at them both, then meaningly at Bean. She spoke.

"I'll say very frankly that I wouldn't marry you myself."

He blinked, then he pretended to search with his eyes for their vanished waiter. But it was no good. He had to face the Demon, helpless.

"But that's nothing to your discredit, and it isn't a question of me," she added dispassionately.

His inner voice chanted, "Play the waiting game; play the waiting game."

"Every woman with a head on her knows what she wants when she sees it. And nowadays, thanks to the efforts of a few noble leaders of our sex, she has the right and the courage to take it. I haven't wasted any time talking to *her.*" She indicated the flapper, who still fixed the implacable look on Bean.

"If she doesn't know at nineteen, she never would —"

"We've settled all *that,*" said the flapper loftily. "Haven't we?"

Bean nodded. All at once that look of the flapper's began to be intelligible. He could almost read it.

"I suppose you expect me to talk a lot of that stuff about marriage being a serious business," continued the Demon evenly. "But I shan't. Marriage isn't half as serious as living alone is. It's what we were made for in my time, and your time isn't a bit different, young man."

She raised an argumentative finger toward him, as if he had sought to contest this.

"I've always —" he began weakly. But the Demon would have none of it.

"Oh, don't tell *me* what you've 'always!' I know well enough what you've 'always.' That isn't the point."

What did the woman think she was talking about? Couldn't he say a word to her without being snapped at?

"What is the point?" he ventured. It was still the waiting game, and it showed he wasn't afraid of her.

"The point is —"

And in that instant Bean read the flapper's look, the look she had puzzled him with from their first meeting. It was like finally understanding an oft-heard phrase in a foreign tongue. How luminous that look was now! The simple look of proud and assured and most determined ownership! It lay quietly on her face now as always. It was the look he must have bestowed on his shell the first time he saw it. Ownership!

"— the point is," the Demon was saying terribly, "I don't believe in long engagements."

He had once been persuaded, yielding out of spineless bravado, to descend the shaft of a mine in a huge bucket. The sensations of that plunge were now reproduced. He looked up to the far circle of light that ever diminished as he went down and down.

"I don't believe in them either," said the flapper firmly. "They're perfectly no good."

"I never did believe in 'em," he heard himself saying. And added with firmness equal to the flapper's, "Silly!" He was wondering if they would ever pull him to the surface again; if the rope would break.

"Just what I think," chanted the flapper. "Silly, and then some!"

"Then some!" repeated the male being in helpless, terrified corroboration.

"Won't he ever come?" queried the Demon. "Oh, here he is!"

The waiter was neatly removing tea and things from the tray. Bean recalled how on that other occasion he had fearfully believed the earth would close upon him, how hope revived as he was precariously drawn upward, and what a novel view the earth's fair surface presented when he again stood firmly upon it.

It was the waiter who raised him from this other abyss where he had been like to perish, the waiter and the things, including tea: plates, forks, napkins, cups and saucers, tea and hot water, jam, biscuit, toast. There was something particularly reassuring about that plate of nicely matched triangles of buttered toast. It spoke of a sane and orderly world where you were never taken off your feet.

"How many lumps?" demanded the pouring flapper.

"Just as you like; I'm not fussy," he answered.

This was untrue. His preference in the matter was decided, but he could not remember what it was. Afterward he knew that he did not take sugar in his tea, but the flapper had sweetened it with three lumps. Grandma again addressed him, engaging his difficult attention with a brandished fragment of toast.

"I can't imagine how you were ever mad enough to think of it," she said, "but you were. I give you credit for that. And just let me tell you that you've won a treasure. Of course, I don't say you won't find her difficult now and then, but you mustn't be too overbearing; give in a bit now and then; 't won't hurt you. Remember she's got a will of her own, as well as you have. Don't try to ride rough-shod —"

"Oh, we've settled all *that*," broke in the flapper. "Haven't we?"

"We've settled all that," said Bean, grateful for the solid feel of a cup in his fingers.

"Don't be too domineering, that's all," warned the Demon. "She wouldn't put up with it."

"I understand all *that*," insisted Bean, resolutely seizing a fork for which he had no use. "I can look ahead!"

He began hurriedly to eat toast, hoping it would seem that he had more to say but was too hungry to say it.

"I know *you*," persisted the Demon. "Brow-beating, bound to have your own way, and, after all, she's nothing but a child."

"I'll *want* him to have his own way," declared the child. "I'll see that he just perfectly gets it, too!"

"Give and take, that's my motto," he muttered, wondering if more toast would choke him.

"Be a row back there, of course," said Grandma, "but Julia's going to marry off the other child after her own heart, and it's only right for me to have a little say about this one. You're a better man than he is. You have a good situation and he's just a waster; couldn't buy his own cigarettes if he had to work for the money, say nothing of his gloves and ties. Born to riches, born to folly, say I. Still, Julia will fuss just about so much. Of course, Jim —"

"Oh, poor old Pops!" The flapper gracefully destroyed him as a factor in the problem.

Bean was feeding toast to Nap, who didn't choke.

"She always has to come around though when the girl makes up her mind. I haven't had that child in my charge for nothing."

"I have a right to choose the —" The flapper broke her speech with tea. "I have the *right,*" she concluded defiantly.

Bean shuddered. He recalled the terrific remainder of that speech.

"I thought we better have this little talk," said Grandma, "and get everything understood."

"'S the only way to do," said Bean, wrinkling his forehead, "have everything clear."

"I had it all perfectly planned out long ago," said the flapper. "I don't *want* a large place."

"Lots of trouble," conceded Bean. "Something always coming up," he added knowingly.

"Nice yard," said the flapper, "plenty of room for flowers and the tennis court, and I'll do the marketing when I motor in for you. They won't let me do it back there," she concluded with some acrimony; "and they get good and cheated and I'm perfectly glad of it. Eighteen cents a head for lettuce! I saw that very thing on a tag yesterday!"

"Rob you right and left," mumbled Bean. "All you can expect."

"Just leave it all to me," said the flapper with four of her double nods. "They'll soon learn better."

"Hardly seems as if it could all be true," ventured Bean in a genial effort at sanity.

"It's just perfectly true and true," insisted the flapper. "I knew it all the time." She placed the old relentless gaze upon him. He was hers.

"The beautiful, blind wants of youth!" said the Demon, who had been silent a long time, for her. "I remember —" But it seemed to come to nothing. She was silent again.

He paid the waiter.

"It was just as well to have this little talk," murmured Grandma as they arose.

The car throbbed before the steps. They were in and away. A reviving breeze swept them as the car gained speed. At least it partially revived one of them.

In the back seat he presently found a hand in his, but his own hand seemed no longer a part of him. He thought the serenity of the flapper was remarkable. She seemed to feel that nothing wonderful had happened. There was something awful about that calm.

*T*he car stopped before the steam-heated apartment. There were but brief adieus before it went on. Cassidy sat at the head of his basement stairs with a Sunday paper. He was reading an article entitled, "My Secrets of Beauty," profusely illustrated.

"I wouldn't have one o' the things did ye give it t' me," said Cassidy. "Runnin' inta telegrapht poles an' trolley cairs."

"Couple of friends of mine took me out for a little spin," said Bean, clutching his stick, his gloves and Nap's leash.

He seemed to be still spinning.

In his own place he went quickly to Its closet, pulled open the door and shouted aloud:

"Well, what do you make of *that?*"

The sound of his own voice was startling as he caught the look of the serene Ram-tah. He softly closed the door upon what his living self had been. He was too violent.

But he could not be cool all at once. He tossed hat, stick, and gloves aside and paced the room.

Engaged to be married! That was all anyone could make of it. All the agreeable iniquity had been extracted from the affair. It was fearsomely respectable. And it was deadly serious. How had he got into it? And yet he had always felt something ominous in that girl's look.

And there would be a row "back there." Julia would make the row. And Jim. They might think Jim wouldn't help in the row, but he knew better. Jim was old Jim Breede, who would of course take Bunker Bean's head off. He had been a fool all the time. In the car he had strained himself to the point of mentioning the Hollins boy. The flapper had laughed unaffectedly. Tommy Hollins was a perfectly darling boy, a good sport and all that, but he couldn't be anything important to the flapper if he were the perfectly last man on earth. How anyone could ever have thought such an absurd thing was beyond the flapper, for one.

And she didn't want a large place: flowers and a tennis court, and she'd do the marketing herself when she motored in for him. Moreover, he was not to be brutally domineering. He was to curb that tendency in himself, at least now and then, and let her have an opinion or two of her own. She was nothing but a child, after all; he mustn't be harsh with her.

He was weak before it. Once more he opened the closet door, feeling the need for new strength. A long time he looked into the still face. He was a king. Was it strange that a woman had fallen before him?

He reduced the event to its rudiments. He was the affianced husband of Breede's youngest daughter, who didn't believe in long engagements.

The thing was incredible, even as he faced Ram-tah.

How had he ever done it?

"Gee!" he muttered, "how'd I ever have the nerve to *do* it!"

Ram-tah's sleeping face remained still. If the wise and good king knew the answer he gave no sign.

X

"*W*here maint'nance f'r both roadway an' 'quipment is clearly surcharged," Breede was exploding, "extent of excess of maintenance over normal 'quirements cannot be taken as present earnin' power, an' this'll haf t' be understood before nex' meetin' d'r'ectors —"

"No need of *you* making any fuss," wrote Bean. "Let Julia do that. I'm as good a man as anybody if you come right down to it."

"— these prior-lien bon's an' receiver's stiff-cuts mus' natchally come ahead of firs'-mortgage bon's —" continued Breede.

"Wouldn't care if she told you right now over that telephone," wrote Bean. "You wouldn't dare touch me, and you know it."

Later he wrote "Poor old Pops!" contemptuously, and put an evil sneer upon Breede's removed cuffs.

At the same time he wished that the flapper and Grandma hadn't been so set against long engagements. And how long had they meant? One day, a week, a month? Would they have *it* done the next time they took him out in that car for tea and things? They were capable of it. Why couldn't they be reasonable and let things stay quiet for a while?

And how about that small place with flowers and a tennis court and a motor to go marketing in? Did they believe he was made of money? About all he could do was to provide a place big enough for a growing dog. And Breede, of course, would cast the girl off penniless, as they always did, telling her never to darken his doors again. And he'd have to find a new job. Breede wouldn't think of keeping on the scoundrel who had lured his child away.

Still, the flapper's mind was set on an early marriage, and, for this once, at least, he would let her have her own way. No good being brutal at the start. They would get along; scrimp and save; even move to Brooklyn, maybe. He looked into the far years and saw his son, greatest of all left-handed pitchers, shutting out Pittsburgh without a single hit. A very aged couple in the grandstand tried to claim relationship with his pitching marvel, saying he was their grandson, but few of the yelling enthusiasts would credit it. One of the crowd would later question the phenomenon's father, who was none other than the owner of the home team, and he would say, "Oh, yes, quite true, but there has been no communication between the two families for more than twenty years."

There would now follow from the abject grandparents timid overtures for a reconciliation, they having at last seen their mistake. These overtures met with a varying response. Sometimes he was adamant and told them no; they had made their bed twenty years before, and now they could lie on it. Again, he would relent, allowing them to come to the house and associate with their superb descendant once every week. He didn't want to be too hard on them.

And he was not penniless. He would continue in the unexciting express business for a while, until he had amassed enough to buy the ball-team.

Out at his typewriter, turning off Breede's letters, his mind kept reverting to those nicely printed stock certificates Aunt Clara had sent to him, five of them for ten shares each, his own name written on them. Of course there were hundreds of shares at the brokers', but those seemed not to mean so much. And they had gone down a point, whatever that was, since his purchase. The broker had explained that this was because of an unexpectedly low dividend, 3 percent. It showed bad management. All the more reason for getting a new man on the Board — a lot of old fossils!

He recalled the indignant-looking old gentleman who was so excessively well dressed. He wore choice gold-rimmed eyeglasses tethered by a black silk ribbon. They were intensely respectable things when adjusted to the nose, but he knew he should clash with that old party the moment he got on the Board. He would find him to be one of the sort that is always looking for trouble.

He wondered if he might not himself some day have sufficient excuse for wearing glasses like those, at the end of a silk ribbon. He thought they set off the face. And the old gentleman's white parted beard flowed down upon a waistcoat he wouldn't mind owning: black silk set with tiny white stars, a good background for a small gold chain. There would be a bunch of important keys on one end of that chain. Bean had yearned to wear one of those key-chains, but he had never had more than a trunk-key and a latchkey, and it would look silly to pull those out on a chain before people; they'd begin to make fun of you!

He worked on, narrowly omitting to have Breede inform the vice-president of an important trunk-line that it wouldn't hurt him any to have those trousers pressed once in a while; also that plenty of barbers would be willing to cut his hair.

Bulger condescendingly wrote at his own typewriter, as if he were the son of a millionaire pretending to work up from the bottom. Old Metzeger was deep in a dream of odd numerals. The half-dozen other clerks wrought at tasks not too absorbing to prevent frequent glances at the clock on the wall.

Tully, the chief clerk, marred the familiarity of the hour by approaching Bean's desk. He walked lightly. Tully always walked as if he felt himself to be on dangerously thin ice. He might get safely across; then again he mightn't. He leaned confidentially on the back of Bean's chair and Bean looked up and through the lenses that so alarmingly magnified Tully's eyes. Tully twitched the point of his blond beard with thumb and finger as if to reassure himself of its presence.

"By the way, Bean, I notice some fifty shares of Federal Express stock in your name. Now it is not impossible that the office would be willing to take them over for you."

That was Tully's way. He was bound to say "some" fifty shares instead of fifty, and of anything he knew to be true he could only aver "it is not impossible." Of a certain familiar enough event in the natural world he would have declared, "The sun sets not infrequently in the west."

Bean was for the moment uncertain of Tully's meaning.

"Shares," he said. "Right there in my desk."

"Quite so, quite so!" said Tully. "I'm not wholly uncertain, you know – this is between us – that I couldn't place them for you. I may say the office would not find even those few shares unwelcome."

"Well, you see, I don't know about that," said Bean. "You see, I had a kind of an idea –"

"I think I may say they would take it not unkindly," said Tully.

"– of holding on to them," concluded Bean.

"Your letting them go for a fair price might not inconceivably react to your advantage," suggested the luminous Tully.

"It is not impossible that I shall want them myself," responded Bean, unconsciously adopting the Tully indirection.

"The office is not unwilling —" began Tully.

"I'll keep 'em a while," said Bean. "I have a sort of plan."

"I should not like to think it possible —"

Bean was tired of Tully. What was the man trying to get at, anyway? He didn't know; but he would shut him off. His mind leaped with an inspiration.

"I can imagine nothing of less consequence," said Bean.

He was at once proud of the snappy way the words came out. Breede, he thought, could hardly have been snappier. He glared at Tully, who looked shocked, hurt, and disgusted. Tully sighed and walked back to his own desk, as if the ice cracked beneath his small feet at every step.

Bean resumed his work, with the air of one forgetting a past annoyance. But he was not forgetting. He might let them have the stock; he had never thought any too well of that express directorship; but let them send someone that could talk straight. He didn't care if he *had* been short with Tully. He was going to lose his job anyway, the day after that wedding, if not before.

He wrote many of Breede's letters, and was again interrupted, this time by Markham, Breede's confidential secretary. Markham's approach to Bean was emphatically footed, as that of a man unable to imagine ice being thin under *his* feet. He was bluff and open, where Tully lurked behind his "not impossibles." He was even jovial now. He smiled down at Bean.

"By the way, Bean, someone was telling me you have some Federal Express."

"Have the shares right there in my desk," admitted Bean, wonderingly. He was suspicious all at once. Tully and Markham had both opened on him with "By the way." He had always felt it a shrewd thing to suspect people who began with "By the way."

"Ah, yes, fifty shares, I believe." Markham smiled again, but seemed to try not to smile. He apparently considered it a rare jest that Bean should own any shares of anything; a thing for smiles even though one must humor the fellow.

"Fifty shares! Well, well, that's good! Now the fact is, old man, I can place those for you this afternoon. Some of the Federal people going to meet informally here, and they happen to want a little block or two of the stuff, for voting purposes, you know. Not that it's worth anything. How'd you happen to get down on such a dead one?"

"Well, you know, I had a sort of a plan about that stock. I don't know —"

"Of course I can't get you what you paid for it," continued the affable Markham, "because it's poor stuff, but maybe they'll stand a point or two above today's quotations. Just let me have them and I'll get your check made out right away; you can go out of here with more money tonight than anyone else will." Markham was prattling on amiably, still trying not to be overcome by the funny joke of Bean owning things.

"I don't want to sell," declared Bean. There had been a moment's hesitation, but that opening, "By the way," of Markham's had finally decided him. You couldn't tell anything about such a man.

"Oh, come now, old chap," cajoled Markham, "Be a good fellow. It's only needed for a technical purpose, you know."

"I guess I'll hold on to it," said Bean. "I've been thinking for a long time —"

"Last quarter's dividend was 3 percent," reminded Markham.

"I know," admitted Bean, "and that's just why. You see I've got an idea —"

"As a matter of fact, I think J.B. doesn't exactly approve of his people here in the office speculating. He doesn't consider it . . . well, you know one of you chaps here, if you weren't all loyal, might very often take advantage — you get my point?"

"I guess I won't sell just now," observed Bean.

"I don't understand this at all," said Markham, allowing it to be seen that he was shocked.

Bean wavered, but he was nettled. He was going to lose his job anyway. You might as well be hung for a sheep as a lamb. To Markham standing there, hurt and displeased, he looked up and announced curtly:

"I can imagine nothing of less consequence!"

He had the felicity to see Markham wince as from an unseen blow. Then Markham walked back to his own room. His tread would have broken ice capable of sustaining a hundred Tullys.

He saw it all now. They were plotting against him. They had learned of his plan to become a director and they were trying to freeze him out. He had never spoken of this plan, but probably they had consulted some good medium who had warned them to look out for him. Very well, if they wanted fight they should have fight. He wouldn't sell that stock, not even to Breede himself —

"Buzz! Buzz! Buzz!" went the electric call over his desk. That meant Breede. Very well; he knew his rights. He picked up his notebook and answered the summons.

Breede, munching an innocent cracker, stared at him.

"How long you had that Federal stock?"

"Aunt bought it five years ago."

"Where?"

"Chicago."

"Want to sell?"

"I think I'd rather —"

"You won't sell?"

"No!"

"'S all!"

Back at his machine he tried to determine whether he would have "let out" at Breede as he had at Tully and at Markham. He had supposed that Breede would of course nag him as the other two had. And would he have said to Breede with magnificent impudence, "I can imagine nothing of less consequence?" He thought he would have said this; the masks were very soon bound to be off Breede and himself. The flapper might start the trouble any minute. But Breede had given him no chance for that lovely speech. No good saying it unless you were nagged.

He became aware that the "Federal people" Markham had mentioned were gathering in Breede's room. Several of them brushed by him. Let them freeze him out if they could. He wondered what they said at meetings. Did everyone talk, or only the head director? Markham had said this was to be an informal meeting.

It is probable that Bean would not have been much enlightened by the immediate proceedings of this informal meeting. The large, impressive, moneyed-looking directors sat easily about the table in Breede's inner room, and said little of meaning to a tyro in the express business.

The stock was pretty widely held in small lots, it seemed, and the agents out buying it up were obliged to proceed with caution. Otherwise people would get silly ideas and begin to haggle over the price. But the shares were coming in as rapidly as could be expected.

Bean would have made nothing of that. He would have been bored, until Markham made a reference to fifty shares that happened to be owned by a young chap in the outer office.

"Take 'em over," said one heavy-jowled director who incongruously held a cigarette between lips that seemed to demand the largest and blackest of cigars.

"He won't sell," answered Markham. "I spoke to him."

"Tell him to," said the director to Breede.

"Tell him yourself," said Breede. "He said he wouldn't sell."

"Um! Well, well!" said the director.

"Exactly what I told him," remarked the conscientious Tully, who was present to take notes, "and he said to me, 'Mr. Tully, I am unwilling to imagine anything of less consequence.' He seemed, uh – I might say – decided."

"Gave me the same thing," said Markham.

"Leak in the office," announced the elderly advanced dresser. "Fifty shares!" he added, twirling the glasses on their silk ribbon. "Hell! Going to let him get away with it?"

"Got to be careful," suggested a quiet director who had listened. "Can't tell who's back of him."

"Call him in," ordered the advanced dresser, fixing the glasses firmly on his purple nose. "Call him in! Bluff him in a minute!"

"Buzz! Buzz! Buzz!" smote fatefully on Bean's ears. He had expected it. If they didn't let him alone, he would tell them all that he could imagine nothing of less consequence.

He entered the room. He hardly dared scan the faces of those directors in the flesh, but they were all scanning him. He stood at the end of the table and fastened his eyes on a railway map that bedecked the opposite wall, one of those mendacious maps showing a trans-continental line of unbroken tangent; three thousand miles of railway without a curve, the opposition lines being mere spirals.

"Here, boy!" It was the advanced dresser of the white parted beard and the constant indignation. Bean looked at him. He had known from the first that he must clash with this man.

"That sort of thing'll never do with *us*, you know," continued the old gentleman, when he had diverted Bean's attention from the interesting map. "Never do at all; not at all; *not-tat-tall*. Preposterous! My word! What rot!"

The last was, phonetically, "Wha' *trawt!*"

Bean was studying the old gentleman's faultless garments. He wore a particularly effective waistcoat of white piqué striped with narrow black lines, and there was a pink carnation in the lapel of the superbly tailored frock coat.

"Wha' trawt!" repeated the ornate director. Bean looked again at the map.

"Here, boy, your last chance. We happen to need those shares in a little matter of voting. I'll draw you a check for the full amount."

He produced the daintiest of check-books and a fountain pen of a chaste design in gold. Bean's look was the look of those who see visions.

"Now then, *now* then!" spluttered the old gentleman, the pen poised. "Don't keep me waiting; don't keep me, I say! What amount? Wha' *tamount?*"

Bean's eyes were withdrawn from the wall. He came briskly to life.

"I'll tell you in a moment. I'll get the shares."

"Shrimp!" said the old gentleman triumphantly, when Bean had gone.

"He told *me,*" began Tully. But the advanced dresser wanted no more of that.

"Shrimp!" he repeated.

Bean reëntered with the certificates. The old gentleman glanced angrily over them.

"Bean!" he exclaimed humorously. "Vegetable after all; not a fish! Funny name that! Bunker Bean! Boston, by gad! Not bad that, I *say!* Come, come, *come!* Want par, of course — all do! There y'are, boy!"

He blotted the check, tore it from the book and waved it toward Bean as he turned to the director of the cigarette.

"About that proposition before us today, Mr. Chairman —" but Bean had gone. Observing this, the old gentleman looked about him.

"Shrimp!" he said contemptuously, with the convinced air of an expert in marine biology.

Bean, outside, once more addressed himself to typewriting. He wondered if he should be seized with a toothache or a fainting spell. Toothache was good, but perhaps Bulger had used that too often. Still Tully would "fall" for a toothache. It gave him a chance to say that if people would only go to a dentist once every three months — Then he remembered that Tully was inside. He wouldn't make any excuse at all.

"Going out a few minutes," he explained to old Metzeger as he swiftly changed from his office coat and adjusted the new straw hat.

Bulger glanced up from his machine, winked at him and shaped a word with his able mouth. An adept in lip-reading could have seen it to be "Chubbins." Bean in response leered confession at him.

The broker's office was in the adjoining block.

"I've just made a little deal," explained Bean to the person who inquired his business. "Here's the check. You know I've got a sort of an idea I'd like a little more of that Federal Express stuff. Just buy me some the same as you did before, as much as you can get on ten margins, er — I mean on ten points."

"Nothing much doing in that stock," suggested the expert. "Why don't you get down on some the live ones. Now there's Union Pacific —"

"I know, but I want Federal Express. That is, you see, I want it merely for a technical purpose." He felt happy at recalling Markham's phrase.

"All right," said the expert resignedly. "We'll do what we can. May take three or four days."

Bean started for the door.

"Say," called the expert, as if on second thought, "you're up at Breede's office, ain't you — old J.B.'s?"

"Oh, I'm there for a few days yet," said Bean.

"Ah, ha!" said the expert. "Have a cigar!"

Bean aimlessly accepted the proffer.

"Sit down and gas a while," urged the expert genially. "Things looking up any over your way?"

"Oh, so-so, only," said Bean. "But I can't stop, thanks! Got to hurry back to see a man."

"Drop in again anytime," said the expert. "We try to make this little den a home for our customers."

"Thanks!" said Bean. "I'll be sure to."

"Ah ha, and ah ha!" said the expert to himself. "Now I wonder."

On his way back to the office Bean suddenly discovered that he was chewing an unlighted cigar. He stopped to observe in a polished window its effect on his face. He rather liked it. He pulled the front of his hat down a bit and held the cigar at a confident angle. He thought it made him look forceful. He wished he might pass the purple-faced old gentleman — the whole Breede gang, for that matter — and chew the cigar at them.

"I'll show them," he muttered, over and around the impeding cigar. "I'll show them they can't keep *me* off that board. I knew what to do in a minute. Napoleon of Finance, eh? I'll show them who's who!"

He was back at his desk finishing the last of Breede's letters for the day. Tully had not discovered his absence. He winked at Bulger to assure him that the worst interpretation could be put upon that absence. He wondered if anything else could happen before the day ended.

"Telephone for Boston Bean," called the wag of an office boy.

This time he closed the double door of the booth, letting Bulger think what he pleased.

"I forgot to ask what you take, mornings," pealed the flapper.

"Take — mornings?"

"For breakfast, silly! Because I think it's best for you to take just eggs and toast; a little fruit of course; not all that meat and things."

"Oh, yes, of course; eggs and — things. Never want much."

"Well, all right, I just perfectly knew you'd see it that way. I'm making up lists. Tell me, do you like a paneled dining room, you know, fumed oak, or something?"

"Only kind I'd ever have."

"I knew you would. What are you doing all the time?"

"Oh, me? I'm getting things into shape. You see, I have an idea —"

"Don't you buy the least little thing until I know. We want to be sure everything harmonizes and I've just perfectly got everything in my head the way it will be."

"That's right; that's the only way."

"You didn't say anything about — you know — to poor old Pops, did you?"

"Why, no. I didn't. You see he's been pretty much thinking about other things all day, and I —"

"Well, that's right. I was afraid you'd be just perfectly impatient. But you leave it all to me. I'll manage. It's the dearest joke! I may not tell them for two or three days. Every time I get alone I just perfectly giggle myself into spasms. Isn't it the funniest?"

"Ha, ha, ha, ha! I should think it was." He was fearfully hoping her keen sense of humor might continue to rule.

"We *do*, don't we?"

"Do what?"

"*You* know, stupid!"

"Yes, *yes* indeed! We just perfectly *do!*"

"More than any two people ever did before, don't we?"

"Well, I should think so; and then some."

"I knew you'd feel that way. Well, good-bye!"

He could fancy her giving the double nod as she hung up the receiver.

During the ride uptown he talked large with a voluble gentleman who had finished his evening paper and who wished to recite its leading editorial from memory as something of his own. They used terms like "the tired business man," "increased cost of living," "small investor," "the common people," and "enemies of the Public Good." The man was especially bitter against the Wall Street ring, and remarked that anyone wishing to draw a lesson from history need look no farther back than the French Revolution. The signs were to be observed on every hand.

Bean felt a little guilty, though he tried to carry it off. Was he not one of that same Wall Street ring? He pictured himself as a tired business man eating boiled eggs of a morning in a dining room paneled with fumed oak, the flapper across the table in some little old rag. He thought it sounded pretty luxurious — like a betrayal of the common people. Still he had to follow his destiny. You couldn't get around that.

He stood a long time before Ram-tah that night, grateful for the lesson he had drawn from him in the afternoon. Back there among those fierce-eyed directors, badgered by the most objectionable of them, nerving himself to say presently that he could imagine nothing of less consequence, there had come before his eyes the inspiring face of the wise and good king. But most unaccountably, as he gazed, it seemed to him that the great Ram-tah had opened those long-closed eyes; opened them full for a moment; then allowed the left eye to close swiftly.

XI

*T*he day began with placid routine. Breede did his accustomed two-hours' monologue. And no one molested Bean. No one appeared to know that he was other than he seemed, and that big things were going forward. Tully ignored him. Markham, who had the day before called him "Old man!" whistled obliviously as they brushed past each other in the hall. No directors called him in to tell him that would never do with *them.*

He was grateful for the lull. He couldn't be "stirred up" that way every day. And he needed to gather strength against Breede when Breede should discover that exquisite joke of the flapper's. He suspected that the flapper wouldn't find it funny to keep the thing from poor old Pops more than a few days longer.

"I'll be drawing my last pay next Saturday," he told himself.

"Telephone for Boston Baked," called the office-boy wit, late in the afternoon.

Bulger looked sympathetic.

"Same trouble I have," he confided as Bean passed him, "Take 'em on once and they bother the life out of you."

"You'd never believe," came the voice of the flapper. "I found the darlingest old sideboard with claw-feet yesterday over on Fourth Avenue. He wants two hundred and eighty, but they're all robbers, and I just perfectly mean to make him come down five or ten dollars. Every little counts. You leave it to me."

"Sure! You fix it all up!"

"And maybe we won't want fumed oak in the dining room — maybe a rich mahogany stain. Would that suit? I'm only thinking of you."

"I'll leave all that to you; you'll perfectly well manage."

"I just perfectly darling well knew you'd say that; and I'm sending you down a car —"

"A what? Car?" This was even more alarming than the darling old sideboard.

"Just a little old last year's car. Poor old Pops would give it to me now if I asked him — but it's just as well to have it away in case Moms could ever make him change his mind, only of course she perfectly well can't do anything of the sort. But anyway I'm sending it to that shop around the corner in the street below you, and they'll hold it there to your order. You never can tell; we might need it suddenly some time, and anyway you ought to have it, don't you see, because I'm just perfectly giving it to you this minute, and you can run about in it with that dearest dog, and it's the very first thing I ever gave you, isn't it? I'll always remember it just for that. It will do us all right for a few weeks, until we can look around. And there never was anyone before, was there? You just needn't answer; you'd have to say 'No,' and anyway Granny says a young — you know what — should never ask silly questions about what happened before she met him, because it perfectly well makes rows, and I know she's right, but there never *was*, was there, and no matter anyway, because it's settled forever now, and we *do*, don't we? My! but I'm excited. Don't forget what I said about the brass andirons and the curtains for your den. Goo'-bye."

"Huh! yes, of course not!" said Bean, but the flapper had gone.

Back at the typewriter he tried to collect his memories of her message: sideboard with darling feet of some kind, no fumed oak, perhaps — brass andirons, curtains for his den. He couldn't recall what she had said about those. Maybe it would come to him. He wished he had told her that he already had a few good etchings. And the car! That was plain in his mind — little old last year's thing — at that shop around the corner. Did one say "garrash" or "garrige?" He heard both.

Anyway, he owned a motorcar; you couldn't get around that. Maybe Bulger wouldn't open his eyes if he knew it. Bulger was an authority on cars, and spoke in detail of their strange insides with the aplomb of a man who has dissected them for years. He had violent disputes with the second bookkeeper about which was the best car for the money. The bookkeeper actually owned a motorcycle, or would, after he had paid five dollars a month a few more times, but Bulger would never allow this minor contrivance to be brought into their discussions. Bulger was intolerant of anything costing under five thou' — eat you up with repairs.

Bean longed to approach Bulger and say:

"Some dame, that! Just sent me a little old last year's car."

But he knew this would never do. Bulger would not only tell him why the car was of an inferior make, but he would want to borrow it to take a certain party, or maybe the gang, out for a spin, and get everybody killed or arrested or something. Bulger dressed fearlessly; no one with eyes could deny that; but he was tactless. Better keep that car under cover.

At seven-thirty that evening, with Nap on a leash, he strolled into the garage. He carried the yellow stick and the gloves, and he was prepared to make all sorts of a nasty row if they tried to tell him the car wasn't there, or so much as hinted that he might not be the right party. He knew how to deal with those automobile sharks.

"I believe you have a car here for me — Mr. Bean," he said briskly. It was the first time in all his life that he had spoken of himself as "Mr. Bean!" He threw his shoulders back even farther when he had achieved it.

The soiled person whom he addressed merely called to another soiled person who, near at hand, seemed to be beating an unruly car into subjection. The second person merely ducked his head backward and over his right shoulder.

"All right, all right!" said the first person, and then to Bean, "All right, all right!"

The car was before him, a large, an alarming car — and red! It was as red as the unworn cravat. Good thing it was getting dark. He wouldn't like to go out in the daytime in one as red as that, not at first.

He ran his eyes critically over it, trying to look disappointed.

"Good shape?" he demanded.

"How about it, Joe? She all right?"

Joe perceptibly stopped hammering.

"Garrumph-rumph!" he seemed to say.

"Well?" said the first person, eying Bean as if this explained everything.

"Take a little spin," said Bean.

"Paul!"

Paul issued from the office, a shock-headed, slouching youth in extreme negligée, a half-burned cigarette dangling from his lower lip. He yawned without dislodging the cigarette.

"Gentleman wants to g'wout." Paul vanished.

Nap had already leaped to a seat in the red car. He had learned what those things were for.

Paul reappeared, trim in leathern cap, well-fitting Norfolk jacket and shining puttees.

"Never know he only had on an undershirt," thought Bean, struck by this swiftly devised effect of correct dressing. He sat in the roomy rear seat beside Nap, leaning an elbow negligently on the arm-rest. He watched Paul shrewdly in certain mysterious preparations for starting the car. An observer would have said that one false move on Paul's part would have been enough.

The car rolled out and turned into the wide avenue half a block away.

"Where to, Boss?" asked Paul.

"Just around," said Bean. "Tea and things!"

They glided swiftly on.

"Oh, just a little old last year's car!" said Bean, frowning royally at a couple of mere foot people who turned to stare.

What would that flapper do next?

He surrendered to the movement. Drunkenly he mused upon a wild inspiration to bring Ram-tah out and give him a ride in this big red car. It appealed to him much. Ram-tah would almost open his eyes at the novelty of that progress. But he felt that this was no safe thing to do. He would be arrested. The whole secret might come out.

He had retained no sense of direction, but he was presently conscious of the river close at his side, and then the car, with warning blasts, curved up to a much lighted building and halted. A large man in uniform came solicitously to help him descend and gave him a fragment of cardboard which he knew would redeem his motor.

He was seated at a table looking down upon the shining river.

"Tea and things," he said to the waiter.

"Yes, sir; black or green, sir?"

"Bottle ginger ale!" How did he know whether he wanted black or green tea. No time to be fussy.

He began a lordly survey of the people at neighboring tables — people who had doubtless walked there, or come in hired cabs, at the best. Hired cabs had yesterday seemed impressive to him; now they were rather vulgar. Of course, there might be circumstances —

He froze like a pointing dog. At a table not twenty feet distant, actually in the flesh, sat the Greatest Pitcher the World Has Ever Known. For a moment he could only stare fixedly. The man was simply *there!* He was talking volubly to two other men, and he was also eating a mere raspberry ice!

It showed how things "worked around," once you got started. Hadn't his whole life been a proof of this? How many times had he wished he might happen upon that Pitcher just as he was now, in street clothes — to look at him, study him! He wished *he* had ordered raspberry ice instead of ginger ale, which he didn't like. He would order one anyway.

It was all Ram-tah. If you knew you were a king, you needn't ever worry again. You sat still and let things come to you. After all, a king was greater than a pitcher, if you came down to it — in some ways, certainly.

He stared until the group left the table. He could actually have touched the Pitcher as he passed. Would wonders never cease?

Two men in uniform helped him into the big red car again, tenderly, as if he were fragile. He had meant to return to the garage, but now he saw the more dignified way was to stop at his own house. Further, Paul should take him to the office in the morning and call for him at four-thirty again. He wouldn't be afraid to ride in the red car even in daylight now. Sitting there not twenty feet from that Pitcher!

"Eight o'clock in the morning," he said curtly to Paul as he descend-ed. And Paul touched his leather cap respectfully as the car moved off.

Cassidy lounged near in shirt sleeves.

"I see three was kilt-up in wan yistaday in th' Bur-ronx," said Cassidy interestedly.

"Good thing for the tired business man, though," said Bean, yawning in a bored way. "And that fellow of mine is careful."

Then his seeming boredom vanished.

"Say, you can't guess who I saw just now. Close to him as I am to you this minute —"

Solitary in the big red car, descending the crowded lanes of the city the next morning, Bean's sensations were conceivably those that had been Ram-tah's at the zenith of his power. There was the fragrant and cherished memory of the Greatest Pitcher, and a car to ride solitary in that simply blared the common herd from before it. People in street-cars looked enviously out at him. He lolled urbanely, with a large public manner. When you were a king you behaved like one, and the world knelt to you. Great pitchers sitting under the same roof with you; red motorcars; fumed oak dining rooms; flappers; brokers; shares. He wished he had thought to chew an unlighted cigar in this resplendent chariot. There seemed to be almost a public demand for it. Certain things were expected of a man!

"Be here at four-thirty," he directed.

And Paul, his fellow, glancing up along the twenty-two stories of the office building, was impressed. He considered it probable that the bored young man owned this building. "The guys that have gits!" thought Paul.

Bean was preposterously working once more, playing the part of a cog on the wheel. Another day, it seemed, of that grotesque nonsense, even after the world's Greatest Pitcher had sat not twenty feet from him the night before, eating raspberry ice. But events could not long endure *that* strain. Before the day was over Breede would undoubtedly "fire" him, with two or three badly chosen words; actually go through the form of discharging a man who had once ruled all Egypt with a kindly but an iron hand!

Of course, the fellow was unconscious of this, as he still must be of the rare joke the flapper was exquisitely holding over his head. His demeanor toward Bean betrayed no recognition of shares or pitchers or big red cars, nor of the ever-impending change in their relationship. He dictated fragments of English words, and Bean reconstructed them with the cunning of a Cuvier. He felt astute, robust, and disrespectful. Just one wrong word from Breede and all would be over between them. The poor old wreck didn't dream that he had nursed a flapper in his bosom, a flapper that would just perfectly have what she wanted — and no good fussing.

In the outer office, however, he was aware that his expansion was subtly making itself felt. Bulger had insensibly altered and was treating him after the manner of a fellow club man. Old Metzeger said "Good morning!" to him affectionately — for Metzeger — and once he detected Tully staring at him through the enlarging glasses as if in an effort to read his very soul. But he knew his soul was not to be read by such as Tully. Tully, back there on the Nile, would have been a dancer — at the most, a fancy skater — if, indeed, he had risen to the human order, and were not still a slinking gazelle. Good name that, for Tully. He would remember it — gazelle!

At three o'clock he glanced aside from his typewriter to see a director enter Breede's room. He did not lift his look above the hem of the man's coat, but he knew him for the quiet one. And yet, when the door closed upon him, he seemed to become as noisy as any of them. Bean heard his voice rising.

Another director came, the big one who gripped a cigarette with an obviously cigar mouth. Once behind the shut door he seemed to approve of the noise and to be swelling its volume.

Three other directors hurried in, the elderly advanced dresser in the lead. He, of course, was always indignant, but now the other two were manifesting choler equal to his own. They puffed and glowered and, when the door had closed, they seemed to help skillfully with the uproar. It was a mob scene.

Bean was reminded of a newspaper line he had once or twice encountered: "The scene was one of indescribable confusion. Pandemonium reigned!" Pandemonium indubitably seemed to reign over those directors. He wondered. He wondered uncomfortably.

"Buzz-z-z-z! Buzz-z-z-z-z! Buzz-z-z-z-z-z!"

He quit wondering. He knew.

Yet for a moment after he stood in their presence they seemed to take no note of him. They were not sitting decorously in chairs as he conceived that directors should. The big one with the cigarette sat on the table, ponderously balanced with a fat knee between fat red hands. Another stood with one foot on a chair. Only the quiet one was properly sitting down. The elderly advanced dresser was not even stationary. With the faultless coat thrown back by pocketed hands, revealing a waist line greater than it should have been, he strutted and stamped. He seemed to be trying to step holes into the rug, and to be exploding intimately to himself.

"Plain enough," said the man who had been studying his foot on the chair. "Someone pulled the plug."

"And away she goes — shoosh!" said the big man dramatically.

"Kennedy & Balch buying right and left. Open at a hundred and twenty-five tomorrow, sure!" said the quiet one quietly.

"Placed an order yesterday for four hundred shares and got 'em," said another, not so quietly. "And today they're bidding Federal Express up to the ceiling."

"Plug pulled!"

The advanced-dressing director strutted to the fore with a visibly purpling face.

"Plug pulled? Want t' know *where* it was pulled? Right in this office. Want to know who pulled it? *That!*" He pointed unmistakably to the child among them taking notes. At another time Bean might have quailed, at least momentarily; but he had now discovered that the advanced-dressing old gentleman used scent on his clothes. He was afraid of no man who could do that in the public nostrils. He surveyed the old gentleman with frank hostility, noting with approval, however, the dignified yet different pattern of his waistcoat. But he knew the other directors were looking hard at him.

"Shrimp! snake!" added the old gentleman, like a shocked naturalist encountering a loathsome hybrid.

"Been plowing with our heifer?" asked Breede incisively.

Bean was familiar with that homely metaphor. He felt easier.

"*Your* heifer!" He would have liked to snort as the old gentleman did, but refrained from an unpracticed effort! "Your heifer? No; I bought a good fat yoke of steers to do my plowing. Took *his* money to buy one of 'em with!" He waved a careless arm at the smoldering-vessel across the table. They were all gasping, in horror, in disgust. He was a little embarrassed. He sought to smooth the thing over a bit with his next words.

"Eagle shot down with its own feather," he said, hazily recalling something that had seemed very poetic when he read it.

"Wha'd I tell you? Wha'd I *tell* you!" shouted the oldest director, doing an intricate dance step.

"Hold 'ny Federal?" asked Breede.

"A block or two; several margins of it," said Bean.

"How many shares?"

"Have to ask Kennedy & Balch; they're my brokers. I guess about some seven or eight hundred shares."

"Wha'd I tell you? Wha'd I *tell* you?" again shouted the oldest director, and, as if despairing of an answer, he swore surprisingly for one of his refined garniture and aroma.

"Find out something in this office?" asked Breede, evenly.

"Why wouldn't I? I found out something the minute you sent people to me with that 'By the way —' stuff. I knew it as quick as you had them breaking their ankles trying to get my fifty shares. Knew it the very minute you sent that — that slinking gazelle to me." He pointed at Tully.

He had not meant to call Tully that. It rushed out. Tully wriggled uneasily in his chair at the desk, blushed well into his yellow beard, then drew out a kerchief of purest white silk and began nervously to polish his glasses.

"Hoo-shaw-Ha-ha-Hooshway!"

It was Breede, with, for the moment, a second purple face on the Board of Directors. Neither Bean nor Tully ever knew whether he had suppressed a laugh or a sneeze.

"Come, come, *come!*" broke in the oldest, sweeping the largest director aside with one finger as he pulled a chair to the table.

"This'll never do with *us*, you know! How much, how much, how much?"

He again poised the chastely wrought fountain pen of gold above the dainty check-book in Morocco leather.

"Have to give 'em up you know; can't allow *that* sort of underhand work; where'd the world be, where'd it be, where'd it *be*? Sign an order; tell me what you paid. Take your word for it!"

He was feeling for Bean the contempt which a really distinguished safe-blower is said to feel for the cheap thief who purloins bottles of milk from basement doorways in the grey of dawn.

"Now, now, *now*, boy!" The pen was still poised.

"Oh, put up your trinkets," said Bean with a fine affectation of weariness.

The old gentleman sat back and exhaled a scented but vicious breath. There was silence. It seemed to have become evident that the unprincipled young scoundrel must be taken seriously.

Then spoke the largest director, removing from his lips a cigarette which his own bulk seemed to reduce to something for a microscope only. He had been silent up to this moment, and his words now caused Bean the first discomfort he had felt.

"You will come here tomorrow morning," he began, slanting his entire facial area toward Bean, "and you will make restitution for this betrayal of trust. I think I speak for these gentlemen here, when I say we will do nothing with you tonight. Of course, if we chose — but no; you are a free man until tomorrow morning. After that all will depend on you. You are still young; I shall be sorry if we are forced to adopt extreme measures. I believe we shall all be sorry. But I am sure a night of sober reflection will bring you to your senses. You will come here tomorrow morning. You may go."

The slow, cool words had told. He tried to preserve his confident front, as he turned to the door. He would have left his banner on the field but for the oldest director, who had too long been silent.

"Snake in the grass!" hissed the oldest director, and instantly the colors waved again from Bean's lifted standard. He did not like the oldest director and he soared into the pure ether of verbal felicity, forgetful of all threats.

He stared pityingly at the speaker a moment, then cruelly said:

"You know they quit putting perfumery on their clothes right after the Chicago fire."

He left the room with faultless dignity.

"*Im*pertinent young whelp!" spluttered the oldest director; but his first fellow-director who dared to look at him saw that he was gazing pensively from the high window, his back to the group.

"No good," said the quiet director to the largest. "A little man's always the hardest to bluff. Bet I could bluff you quicker than you could bluff him!"

"Well, I didn't know what else," answered the largest director, who was already feeling bluffed.

"Why didn't J.B. here assert himself then?"

"'Fraid he'd get mad's 'ell an' quit me," said Breede. "Only st'nogfer ever found gimme minute's peace. Dunno why — talk aw ri'. He un'stan's me; res' drive me 'sane."

"Plug's pulled, anyway," commented the quiet director. "Only thing to do is haul in what we can on a rising market. God knows where she'll stop."

"Pound her down," said the largest director sagely.

"Any pounding now will pound her up."

"Hold off and let it die down."

"Only make it worse. No use; we've got to cut that money up."

"Seven hundred shares, did he say?" asked the large director. "Very pretty indeed! J.B., I'll only give you one guess whether he quits his job or not."

"Thasso!" admitted Breede dejectedly.

"He'll show up all right in the morning, mark me," said the largest director, regaining confidence.

"Sneaking snake in the grass," muttered the oldest director, yet without his wonted vim.

"I'll telephone to McCurdy, right in the next block here," continued the largest director. "Might as well have this chap watched tonight and keep tight to him tomorrow until he shows up. We may find somebody's behind him."

"'S my idea," said Breede, "someone b'ind him."

"Grinning little ape!" remarked the oldest director bitterly.

To Bean in the outer office came the facetious boy.

"Telephone for Perfesser Bunker Hill Monument," he said, but spoiled it by laughing himself. It was extempore and had caught him unawares. The harried Bean fled to the telephone booth.

"I wanted to tell you," began the flapper, "not to eat anything out of cans unless I just perfectly have it on my pure-food list. They poison people, but the dearest grocer gave me a list of all the safe things, made up by a regular committee that tells how much poison each thing has in it, so you can know right off, or alcohol either. Now, remember! Oh, yes, what was I going to say? Granny says the first glamour soon fades, but after that you just perfectly settle down to solid companionship. And oh, yes, I want you to let me just perfectly have my own way about those hangings for the drawing room, because you see I know, and, oh, I had something else. No matter. Won't I be glad when the deal is adjusted in the interests of all concerned, as poor old Pops says. Why don't you tell me something? I'm just perfectly waiting to hear."

"Uh, of course, of course; you're just perfectly a slinking gazelle. Ha, ha, ha!" answered Bean, laughing at his own jest after the manner of the office-boy.

He was back making a feeble effort to finish the last of Breede's letters. He glanced mechanically at his notes. Above that routine work he had so many things to think about. He'd fixed Tully for good. Tully wouldn't try that "by the way" and "not impossible" stuff with *him* anymore. And that little old man — perfumery not used since the Chicago fire, or had he said the Mexican War? No matter. And talked to Breede about heifers. But there was the big-faced brute, speaking pretty seriously. Let him go free *tonight!* State's prison offence, maybe! Might be in jail this time tomorrow. Would the flapper telephone to him there? Send him unpoisoned canned food? Would he be disgraced? Breede — directors — glamour wearing off — slinking gazelles with yellow whiskers — rotten perfumery. So rushed the turbulent flood of his mind. But the letter was finished at last.

Two days later a certain traffic manager of lines west of Chicago read a paragraph in this letter many times:

"The cramped conditions of this terminal have been of course appreciably relieved by the completion of the westside cut-off. Nevertheless our traffic has not yet attained its maximum, and new problems of congestion will arise next year. I am engaged to that perfectly flapper daughter of yours, and we are going to marry each other when she gets perfectly good and ready. Better not fuss any. Let Julia do the fussing. To meet this emergency I dare say it will come to four-tracking the old main line over the entire division. It will cost high, but we must have a first-class freight-carrier if we are to get the business."

The traffic manager at first reached instinctively for his telegraphic cipher code. But he reflected that this was not code-phrasing. He read the paragraph again and was obliged to remind himself that his only daughter was already the wife of a man he knew to be in excellent health. Also he was acquainted with no one named Julia.

He copied from the letter that portion of it which seemed relevant, and destroyed the original. He had never heard it said of Breede; but he knew there are times when, under continued mental strain, the most abstemious of men will relax.

XII

*W*hen Bean emerged from the office-building that afternoon he was closely scrutinized by an inconspicuous man who, just inside the door by the cigar-stand, had been conversing with Tully. Bean saw Tully, but strode by that gentleman with head erect, chest expanded, and waist drawn in. Tully was cut. And Bean did not, of course, notice the inconspicuous man with whom Tully talked.

This person, however, followed Bean to the street, where he seemed a little taken aback to observe the young man very authoritatively enter a large red touring car and utter a command to its driver with an air of seasoned ownership. The red car moved slowly up Broadway. The inconspicuous man surveyed the passing vehicles, and seemed relieved when he discovered an empty taxi-cab going north. He hailed it and entered, giving directions to its guide that entailed much pointing to the large red touring car now a block distant.

Thereafter, until late at night, the red car was trailed by the taxi-cab. At six o'clock the car stopped at a place of refreshment overlooking the river, where the trailed youth consumed a modest dinner, which he concluded with a radiant raspberry ice. A little later he reëntered the red car and was driven aimlessly for a couple of hours through leafy byways. The inconspicuous man became of the opinion that the occupant of the red car was cunningly endeavoring to conceal his true destination.

The car returned to the place of refreshment at nine-thirty, where the young man again ordered a raspberry ice, with which he trifled for the better part of an hour. He betrayed to the alert but inconspicuous person who sat near him, by his expectant manner of scanning newcomers' faces, that he had hoped to meet someone here.

This expectation was disappointed. The watchful person suspected that the youth's confederates might have been warned. The quarry at length departed, in obvious disappointment, and was driven to his abode in a decent neighborhood. The taxi-cab was near enough to the red car when this place was reached to enable its occupant to hear the young man request it for eight the following morning. The young man entered what a sign at the doorway declared to be "Choice Steam-heated Apartments," and the occupant of the taxi-cab was presently overheard by the janitor of the apartments expostulating with the vehicle's driver about the sum demanded for his evening's recreation. He was heard to denounce the fellow as "a thief and a robber!" and to make a vicious threat concerning his license.

Bean was face to face with Ram-tah, demanding whatever strength might flow to him from that august personage. A crisis had come. Either he was a king, or he was not a king. If a king, he must do as kings would do. If not a king, he would doubtless behave like a rabbit.

But strength flowed to him as always from that calm, strong face. In Ram-tah's presence he could believe no weakness of himself. Put him in jail, would they? A man who had not only once ruled a mighty people in peace, but who had, some hundreds of centuries later, made Europe tremble under the tread of his victorious armies. Ram-tah had been no fighter – but Napoleon! He, Bunker Bean, was a wise king, yet a mighty warrior. Beat him down, would they? Merely because he wanted to become a director in their company! Well, they would find out who they were trying to keep off that Board. What if they did put him in jail? A good lawyer would get him out in a few minutes with a writ of something or other, a stay of proceedings, a demurrer, a legal technicality. He read the papers. Lawyers were always getting Wall Street speculators out of jail by someone of those devices; and if every other means failed a legal technicality did the work. And the papers always called the released man a Napoleon of Finance. It wasn't going to be so bad.

He hauled Ram-tah out of the closet and stood him at the foot of the bed for the night, so that courage might come to him as he slept. The plan proved to be an excellent one after Nap grew quiet. Nap had always been excited in Ram-tah's immediate presence, and now he insisted upon sniffing about the royal cadaver in a manner atrociously suggestive. Being dissuaded from this and consenting to sleep, Bean sank into dreams of mastery beneath Ram-tah's lofty aspect.

He awoke with a giant's strength. He arrayed himself in the newest check suit, and an especially beautiful shirt with a lavender stripe that bore his embroidered initials on one sleeve. He thought he would like to face them in his shirtsleeves, and give Breede and the fussy old gentlemen a good look at that lettered arm. He was almost persuaded to don the entirely red cravat, let the consequences be what they might. His refreshed spirit was equal to this audacity – but the red car. Wearing a red cravat in a very red car was just a little *too* loud – "different" enough, to be sure, but hardly "dignified." Too advanced, in short. At eight o'clock he went out upon the world, grasping his yellow stick and gloves. Most heroically would he enter the office with stick and gloves. Make Bulger stare! And if they put him in jail he must look right – papers get his picture, of course!

On the curb, before the car that vibrated so excitingly he had a happy thought. Was he to go down there and wait, pallid, perhaps trembling, until they came in and did things with him? Not he! A certain Corsican upstart would let them assemble first, let them miss him – wonder if he would come at all. Then he would saunter in, superbly define the extreme limits of his imagination, and coolly ask them what they were going to do about it. This would irritate them. It would irritate them all, and especially the little oldest director. He would swell up and grow purple. Perhaps he would have a stroke right there on the rug. Good work!

"Can't go to business this early," he said genially to the ever respectful Paul. "Too fine a day. And I got a deal on hand; have to think it over. Go on out that way for a nice little spin."

Paul directed the car out that way, spinning it nicely. It was a monstrous performance, to spin at that hour in a direction quite away from the place where you are expected by all the laws of business and common decency. This seemed to be the opinion of an inconspicuous man who followed discreetly in a taxi-cab. But Bean enjoyed it, thinking that the night might find him in a narrow cell. He looked with new interest on the street-cars full of office-bound people. They were meekly going to their tasks while he was affronting men with more millions than he had checks on the newest suit.

As they left the city and came to outlying villages, he saw that he was going in the direction of Breede's place. He thought it would be a fine thing to get the flapper and go and be just perfectly married. Then he could send a telegram to the office, telling them he could imagine nothing of less consequence, and that they might all go to the devil. It was easy to be "snappy" in a telegram. But he remembered that the flapper just perfectly wished to manage it herself; probably she wouldn't like his taking a hand in the game. Better not be rough with the child at the start.

They were miles away. The person in the taxi-cab might have been observed searching his pockets curiously, and to be counting what money he found therein as he cast anxious glances toward the dial of the taxi-meter.

Bean surveyed the landscape approvingly. Anyway, it was a fine enough performance to keep them waiting there. They would all be enraged. Perhaps the old one would have his stroke before the arrival of the spectator to whom it would give the most pleasure. They might be taking him out to the ambulance, and all the other directors would stand there and say, "This is *your* work. Officer, do your duty!" Well, it would be worth it. He'd tell them so, too!

Looking ahead, he became aware that an electric car had suffered an accident. The passengers streamed out and gathered around the motorman who was peering under the car. As Paul slowed down and turned aside to pass, the motorman declared, "She's burned out. Have to wait for the next car to push us."

There were annoyed stirrings in the group. A few passengers started for a suburban railway station that could be seen a half-mile distant. Bean looked down upon these delayed people with amused sympathy.

Then, astoundingly, his eye fell upon one of the passengers a little aloof from the group about the motorman. He, too, after a last look at the car, seemed to be resolving on that long tramp to the station. He was a sightly young man, tall, heavily built, and dressed in garments that would on any human form have won Bean's instant respect. But on the form of the Greatest Pitcher the World Has Ever Seen — !!

His mind was at once vacant of all the past, of all the future. There was no more a Breede, male or female, no more directors or shares or jails. There was only a big golden Present, subduing, enthralling, limitless!

"Stop car!" hissed Bean. The car halted three feet from the young man on foot.

"Jump in!" gasped Bean.

"Thanks," said the young man; "I'm going the other way."

"Me, too! I was turning around just here."

The young man hesitated, surveying his interlocutor.

"Well," he said, "if it won't be too much trouble?"

"Trouble!" The word was a caress as Bean uttered it. He pushed a door open, clumsy with excitement, and the World's Greatest Pitcher stepped in to sit beside him.

"Grounds?" asked Bean.

"Yes," said the Pitcher, "if it's convenient."

"Polo Grounds," called Bean to Paul. "Hurry and turn around there, someway." He was afraid his guest might reconsider.

But the guest sat contentedly enough, the car was turned, and presently was speeding back toward town. The person in a taxi-cab which made the same turn a moment later was heard to say, "What the devil now?" with no discernible relevance.

"Living out this way?" asked Bean when he was again certain of his voice-control.

"No; only went out to stay over night with some friends. Had to get back this morning. They told me to take that car and change at —"

"Ought to have one these," said Bean, "then you know where you are."

"This runs well," said the Pitcher affably.

"'S little old last year's car," said Bean with skilled ennui.

He was trying to remember — mustn't talk to a ball-player about ball; they're sick of it.

"Got a busy day ahead of me in the Street," he said brightly. "I was only taking a little spin to get my head cleared out. Have to keep your head clear down there!"

"Say, that's some suit you have on," said the Pitcher with frank admiration. "I like that check."

"Do you?" asked Bean, trying not to choke. Then, "Where'd you get yours? I was noticing that suit the other night; saw you up at Claremont —"

"Couple of pals of mine when I'm in town —"

"That white line against the blue comes out great in the day time. Cut well, too. I see you got one those patent neck-capes that prevents wrinkling below the coat-collar. And extension safety pockets, I suppose?"

"Match pockets, change pockets, pencil pockets, fountain pen pockets, improved secret money pocket, right here; see?" The speaker indi-

cated the last mentioned item. "Flower holder up here under the lapel."
He revealed it.

"I have 'em make a vestee," said Bean; "goes on with gold pins; adds
dressiness, the man says."

The Pitcher revealed a vestee, adjusted with gold pins.

The red car moved as smoothly as if nothing had happened.

Next was made the momentous discovery that each wore a shirt with
the identical lavender stripe.

"Initials!" said Bean, pulling up the sleeve of his coat and rotating
his fore-arm under the Pitcher's approving glance.

"Got mine tattooed the same way," said the Pitcher, pulling up the
sleeve of his coat in turn.

They discussed shirts.

"Funny thing," said Bean. "Chap down in the office with me, worth
about a hundred million if he's worth a cent, wears separate cuffs; fastens
'em on with those nickel jiggers."

"Had a fellow on the team last year did the same thing," said the
Pitcher. "He's back to the bush now, though. The hick used to wear a
made-up neck tie, too, till the other lads kidded him out of it."

"You must get a lot of those Silases, one time and another," said Bean
sympathetically. He was wondering; the fellow had referred at least
indirectly to his calling.

"In the box, today?" he asked, feeling brazen.

The Pitcher nodded.

"You certainly pitched some air-tight ball last time I saw you. Say, I'll
tell you something. If I ever have a kid, you know what's going to
happen? Nothing used but his left hand from the cradle up; and, for
toys one league ball and a light bat. That's all."

"Right way," said the Pitcher approvingly.

"I'm only afraid the managers will get wise to him and not let him
finish out his college course," said Bean. "I don't know, though. I'll be
in the business myself by that time; may sign him on myself."

"Like it?" asked the Pitcher, interestedly.

"*Like* it! Say, what else is there? *Like* it! I'm only keeping on down
there in the Street till I put a certain deal through; then nothing but old
Base B. Ball for mine! You'll see. I'll pick up one the big clubs somewhere
if *money'll* do it!"

"Well, it's the one branch of the business where you don't have to
treat your arm like a sick baby," said the Pitcher. "Say, you want to come
inside a while?"

To Bean's amazement the car had stopped before the players' entrance. He had supposed himself miles back in the country. Did he want

to go inside for a while! He was out of the car as quickly as Nap could have achieved it.

"What did you say your name was?" asked the Pitcher.

He was in a long room lined with lockers. He recognized several players lounging there. A big man with a hard face, half in a uniform, was singing, "Though Silver Threads Are 'Mong the Gold, I Love You Just the Same." These men were requested to shake hands with the Pitcher's friend, Mr. Bean. They were also told informally that his new check suit was some suit.

"I'll soon have one coming off the same piece," said the Pitcher.

They went through a little door and out upon the grounds. A few players were idling there, only two of the pitchers being in uniform. The vast empty stands and bleachers seemed to confer privacy upon an informal and friendly gathering.

Several more players shook hands with the Pitcher's friend, Mr. Bean, and the circumstance of his presence was explained.

"I found your twist-paw out in the brush with nothing but a bum trolley car between him and a long walk," said Bean jauntily.

"He's got the prettiest red car that ever made you jump at a crossing," added the Pitcher.

They sat on the bench together.

"He winds up like old Sycamore," said Bean expertly of a young pitcher who was working nearby.

"He does for a fact," testified one of the players. "Did you know old Syc?"

"Chicago," said Bean. "Down and out; coming in from some tank-team and having to wear his uniform for underclothes all winter."

They regarded him with respectful interest.

"Poor Syc could never learn to take water in it," said one.

"He lived in a boarding-house two doors away from me," said Bean. "And when he'd taken about six or seven in at Frank's Place, he'd start singing 'My Darling Nellie Grey,' only he'd have to cry at about the third verse; then he'd lick some man that was laughing at him."

"That's old Syc, all right. You *got* him, pal!"

The talk went to other stars of the past. Bean mostly listened, but when he spoke they heard one who knew whereof he spoke. He was familiar with the public performance of every player of prominence for ten years. He was at home, among equals, and easy in his mind.

An inconspicuous man who had gained admittance to the grounds, by alleging his need to inspect a sign that was to be "done over," above the fence beyond the outfield, passed closely to Bean and detected the true situation with one sweep of his eagle eyes.

Fifteen minutes later this man was saying over a telephone to the largest director who sat in Breed's office:

"Nothing doing last night but riding around in a big red car that was waiting for him down in front. This morning at eight he starts north and picks up a man just this side Fordham, from a trolley car that breaks down. They turn around and go to the baseball park. He's setting there now, gassing with a lot of the players, telling funny stories and the like. He looks as if he didn't have a trouble on earth. My taxi-cab bill is now, for last night and today, forty-six eighty-five. Shall I keep on him?"

"No!" shouted the largest director. "Let him go to — let him alone and come in."

"I forgot to say," added the inconspicuous man, "that the party he picked up on the road and brought back here looks like he might be a ball player himself."

"Come in," repeated the largest director; "on a street-car!"

"Looks to me," ventured the quiet director to the largest, "as if you didn't bluff him quite to death last night."

"Aut'mobile!" said Breede. "Knew he had someone b'ind him."

"Let's get to business. No good putting it off now," said the quiet director.

"Seven hundred shares! My God! This is monstrous!" said the little eldest director, who had been making noises like a heavy locomotive.

Bean would have sat forever on that bench of the mighty, world-forgetting, if not world-forgot. But the departure of several of the men drew his attention to the supreme obligation of a guest.

"Well," he said, rising.

"Look in on us again some day," urged the Pitcher cordially.

"Thanks, I surely will," said Bean. "I like to forget business this way, now and then. Good day!"

They waved him friendly adieus, and he was out where Paul waited.

"Forget business!" He had indeed for two hours forgotten business and people. Not once had he thought of those waiting directors.

Well, they could do their worst, now. He was ripe to laugh at any fate. What was prison? "The prisoner," he seemed to read, "betrayed no consciousness of the enormity of his crime, and had, indeed, spent the morning at the Polo Grounds, chatting with various members of the Giants, with which team he is a great favorite."

Let them bring their gyves. Let the barred door clang shut!

"Office!" he said to Paul. There was no doubt in Paul's mind as to the quality of his patron. He had at once recognized the Greatest Pitcher. He ceased to speculate as to whether this assured young man owned the high office-building. That was now of minor consequence.

On the way downtown he tried to remember what day it was. He thought it was Friday, but again it seemed to be Monday. He stopped the car and bought an afternoon paper to find out.

At the entrance to the big office-building he debated a moment.

"Wait!" he directed Paul.

He was uncertain how long he might be permitted to remain in that building. If he must go to jail, he would ride. He wondered if Paul knew the address of the best jail. He could have things sent in to him — magazines and fruit.

Inside the entrance he paused before the cigar-stand. He must think carefully what he would say to those men of round millions. He must keep up his front. His glance roamed to the beautifully illustrated boxes of cigars. A good idea!

"Gimme one those," he said to the clerk, indicating a box that flaunted the polychrome portrait of a distinguished-looking Spaniard. He was surprised at the price, but he bit the tip off violently and began to mouth it.

"I'm no penny-pincher," he muttered, thinking of the cigar's cost. He tilted the cigar to a fearless angle and slanted his hat over his left eye. He lolled against the cigar-case, gathering resolution for the ordeal.

The door of an elevator down the corridor shot open, and there emerged, in single file, a procession, headed by the little oldest director, who had allowed him to go free overnight. They marched toward the door, looking straight ahead. They must pass in front of him. He felt a sudden great relief. Something in their bearing told him they were powerless to restrict his liberty.

The oldest director deigned him no glance, but snorted accurately in his direction, nevertheless. The quiet one grinned faintly at him, but the two neutral directors passed him loftily, as if they were Virtue scorning Vice in a morality play. The largest director frowned at the stripling who was savagely chewing a fifty-cent cigar at the procession.

The moment was incontestably the stripling's. He was cool and meant to take the fullest advantage of it. He meant to say, contemptuously, "I can imagine nothing of less consequence!"

But the officious cigar-clerk held a lighted match to the choice cigar and the magnificent defiance was smothered by a cough. He was obliged to content himself with glaring at the expansive and well-rounded back of the biggest director.

He was alone on the field, pretending enjoyment of a cigar which was now lighted and loathsome.

Bulger entered from the street and viewed him with friendly alarm.

"Say, where you been?" demanded Bulger. "Old Pussy-foot's got a sore thumb right now from pounding that buzzer of yours all morning. He's hot at everyone. I heard him call Tully a slinking something or other; couldn't get the word, but Tully got it. Say, you better get busy — regular old George W. Busy — if you want to hold that job."

"Job!" laughed Bean bitterly, and waved the expensive and lighted cigar in Bulger's face. "Job! Well, I may get busy, and then again I may not. All depends!"

"Gee!" said Bulger, profoundly moved by this admirable spirit of insubordination. "Well, I got to get back; I'm five minutes late myself."

Bean waited until he had gone. Then he strolled out to the street and furtively dropped an excellent and but slightly burned cigar into the gutter. He wished those fellows at cigar-stands would do only what they were put there for. Taking liberties with people!

He decided to go back as if nothing had happened. Let Breede do the talking, and if he talked rough, then tell him very simply that nothing of less consequence could be imagined. Continue to play the waiting game. That was it!

He entered the office, humming lightly. He seemed to be annoyed by the people he found there. He glared at Bulger, at old Metzeger, at the other clerks, and especially at Tully. Tully looked uncomfortable. He wasn't a gazelle after all. He was a startled fawn.

"Telephone for —" began the office boy humorist, but Bean was out of hearing in the direction of the telephone booth before the latest *mot* could be delivered.

"Been trying to get you all the morning," began the flapper in eager tones. "I should think you would stay there, when I may have to call you any minute. That grocer gave me the nicest little book, 'Why Did Your Husband Fail in Business?' with a picture of the poor man that failed on the cover. It's because he didn't get enough phosphorous to make him 100 percent efficient, and if he'd eaten 'Brain-more' mush for breakfast, nothing would have happened. We'll try it, anyway, and there's a triple-plate spoon in every package, so if I order a dozen . . . and oh, yes, what was I going to say? Why, I'm perfectly going to pull off the funniest stunt this afternoon; you'd just deliciously die laughing if I told you, but it will be still funnier if you don't know. Are you paying attention? It's because I'd already spent my allowance for three years and seven months ahead — I figured it all out like a statement — and I've perfectly just got to have some money of my real own. I've enough to worry about without bringing money into it, with proper food for you and those patent laundry tubs I told you about, and the man says he wouldn't think of letting it go for less than two seventy-five, but that's five dollars saved. Well, good-bye! I'll manage everything, and Granny says always to conceal little household worries from him, and just perfectly keep the future looking bright and interesting . . . she says that's the secret. Good-bye! What am I?"

"Startled fawn," said Bean.

"Well, don't forget."

"I won't. I'll attend to my part all right."

He heard the fateful buzzing even before he opened the door of the telephone booth. Breede was at it again. He walked coolly to his desk for a notebook. Everyone else in the office was showing nervousness. He was the only man who could still the troubled waters. He would play the waiting game; keep the future looking "bright and interesting." Breede could do the rest.

"Buzz! Buzz-z-z-z! Buzz-z-z-z-z!" It sounded pretty vicious.

He entered Breede's room with his accustomed air of quiet service. Breede did not glance at him. He began, as usual, to dictate before Bean was seated.

"Letter T.J. Williams 'sistant sup'ntendent M.P. 'n' C. department C. 'n' L.M. rai'way Sh'-kawgo dear sir please note 'closed schej'l car 'pairin' make two copies send one don't take that an' let me have at y'r earles c'nvenience —"

Apparently nothing at all had happened. He was at his old post, and Breede did nothing but explode fragments of words as ever. No talk of jail or betrayal of trust or of his morning's flagrant absence.

One might have thought that Breede himself played the waiting game. Or perhaps Breede only toyed with him. He fastened his gaze on the criminal cuffs. They were his rock of refuge in any cataclysm that might impend. If only he could keep those cuffs within his range of vision he would fear nothing. Patent laundry tubs; five dollars saved; why your husband failed in business; bright and interesting future —

"'Lo! 'Lo!" Breede was detonating into the desk-telephone which had sounded at his elbow.

"'Lo! Well? What? Run off! Stop nonsense! Busy!" He hung up the receiver.

"— also mus' be stipulated that case of div'dend bein' passed —"

The desk telephone again rang, this time more emphatically. Bean was chilled by a premonition that the flapper meant to pull off that funny stunt which was to cause him quite deliciously to die laughing.

Breede grasped the receiver again impatiently.

"Busy, tell you! No time nonsense! What! *What.* W-H-A-T!!!"

He listened another moment, then lessening his tone-production but losing nothing of intensity, he ripped out:

"Gur – reat Godfrey!"

His eyes, narrowed as he listened, now widened upon Bean who stared determinedly at the cuffs.

"You know what she *says?*"

"Yes," said Bean doggedly.

Then his eyes met Breede's and gave them blaze for blaze. The Great Reorganizer knew it not, but he no longer looked at Bunker Bean. Instead, he was trying to shrivel with his glare a veritable king of old Egypt who had enjoyed the power of life and death over his remotest subject. Bean did not shrivel. Breede glared his deadliest only a moment. He felt the sway of the great Ram-tah without identifying it. He divined that mere glaring would not shrivel this presumptuous atom. In truth, Bean outglared him. Breede leaned again to the telephone, listening. Bean lowered his eyes to the cuffs. He sneered at them now. The intention of the lifted upper lip was too palpable.

"Gur-reat stars above!" murmured Breede. "She says she's got it all reasoned out!" There was something almost plaintive in his tones; he shuddered. Then he rallied bravely once more.

"Tell you, no time nonsense. Busy."

But he seemed to know he was beaten. He listened again, then wilted.

"What next?" he demanded of Bean.

"Ask *her!*"

"Nice mess you got *me* into!"

Bean sneered resolutely at the cuffs. Again the telephone tinkled.

Breede listened and horror grew on his face.

"Now she's told her mother," he muttered. "My God!"

The transmitter was an excellent one, and Bean caught notes of hysteria. Julia was fussing back there.

"Now, now!" urged Breede. "No good. Better lie down. She says she's got it all reasoned *out*, don't I tell you?" He put a throttling hand over the anguished voice, and looked dumbly at Bean. He noted the evil sneer and traced it to the cuffs. Slowly he hung up the receiver and took one of the cuffs in his hands.

"Wha's matter these cuffs?" he demanded with a show of his true spirit.

"Right enough. Cuffs all right, if you like that kind. But why don't you wear 'em *on* — like this?" He luminously exposed his left forearm. It was by intention the one that carried the purple monogram.

"Sewed on, like that!" he added almost sharply.

Breede seemed to be impressed by the exhibit.

"Well," he began, awkwardly, as a man knowing himself in the wrong but still defiant, "I won't do it. *That's* all! Not for anybody."

Still, he seemed to consider that something more than mere apparent perverseness would become him.

"They get down 'round m' hands all the time. Can't think when they get down that way. Bother me. Take m' mind off. I won't do it, that's all. I don't care. Not for anybody't all!" He replaced the cuff beside its mate. He seemed to be saying that he had settled the matter — and no good talking anymore about it.

Bean was silent and dignified. His own air seemed to disclose that when once you warned people in plain words, you could no longer be held responsible. For a moment they made a point of ignoring the larger matter.

"Say," Breede suddenly exploded, "I wish you'd tell me just how many kinds of a — no matter! Where was I? This reserve fund may be subject to draft f'r repairs an' betterment durin' 'suin' quarter or 'ntil such time as —"

The telephone again rang its alarm. Breede took the receiver and allowed dismay to be read on his face as he listened.

"Well, well, well," he at length began, soothingly, "go lie down; take something; take *something*; well, send over t' White Plains f'r s'more. Putcha t' sleep. What can *I* do?" Again the throttling hand.

He ruefully surveyed his littered desk, then drew the long sigh of the baffled.

"Take telegram m' wife. Sorry can't be home late, 'port'n board meet'n'. May be called out of town."

The telephone rang, but was ignored.

"Send it off," he directed Bean above the bell's clear call. "Then c'mon; go ball game. G'wup 'n subway."

"Got car downstairs," suggested Bean.

"You got your work cut out f'r you; 'sall I got t' say," growled Breede.

"'S little old last year's car," said Bean modestly.

XIII

*A*s the little old last year's car bore them to the north, some long sleeping-image seemed to stir in Breede's mind.

"Got car like this m'self somewheres," he remarked.

Bean was relieved. He didn't want the name of a woman to be brought into the matter just then.

"'S all right for town work," he said. "Good enough for all I want of a car."

"'S awful!" said Breede, obviously forgetting the car for another subject.

"What can I do? She says she's got the right," suggested Bean.

"She'd take it anyway. *I* know her. Pack a suit-case. Had times with her already. Takes it from her mother."

"Can't be too rough at the start," declared Bean. "Manage 'em of course, but 'thout their finding it out — velvet glove." He looked quietly confident and Breede glanced at him almost respectfully.

"When?" he asked.

"Haven't made up my mind yet," said Bean firmly. "I may consult her, then again I may not; don't believe in long engagements."

Breede's glance this time was wholly respectful.

"You're a puzzle to me," he conceded.

Bean's shrug eloquently seemed to retort, "that's what they all say, sooner or later."

They were silent upon this. Bean wondered if Julia was still fussing back there. Or had she sent to White Plains for some more? And what was the flapper just perfectly doing at that moment? Life was wonderful! Here he was to witness a ball game on Friday!

They were in the grandstand, each willing and glad to forget, for the moment, just how weirdly wonderful life was. A bell clanged twice, the plate was swept with a stubby broom, the home team scurried to their places.

"There he is!" exclaimed Breede; "that's him!" Breede leaned out over the railing and pointed to the Greatest Pitcher the World Has Ever Seen. Bean sat coolly back.

The Pitcher scanned the first rows of faces in the grandstand. His glance came to rest on a slight, becomingly attired young man, who betrayed no emotion, and, in the presence of twenty thousand people, the Pitcher unmistakably saluted Bunker Bean. Bean gracefully acknowledged the attention.

"He know *you?*" queried Breede with animation.

"*Know* me!" He looked at Breede almost pityingly, then turned away. The Pitcher sent the ball fairly over the plate.

"Stur-r-r-ike one!" bellowed the umpire.

"With him all morning," said Bean condescendingly to his admiring companion. "Get shirts same place," he added.

His cup had run over. He was on the point of confiding to his companion the supreme felicity in store for Breede as a grandfather. But the batter struck out and the moment was only for raw rejoicing. They forgot. Bean ceased to be a puzzle to anyone, and Breede lapsed into unconsciousness of Julia.

The game held them for eleven innings. The Greatest Pitcher saved it to the home team.

"He was saying to me only this morning —" began Bean, as the Pitcher fielded the last bunt. But the prized quotation was lost in the uproar. Pandemonium truly reigned and the scene was unquestionably one of indescribable confusion.

Outside the gate they were again Breede and Bean; or, rather, Bean and Breede. The latter could not so quickly forget that public recognition by the Greatest Pitcher.

"You're a puzzle t'me," said Breede. "Lord! I can't g'ome yet. Have't take me club."

"Can't make y'out," admitted Breede once more, as they parted before the sanctuary he had indicated.

"Often puzzle myself," confessed the inscrutable one, as the little old last year's car started on. Breede stood on the pavement looking after it. For some reason the car puzzled him, too.

Bean was wondering if Julia herself wouldn't have been a little appeased if she could have seen the Pitcher single him out of that throng. Some day he might crush the woman by actually taking the Pitcher to call.

At his door he dismissed the car. He wanted quiet. He wanted to think it all out. That morning it had seemed probable that by this time he would have been occupying a felon's cell, inspecting the magazines and fruit sent to him. Instead, he was not only free, but he was keeping a man worth many millions from his own home, and perhaps he had caused that man's wife to send over to White Plains for some more. It was Ram-tah. All Ram-tah. If only everyone could find his Ram-tah —

Cassidy was reading his favorite evening paper, the one that shrieked to the extreme limits of its first page in scarlet headlines and mammoth type. It was a paper that Bean never bought, because the red ink rubbed off to the peril of one's eighteen-dollar suit.

Cassidy, who for thirty years had voted as the ward-boss directed, was for the moment believing himself to be a rabid socialist.

"Wall Street crooks!" he began, in a fine orative frenzy. "Dur-r-rinkin' their champagne whilst th' honest poor's lucky t' git a shell av hops! Ruh-hobbin' th' tax-pay'r f'r' t' buy floozie gowns an' jool bresslets f'r their fancy wives an' such. I know th' kind well; not wan cud do a day's bakin' or windy-washin'!"

He held the noisy sheet before Bean and accusingly pointed a blunt forefinger. "Burly Blonde Divorcée, Routed Society Burglar," across the first two columns, but the proceeding was rather tamely typed and the Burly Blonde's portrait in evening dress was inconspicuous beside the headlines "Flurry in Federal Express! Wild Scenes on Stock Exchange. Millions made by Gentlemen's Agreement."

"Gentlemin!" hissed Cassidy. "The sem agreemint that two gentlemin porch-climbers has whin wan climbs whilst th' other watches t' see is th' cop at th' upper ind av th' beat! Millions med whilst I'm wur-r-kin' f'r twinty per month an' what's slipped me — th' sem not buyin' manny jools ner private steamboats! Millions med! I know th' kind well!" Bean felt his own indignation rise with Cassidy's. He was seeing why they had feared to have him on the board of directors. Apparently they were bent on wrecking the company by a campaign of extravagance. The substance of what he gleaned from Cassidy's newspaper was that those directors had declared a stock dividend of 200 percent and a cash dividend of 100 percent.

They were madly wrecking the company in which he had invested his savings. Such was his first thought. And they were crooks, as Cassidy said, because for two years they had been quietly, through discreet agents, buying in the stock from unsuspecting holders.

"Rascals," agreed Bean with Cassidy, leaving but slight gifts for character analysis.

"Tellin' th' poor dubs th' stock was goin' down with one hand an' buyin' it in with th' other," said the janitor, lucidly.

Bean was suddenly troubled by a cross-current of thought. When you wrecked a company you didn't buy in the stock — you *sold*. He viewed the headlines from a new angle. Those directors were undoubtedly rascals, but was he not a rascal himself? What about his own shares?

"Maybe there's something we don't understand about it," he ventured to Cassidy.

"I know th' kind well," persisted Cassidy. "Th' idle rich! Small use have they f'r th' wur-r-r-kin' man! Souls no wider than th' black av y'r nail!"

"Might have had good reasons," said Bean, cautiously.

"Millions av thim," assented Cassidy with a pointed cynicism. "An' me own father dyin' twinty-three years ago fr'm ixposure contracted in County Mayo!"

Bean returned the paper to its owner and went slowly in to Ram-tah. One of the idle rich! Well, that is what kings mostly were, if you came down to it. At least they had to be rich to buy all those palaces. But not necessarily idle. The renewed Ram-tah would not be idle. It was not idleness to own a major-league club.

For the first time in their intercourse he felt that he faced the dead king almost as an equal. He was confronted by problems of administration, as Ram-tah must often have been. He must think.

If the flapper quite madly brought about an immediate marriage they would, for their honeymoon, follow the home club on its Western trip, and the groom would not be idle. He would be "looking over the ground." Then he would buy one of the clubs. If he proved to be not rich enough for that, not quite as rich as one of the idle rich, he would buy stock and become a director. He was feeling now that he knew how to be a director; that his experience with the express company had qualified him. He wondered how rich he would prove to be. Maybe he would have as much as thirty thousand dollars.

And he was a puzzle to Breede. He looked knowingly at Ram-tah when he remembered this. Ram-tah had probably puzzled people, too.

*H*e went to the office in the morning still wondering how rich he might be. The newspaper he read did not enlighten him, though it spoke frankly of "Federal Express Scandal." If the thing was *very* scandalous, perhaps he had made a lot of money. But he could not be sure of this. It might be merely "newspaper vituperation," which was something he knew to be not uncommon. The paper had declared that those directors had juggled a twenty-million dollar surplus for years, lending it to one another at a low rate of interest, until, alarmed by clamoring stockholders, they had declared this enormous dividend, taking first, however, the precaution to buy for a low price all the stock they could. But the newspaper did not say how rich anyone would be that had a whole lot of margins on that stock at Kennedy & Balch's. Maybe you had to hire a lawyer in those cases.

Entering the office, he was rudely shocked by Tully.

"Good-morning, Mr. Bean!" said Tully distinctly.

"Good-morning!" returned Bean, stunned by Tully's "Mr." "Uh! pleasant day," he added.

"Yes, sir!" said Tully, again distinctly.

Bean controlled himself and went to his desk.

"'Mr.' and 'Sir'! Gee! Am I as rich as *that??*" he thought.

Half an hour later it no longer seemed to him that he was rich at all. He was seated opposite Breede taking letters in shorthand as if he were merely a thirty-dollar-a-week Bunker Bean. Breede was refusing to recognize any change in their relationship. He made no reference to their talk of the day before and his detached cuffs stubbornly occupied their old position on the desk. Was it all a dream — and the flapper, too?

But the flapper soon called him to the telephone.

"Poor old Pops came home late, and he says you're just perfectly a puzzle to him," she began.

"I know," said Bean; "he says he can't make me out."

"And Moms began to say the silliest things about you, until I just had to take her seriously, so I perfectly told her that woman had come into her own in this generation, thanks to a few noble leaders of our sex — it's in Granny's last speech at the league — and that sent her up in the air. I don't think she can be as well as she used to be; and I told Pops he had to give me some money, and he said he knew it as well as I did, so what was the use of talking about it, and so he just perfectly gave me fifty or sixty thousand dollars and told me to make it go as far as I could, but I don't know, that grocer says the cost of living is going up every day because the Senate isn't insurgent enough; and anyway I'll get the tickets and a suite on that little old boat that sails Wednesday. I thought you'd want a day or two; and everything will be very quiet, only the family present, coming into town for it, you know, Wednesday morning, and the boat sails at noon, and I'll be so perfectly glad when it's all over because it's a very serious step for a young girl to take. Granny herself says it should never be taken lightly, unless you just perfectly know, but of course we do, don't we? I think you'll like fumed oak better, after all — and poor old Pops saying you're such a puzzle to him. He says he can't make out just how many kinds of a perfectly swear-word fool you are, but I can, and that's just deliciously enough for anybody. And you're to come out tomorrow and have tea and things in the afternoon, and *I'm* going to be before sister is, after all. She's perfectly furious about it and says I ought to be put back into short skirts, but I just perfectly knew it the very first time I ever looked at you. Stay around there, in case I think of something I've forgotten. G'bye."

Wednesday — a little old steamer sailing at noon! A steamer, and he couldn't swim a stroke and was always terrified by water. And the trip West with the home team! What about that? Why had he not the presence of mind to cut in and just perfectly tell her where they were going? But he had let the moment pass. It was too late. He didn't want to begin by making a row. And Breede was puzzled by him *that* way, was he? Couldn't make out how many kinds of perfectly swear-word fool he was?

He regretted that he had not been more emphatic about those cuffs. And Breede had said it after witnessing that salute from the pitcher's box! He must be a hard man to convince of anything. What more proof did he want?

Buzz! Buzz! Buzz!

The man who couldn't make him out was calling for him. For an hour longer he took down the man's words, not sneering pointedly at the cuffs, yet allowing it to be seen that he was conscious of them. A puzzle was he?

"— Hopin' t'ave promp' action accordin' 'bove 'structions, remain yours ver' truly she's got it all reasoned out," concluded Breede.

"She just told me," said Bean; "little old steamer sailing Wednesday."

"Can't make y' out," said Breede.

That thing was getting tiresome.

"You're a puzzle to me, too," said Bean.

"Hanh! Wha's 'at? What kinda puzzle?"

"Same kind," said Bean, brightly.

"Hum!" said Breede, and pretended to search for a missing document. Then he eyed Bean again.

"Know how much you made on that Federal stuff?"

"I was going to ask a lawyer," confessed Bean. "I got a whole lot of margins or whatever you call 'em around at that broker's. Maybe he wouldn't mind letting me know."

"Stock'll be up t' six hundred before week's out; net you 'round four hund' thous'n'," exploded Breede in his most vicious manner.

"Four hundred thousand margins?" He wanted to be cautious.

"*Dollars,* dammit!" shouted Breede.

Bean was able to remain cool. That amount of money would have meant nothing to him back on the Nile. Why should it now?

"It wasn't the money I was after," he began, loftily.

"*Hanh!*"

"Principle of the thing!" concluded Bean.

Breede had lost control of his capable under jaw. It sagged limply. At last he spoke, slowly and with awe in his tone.

"You don't puzzle me anymore." He shook his head solemnly. "Not anymore. I *know* now!"

"Little old steamer — can't swim a stroke," said Bean.

"'S all," said Breede, still shaking his head helplessly.

At his desk outside Bean feigned to be absorbed in an intricate calculation. In reality he was putting down "400,000," then "$400,000," then "$400,000.00" By noon he had covered several pages of his notebook with this instructive exercise. Once he had written it $398,973.87, with a half-formed idea of showing it to old Metzeger.

As he was going out Tully trod lightly over a sheet of very thin ice and accosted him.

"The market was not discouraging today," said Tully genially.

"'S good time to buy heavily in margins," said Bean.

"Yes, sir," said Tully respectfully.

In the street he chanted "four hundred thousand dollars" to himself. He was one of the idle rich. He hoped Cassidy would never hear of it. Then, passing a steamship office, he recalled the horror that lay ahead of him. Little old steamer. But was a financier who had been netted four hundred thousand dollars to be put afloat upon the waters at the whim of a flapper? She was going too far. He'd better tell her so in plain words; say, "Look here, I've just netted four hundred thousand dollars, and no little old steamer for mine. I don't care much for the ocean. We stay on land. Better understand who's who right at the start."

That is what he would tell the flapper; make it clear to her. She'd had her own way long enough. Marriage was a serious business. He was still resolving this when he turned into a shop.

"I want to get a steamer trunk — sailing Wednesday," he said in firm tones to the clerk.

*I*t was midnight of Tuesday. In the steam-heated apartment Bean paced the floor. He was attired in the garments prescribed for gentlemen's evening wear, and he was still pleasantly fretted by the excitement of having dined with the Breede family at the ponderous town house up east of the park.

He tried to recall in their order the events of those three days since he had left the office on Saturday. His coolest efforts failed. It was like watching a screen upon which many and diverse films were superimposing scenes in which he was an actor of more or less consequence, but in which his figure was always blurred. It was confounding.

Yet he had certainly gone out to that country place Sunday for tea and things, taking Nap. And the flapper, with a sinful pride, had shown him off to the family. He and the flapper had clearly been of more consequence than the big sister and the affianced waster, who wouldn't be able to earn his own cigarettes, say nothing of his ties and gloves. Sister and the waster, who seemed to be an agreeable young man, were simply engaged in a prosaic way, and looked prosaically forward to a church wedding. No one thought anything about them, and sister was indeed made perfectly furious by the airs the flapper put on.

Mrs. Breede, from one of the very oldest families of Omaha, had displayed amazing fortitude. She had not broken down once, although she plainly regarded Bean as a malignant and fatal disease with which her latest-born had been infected. "I must be brave, brave!" she had seemed to be reminding herself. And when Nap had chased and chewed her toy spaniel, named "Rex," until it seemed that Rex might pass on, she had summoned all her woman's resignation and only murmured, "Nothing can matter now!"

There had seemed to be one fleeting epoch which he shared alone with the flapper, feeling the smooth yielding of her cheek and expanding under her very proudest gaze of ownership. And a little more about fumed oak panels and the patent laundry tubs.

Monday there had been a mere look-in at the office, with Tully saying "Sir"; with Breede exploding fragments of words to a middle-aged and severely gowned woman stenographer who was more formidable than a panorama of the Swiss Alps, and who plainly made Breede uncomfortable; and with Bulger saying, "Never fooled your Uncle Cuthbert for a minute. Did little old George W. Wisenham have you doped out right or not? Ask me, *ask* me; wake me up anytime in the night and ask me!"

Tuesday afternoon he had walked with the flapper in the park and had learned of many things going forward with solely his welfare in view — little old house surrounded on all sides by just perfectly scenery — little old next year's car — little old going-away rag — little old perfectly just knew it the first moment she saw him — little old new rags to be bought in Paris — and sister only going to Asheville on *hers.*

And the dinner in town, where he had seemed to make an excellent impression, only that Mrs. Breede persisted in behaving as if the body was still upstairs and she must be brave, brave! And Grandma, the Demon, confiding to him over her after-dinner cigarette that he was in for it now, though she hadn't dared tell him so before; but he'd find that out for himself soon enough if he wasn't very careful about thwarting her. It made her perfectly furious to be thwarted.

Nor did he fail to note that the stricken mother was distinctly blaming the Demon for the whole dreadful affair. Her child had been allowed to associate with a grandmother who had gone radical at an age when most of her sex simmer in a gentle fireside conservatism and die respectably. But it was too late now. She could only be brave, brave!

And he was to be there at nine sharp, which was too early, but the flapper could be sure only after he came that nothing had happened to him, that he had neither failed in business, been poisoned by some article of food not on her list, nor diverted by that possible Other One who seemed always to lurk in the flapper's mental purlieus. She just perfectly wanted him there an hour too early; all there was about it!

These events had beaten upon him with the unhurried but telling impact of an ocean tide. Two facts were salient from the mass: whatever he had done he had done because of Ram-tah; and he was going to Paris, where he would see the actual tomb of that other outworn shell of his.

He thought he would not be able to sleep. He had the night in which to pack that steamer trunk. Leisurely he doffed the faultless evening garments — he was going to have a waistcoat pointed like the waster's, with four of those little shiny buttons, and studs and cuff-links to match — and donned a gaily flowered silk robe.

With extreme discomfort he surveyed the new steamer trunk. Merely looking at a steamer trunk left him with acute premonitions of what the voyage had in store for him. But the flapper was the flapper; and it was the only way ever to see that tomb.

The packing began, the choice garments were one by one neatly folded. A light tan overcoat hung in Ram-tah's closet, back of the case. Ram-tah was dragged forth and for the moment lay prone. He was to be left in the locked closet until a more suitable housing could be provided, and Cassidy had been especially warned not to let the steam-heated apartment take fire.

He found the coat and returned to the half-packed trunk in the bedroom where he resumed his wonderful task, stopping at intervals for always futile efforts at realization of this mad impossibility. It was all Ram-tah. Nothing but that kingly manifestation of himself could have brought him up to the thing. He dropped a choice new bit of haberdashery into the trunk and went for another look at It prone on the floor in that other room.

A long time he gazed down at the still face — his own still face, the brow back of which he had once solved difficult problems of administration, the eyes through which he had once beheld the glories of his court, the lips that had kissed his long dead queen, smiled with rapture upon his first-born and uttered the words that had made men call him wise. It was not strange — not unbelievable. It was sane and true. He was still a king.

He reached down and laid a tender, a fraternal hand upon the brow. The contact strengthened him, as always. He could believe anything wise and good of himself. He could be a true mate to that bewildering flapper, full of understanding kindness. He saw little intimate moments of their life together, her perplexities over fumed oak and patent tubs and marketing for pure food; always her terrific earnestness. Now and then he would laugh at that, but then she would laugh too; sometimes the flapper seemed to show, with an engaging little sense of shame, that she just perfectly knew how funny she was.

But she was staunch; she had perfectly well known the very first moment she saw him. And she had never spoiled it all, like that other one in Chicago, by asking him if he was fond of Nature and Good Music and such things. The flapper was capable but quiet. With his hand still upon Ram-tah's brow in that half-timid, strange caress, he was flooded with a sudden new gladness about the flapper. She was *dear,* if you came right down to it. And Ram-tah had brought her to him. He erected himself to look down once more. They *knew,* those two selves; understood each other and life.

It occurred to him for the first time that Ram-tah, too, must have liked dogs, must have been inexpressibly moved by the chained souls that were always trying to speak from their brown eyes. He looked over to Nap, who fiercely battled with a sofa cushion, and was now disemboweling it through a rent in the cover. He wondered what Ram-tah's favorite dog had been like.

He went back to the bedroom to finish his packing. Ram-tah could lie until the moment came to lock him again in the closet, to leave him once more in a seclusion to which he had long been accustomed.

He worked leisurely, stowing those almost advanced garments so that they should show as few wrinkles as possible after their confinement. Occasionally Nap diverted his thoughts by some louder growl than usual in the outer room, or by some noisier scramble.

The trunk was packed and locked for the final time. Thrice had it been unlocked and opened to receive slight forgotten objects. The last to be placed directly under the lid was the entirely scarlet cravat. He was equal to wearing it now, but a sense of the morrow's proprieties deterred him. The stricken mother! In deference to her he laid out for the morning's wear the nearest to a black cravat that he possessed, an article surely unassuming enough to be no offence in a house of mourning.

He fastened the straps of the trunk and sighed in relief. It was a steamer trunk, and he was to sail on a little old steamer, but other people had survived that ordeal. Ram-tah would have met it boldly. Ram-tah!

He stood in the doorway, his attention attracted to Nap, who had for some moments been more than usually vocal. In a far corner Nap had a roundish object between his paws and his sharp teeth tore viciously at it. He looked up and growled in fierce pretence that his master also wished to gnaw this delectable object.

A moment Bean stood there, looking, looking. Slowly certain details cleared to his vision: the details of an unspeakable atrocity. He felt his knees grow weak, and clutched at the doorway for support.

The body of Ram-tah was out of its case and half across the room, yards of the swathed linen unfurled; but, more terrible than all, the head of Ram-tah was not where it should have been.

In the far corner the crouching Nap gnawed at that head, tearing, mutilating, desecrating.

"Napoleon!" It was a cry of little volume, but tense and terrible. Napoleon, destroyer of kings! In this moment he once more put the creature's full name upon him. The dog found the name alarming; perceived that he had committed someone of those offences for which he was arbitrarily punished. He relaxed the stout jaws, crawled slinkingly to the couch, and leaped upon it. Once there, he whimpered protestingly. One of the few clear beliefs he had about a perplexing social system was that nothing hurtful could befall him once he had gained that couch. It was sanctuary.

Bean's next emotion was sympathy for the dog's fright. He tottered across to the couch, mumbling little phrases of reassurance to the abject Nap. He sat down beside him, and put a kindly arm about him.

"Why, why, Nappy! Yes, 'sall right, yes, he *was* — most beautiful doggie in the whole world; yes, he *was.*"

He hardly dared look toward the scene of the outrage. The calamity was overwhelming, but how could dogs know any better? Timidly, at length, he raised his eyes, first to where the fragmentary head lay, then to the torn body.

Something about the latter electrified him. He leaped from the couch and seized an end of the linen that bound the mummy. He pulled, and the linen unwound. He curiously surveyed something at his feet. It was a tightly rolled wad of excelsior. The swathing of linen — he had unwound it to where the hands should have been folded on the breast — had enclosed excelsior.

Dazedly he looked into the empty case. Upon one of the new boards he saw marked with the careless brush of some shipping-clerk, "Watkins & Co., Hartford, Conn."

Again, as with the unstable lilac-bushes, his world spun about him; it drew in and darkened. He had the sensation of a grain of dust sucked down a vast black funnel.

Outside the quiet room, the city went on its ruthless, noisy way. In there where dynasties had fallen and a monarch lay prone, a spotted dog sporting with a *papier-mâché* something, came suddenly on a cold hand flung out on the rug. Nap instantly forsook the sham for the real, deserted the head of Ram-tah, and laved Bean's closed eyes with a lolloping pink tongue.

XIV

*T*he next morning at eight-thirty the door of the steam-heated apartment resounded to sharp knocking. There being no response, the knocking was repeated and prolonged. Retreating footsteps were heard in the hallway. Five minutes later a key rattled in the door and Cassidy entered, followed by the waster.

Bean was discovered in a flowered dressing gown gazing open-eyed at the shut door of a closet. He sat on the couch and one of his arms clasped a sleeping dog. The floor was littered with wisps of excelsior.

"My word, old top, had to have the chap let me into your diggin's you know. You were sleeping like the dead." The waster was bustling and breezy.

"Busy," said Bean. He arose and went into the hall where Cassidy stood.

"He *would* have in," explained Cassidy. "Say th' wor-r-d if he's no frind, an' he'll have out agin. I'll put him so. 'T would not be a refined thing to do, but nicissary if needed."

"'S all right," said Bean. "Friend of mine." He closed the door on Cassidy.

Inside, he found the waster interestedly poking with his stick at a roundish object on the floor.

"Dog's been at it," explained the waster brightly. "What's the idea? Private theatricals?"

"Yes," said Bean, "private theatricals," and resumed his place on the couch, staring dully at the closet door.

"But, look here, old chap, you must liven up. She would have it I should come for you. My word! I believe you're funking! You look absurdly rotten like it, you know."

"Toothache, right across here," muttered Bean. "Have to put it off."

"But that's not done, old top; really it's not done, you know. It . . . it . . . one doesn't do it at all, you know."

"Never?" asked Bean, brightening a little with alarm.

"Jolly well never," insisted the waster; "not for anything a dentist-fellow could manage. Come now!"

Bean was listless once more, deaf, unseeing.

"Righto," said the waster. "Bachelor dinner last night . . . yes?"

The situation had become intelligible to him. He found the bathroom, and from it came the sound of running water. He had the air of a Master of Revels.

"Into it — only thing to do!"

He led Bean to the brink of the icy pool and skillfully flayed him of the flowered gown. He was thorough, the waster. He'd known chaps to pretend to get in by making a great splashing with one hand, after they were left alone. He overcame a few of the earlier exercises in jiu-jitsu and committed Bean's form to the deep.

"Righto!" he exclaimed. "Does it every time. Shiver all you like. Good for you! Now then — clothes! Clothes and things, Man! Oh, here they are to be sure! How stupid of me! Feel better already, yes? Knew it. Studs in shirt. My word! Studs! Studs! There! Let me tie it. Here! Look alive man! She would have it. She must have known you. There!"

He had finished by clamping Bean's hat tightly about his head. Bean was thinking that the waster possessed more executive talent than Grandma had given him credit for; also that he would find an excuse to break away once they were outside; also that Balthasar was keenly witty. Balthasar had *said* it would disintegrate if handled.

He would leave Nap with Cassidy. He would return for him that night, then flee. He would go back to Wellsville, which he should never have left.

The waster had him in the car outside, a firm grasp on one of his arms.

"I'll allow you only one," said the waster judicially as the car moved off. "I know where the chap makes them perfectly — brings a mummy back to life —"

"A mum — what mummy?" asked Bean dreamily.

"Your own, if you had one, you silly juggins!"

Bean winced, but made no reply.

The car halted before an uptown hotel.

"Come on!" said the waster.

"Bring it out," suggested Bean, devising flight.

The waster prepared to use force.

"Quit. I'll go," said Bean.

He was before a polished bar, the white-jacketed attendant of which not only recognized the waster but seemed to divine his errand.

"Two," commanded the waster. The attendant had already reached for a bottle of absinthe, and now busied himself with two eggs, a shaker, and cracked ice.

"White of an egg, delicate but nourishing after bachelor dinners," said the waster expertly.

Bean, in the polished mirror, regarded a pallid and shrinking youth whom he knew to be himself — not a reincarnation of the Egyptian king, but just Bunker Bean. He could not endure a long look at the thing, and allowed his gaze to wander to the paneled woodwork of the bar.

"Fumed oak," he suggested to the waster.

But the waster pushed one of the slender-stemmed glasses toward him.

"There's the life-line, old top; cling to it! Here's a go!"

Bean drank. The beverage was icy, but it warmed him to life. The mere white of an egg mixed with a liquid of such perfect innocence that he recalled it from his soothing-syrup days.

"Have one with me," he said in what he knew to be a faultless bar manner.

"Oh, I say old top," the waster protested.

"One," said Bean stubbornly.

The attendant was again busy.

"Better be careful," warned the waster. "Those things come to you and steal their hands into yours like little innocent children, but —."

They drank. Bean felt himself bold for any situation. He would carry the farce through if they insisted on it. He no longer planned to elude the waster. They were in the speeding car.

"Fumed eggs!" murmured Bean approvingly.

They were inside that desolated house, the door closed fatefully upon them. The waster disappeared. Bean heard the flapper's voice calling cheerily to him from above stairs. A footman disapprovingly ushered him to the midst of an immense drawing room of most ponderous grandeur, and left him to perish.

He sat on the edge of a chair and tried to clear his mind about this enormity he was going to commit. False pretenses! Nothing less. He was not a king at all. He was Bunker Bean, a stenographer, whose father drove an express wagon, and whose grandmother had smoked a pipe. He had never been anything more, nor ever would be. And here he was . . . pretending.

No wonder Julia had fussed! She had seen through him. How they would all scorn him if they knew what that scoundrelly Balthasar knew. He'd made money, but he had no right to it. He had made that under false pretenses, too, believing money would come naturally to a king. Would they find him out at once, or not until it was too late? He shudderingly recalled a crisis in the ceremony of marriage where someone is invited to make trouble, urged to come forward and say if there isn't some reason why this man and this woman shouldn't be married at all. Could he live through that? Suppose a policeman rushed in, crying, "I forbid the banns! The man is an impostor!" He seemed to remember that banns were often forbidden in novels. Then would he indeed be a thing for contemptuous laughter.

Yet, in spite of this dismal foreboding, he was presently conscious of an unusual sense of well-being. It had been growing since they stopped for those eggs, in that fumed oak place. What about the Corsican? Better have been him than no one! He would look at that tomb. Then he would know. He was rather clinging to the idea of the Corsican. It gave him courage. Still, if he could get out peacefully . . .

He stepped lightly to the hall and was on the point of seizing his hat when the flapper called down to him.

"You just perfectly don't leave this house again!"

"Not going to," he answered guiltily. "Looking to see what size hat I wear. Fumed eggs," he concluded triumphantly.

He was not again left alone. The waster came back and supposed he would do some golfing "over across."

Bean loathed golf and gathered the strange power to say so.

"Sooner be a mail-carrier than a golf-player," he answered stoutly. "Looks more fun, anyway."

"*My* word!" exclaimed the waster, "aren't you even keen on watching it?"

"Sooner watch a lot of Italians tearing up a street-car track," Bean persisted.

"Oh, come!" protested the waster.

"Like to have another fumed egg," said Bean.

"You've had one too many," declared the waster, knowing that no sober man could speak thus of the sport of kings.

Grandma, the Demon, entered and portentously shook hands with him. She seemed to have discovered that marriage was very serious.

"Fumed eggs," said Bean, regarding her shrewdly.

"What?" demanded Grandma.

"Fumed eggs, hundred p'cent efficient," he declared stoutly.

The Demon eyed him more closely.

"My grandmother smoked, too," said Bean, "but I never went in for it much."

"U-u-u-mmm!" said the Demon. It was to be seen that she felt puzzled.

Breede slunk into the room, garbed in an unaccustomed frock coat. He went through the form of shaking hands with Bean.

Bean felt a sudden necessity to tell Breede a lot of things. He wished to confide in the man.

"Principle of the thing's all I cared about," he began. "Anybody make money that wants to be a Wall Street crook and take it away from the tired business man. What I want to be is one of the idle rich . . . only not idle much of the time, you know. Good major league club for mine. Been looking the ground over; sound 'vestment; keep you out of bad company, lots time to read good books."

"Hanh! Wha's 'at?" exploded Breede.

"Fumed eggs," said Bean, feeling witty. He affected to laugh at his own jest as he perceived that the mourning mother had entered the room. Breede drew cautiously away from him. Mrs. Breede nodded to him bravely.

He mentioned the name of the world's greatest pitcher, with an impulse to take the woman down a bit.

"Get our shirts same place; he's going to have a suit just like this — no, like another one I have in that little old steamer trunk."

He was aware that they all eyed him too closely. The waster winked at him. Then he found himself shaking hands with a soothing old gentleman in clerical garb who called him his young friend and said that this was indeed a happy moment.

The three Breedes and the waster stood apart, studying him queerly. He was feeling an embarrassed need to make light conversation, and he was still conscious of that strange power to make it. He was going to tell the old gentleman, whose young friend he was, that fumed eggs were a hundred p'cent efficient.

But the flapper saved him from that. She came in, quiet but business-like, and in a low yet distinct voices aid she wished it to be perfectly over at once. She did not relax her grasp of Bean's arm after she approached him, and he presently knew that something solemn was going on in which he was to be seriously involved.

"Say, 'I do,'" muttered the old gentleman, and Bean did so. The flapper had not to be told.

There followed a blurred and formal shaking of his hand by those present, and the big sister whom he had not noticed before came up and kissed him.

Then he was conscious of the flapper still at his side. He turned to her and was amazed to discover that she was blinking tears from her eyes.

"There, *there!*" he muttered soothingly, and took her in his arms quite as if they were alone. He held her closely a moment, with little mumbled endearments, softly patting her cheek.

"There, there! No one ever going to hurt *you.* You're *dear,* yes, you are!"

He was much embarrassed to discover those staring others still present. But the flapper swiftly revived. It seemed to be perfectly over for the flapper. She announced that everyone must hurry.

Hurriedly, with everyone, it seemed, babbling nonsense of remote matters, they sat at a table, and ate of cold food from around a bed of flowers. Bean ate frankly. He was hungry, but he took his part in the talk as a gentleman should.

They were toasting the bride in champagne.

"Never drink," protested Bean to the proffered glass.

"Won't happen every day, old top," suggested the waster.

He drank. The sparkling stuff brought him new courage. He drained the glass.

"I knew they were trying to keep me off that board of directors," he confided to Breede, "specially that oldest one."

"That your first drink s'morning?" asked Breede in discreet tones.

"First drink I ever took. Had two eggs's morning."

"What board of directors?" asked Breede suspiciously.

"Fed'l Express. I wanted that stock for a technical purpose — so I could get on board of directors."

Breede looked across the table to Grandma. There seemed to be alarm in his face.

"Given it up, though," continued Bean. "Can't be robbing tired business men. Rather be a baseball king if you come down to that. I'll own three four major league clubs before year's out. See 'f I don't! 'S only kind of king I want to be — wake me up anytime in the night and ask me — old George W. Baseball King. 'S my name. I been other kings enough. Nothing in it. You wouldn't believe it if I told you I was a king of Egypt once, 'way back, thous'n's years before you were ever born. I had my day; pomps and attentions and powers. But I was laid away in a mummy case — did that in those days — thous'n's and thous'n's of years before you were ever born — an' that time I was Napoleon . . ."

He stopped suddenly, feeling that the room had grown still. He had been hearing a voice, and the voice was his own. What had he said? Had he told them he was nothing, after all? He gazed from face to face with consternation. They looked at him so curiously. There was an embarrassing pause.

The flapper, he saw, was patting his hand at the table's edge.

"No one ever hurt you while I'm around," he said, and then he glared defiantly at the others. The old gentleman, whose young friend he was, began an anecdote, saying that of course he couldn't render the Irish dialect, also that if they had heard it before they were to be sure and let him know. Apparently no one had heard it before, although Breede left the table for the telephone.

Bean kept the flapper's hand in his. And when the anecdote was concluded everybody arose under cover of the applause, and they were in that drawing room again where the thing had happened.

The waster chattered volubly to everyone. Grandma and the bride's mother were in earnest but subdued talk in a far corner. Breede came to them.

"Chap's plain dotty," said Breede. "Knew something was wrong."

"Your mother's doing," said Mrs. Breede.

"U-u-u-mm!" said the Demon. "I'll go with them."

"I shall also go with my child," said the mother. "James, you will go too."

But Breede had acted without waiting to talk.

"Other car'll be here, 'n' I telephoned for quarters on boat. 'S full up, but they'll manage. Chap might cut her throat."

"U-u-u-mm!" said the Demon.

"Half pas' ten," reminded Breede. "Hurry!"

Bean had accosted the waster.

"Always take fumed eggs for breakfast," he cautioned. "Of course, little fruit an' tea an' things."

"Your father's had a sudden call to Paris. We're going with him," said the Demon, appearing bonneted.

"What boat?" demanded the flapper in quick alarm.

"Your's," said the Demon.

"Jolly party, all together," said Bean cordially. "He coming, too?" He pointed to the old gentleman, but this it seemed had not been thought of.

"He better come too," insisted Bean. "I'm his young friend, and this is indeed a happy moment. Jus' little ol' las' year's steamer."

"You're tagging," accused the flapper viciously, turning to the Demon.

*B*ean awoke late that night, believing he was dead — that he had fallen in sleep and been laid unto his fathers. But the narrow grave was unstable. It heaved and rolled as if to expel him.

Slowly he remembered. First he identified his present location. He was in an upper berth of that little old steamer. Outside a little round window was the whole big ocean and beneath him slept a man from Hartford, Conn. He had caught the city's name on the end of the man's steamer trunk and been enraged by it. Hartford was a city of rascals. The man himself looked capable of any infamy. He was tall and thin, and wore closely trimmed side-whiskers of a vicious iron grey. He regarded Bean with manifest hostility and had ostentatiously locked a suit-case upon his appearance.

So much for his whereabouts. How had he come there? Laboriously, he went over the events of the afternoon. They were hazy, but certain peaks jutted above the haze. They were "tagged," as the flapper had surmised they were going to be. Aboard the little old steamer had appeared Breede and Julia and the Demon. They had called the flapper aside and apparently told her something for her own good, though the flapper had not liked it, and had told them with much spirit that they were to perfectly mind their own affairs.

Bean had fled into the throng on deck. His hat had received many dents, and when he emerged to a clear space at the far end of the boat he had discovered that his perfectly new watch was gone. He was being put upon, and meekly submitting to it as in that other time when he had not believed himself to be somebody. He stared moodily over the rail as the little old steamer moved out. Thousands of people on the dock were waving handkerchiefs and hats. They seemed to be waving directly at him and yelling. Above it all, he was back in the bird-and-animal store, hearing the parrot shriek over and over, "Oh, what a fool! Oh, what a fool!"

He made an adventurous way through all kinds of hurried people, back to that group of queerly behaving Breedes. The flapper was showing traces of tears, but also a considerable acrimony. She was threatening to tell the captain to just perfectly turn the little old steamer back. But it came to nothing. At least to nothing more than Bean's sharing the stateroom of the Hartford man, who had covered the lower berth with his belongings so that there might be no foolish mistake.

And that was because there had been no provision made on the little old steamer for this invasion of casual Breedes. Pops and Moms had secured an officer's room; the Demon, rather than sit up in the smoking-room of nights, had consented to share the flapper's suite; and Bean had been taken in charge by a cold-blooded steward who left him in the narrow quarters of the Hartford person.

And there, in the far night, he was wishing he might be back in the steam-heated apartment with Nap. He had a violent headache, and he had awakened from a dream of falling into a well of cool, clear water of which he thirstily drank. His narrow bed behaved abominably, rolling him from side to side, then letting his head sink to some far-off terrifying depth. And there was no way of leaving that little old steamer . . . not for a man who couldn't swim a stroke.

So he suffered for long miserable hours. Light broke through the little round windows, and outside he could see the appalling waste of water, foaming, seething, rising to engulf him. He couldn't recall mounting to that high place where he had slept. He wondered if the callous steward would sometime come to take him down. Perhaps the steward would forget.

The man from Hartford bestirred himself and was presently shaving before the small glass. Bean looked sullenly down at him. The man was running a wicked-looking razor perilously about his restless Adam's apple. He was also lightly humming "The Holy City."

"Watkins," said Bean distinctly, recalling the name that had revealed the fictitious and Hartford origin of It.

"Adams," said the man, breaking off his song and tightening a leathery cheek for the razor.

"Adam's apple," said Bean, scornfully. "Watkins!"

The man glanced at him and painfully twisted up a corner of his mouth while he applied the razor to the other corner. But he did not speak.

"Think there's a doctor on this little old steamer?" demanded Bean.

The man from Hartford laid down his weapon and began to lave his face.

"I believe," he spluttered, "that medical attendance is provided for those still in mortal error."

"'S'at *so?*" demanded Bean, sullenly.

The man achieved another bar of "The Holy City," and fondly dusted his face with talcum powder, critically observing the effect.

"If you will go into the silence," he at length said, "and there hold the thought of the all-good, you will be freed from your delusion."

"Humph!" said Bean and turned his face from the Hartford man.

The latter locked his razor into a toilet-case, locked the toilet-case into a suit-case, and seemed to debate locking the suit-case into a little old steamer trunk. Deciding, however, that his valuables were sufficiently protected, and that nothing was left out to excite the cupidity of a man to whom he had not been properly introduced, the person from Hartford went forth with a final retort.

"'As a man thinketh in his heart, so is he!'"

"'S'at *so?*" said Bean insolently to the closed door.

He roused himself and descended precariously from his shelf. Once upon his feet he was convinced that the ship was foundering. He hurriedly dressed and adjusted a life-belt from one of a number he saw behind a rack. Over the belt he put on a serviceable rain-coat. It seemed to be the coat to wear.

Outside he plunged through narrow corridors until he came to a stairway. He mounted this to be as far away from the ocean as possible. He came out upon a deck where people were strangely not excited by the impending disaster. Innocent children romped, oblivious to their fate, while callous elders walked the deck or reclined in little old steamer chairs.

He poised a moment, trying to prevent the steamer's deck from mounting by planting one foot firmly upon it. The device, sound enough in mechanical theory, proved unavailing. The vast hulk sank alternately at either end, and to fearsome depths of the sea. There would come a last plunge. He tightened the life-belt.

Then, through the compelling force of associated ideas, there seemed to come to him the faint sweet scent of lilac blossoms . . . the vision of a lilac clump revolving both vertically and horizontally . . . the noisome fumes of Grammer's own pipe.

"Too much for you, eh? Ha, ha, ha!" It was the scoundrel from Hartford, malignantly cheerful. He was inhaling a cubeb cigarette.

"Lumbago!" said Bean, both hands upon the life-belt.

"'As a man thinketh, so is he!' As simple as that," admonished the other.

Bean groped for the door and for ages fled down blind corridors, vainly seeking that little old stateroom. He did not find it as quickly as he should have; but he was there at last, and a deft steward quickly divested him of the life-belt and other garments for which there no longer seemed to be any need.

He lay weakly reflecting, with a sinister glee, that the boat was bound to sink in a moment. He wanted it to sink. Death was coming too slowly.

Later he knew that the flapper was there. She had come to die with him, though she was plainly not in a proper state of mind to pass on. She was saying that something was the nerviest piece of work she'd ever been up against, and that she would perfectly just fix them . . . only give her a little time — they were snoop-cats!

"You'll perfectly manage; jus' leave it to you," breathed her moribund husband.

"If you'd try some fruit and two eggs," suggested the flapper.

He raised a futile hand defensively, and an expression of acute repugnance was to be seen upon his yellowed face.

"Please, please go 'way," he murmured. "Let Julia do fussing. Go way off to other end of little old steamer; stay there."

The flapper saw it was no time for woman's nursing. Sadly she went.

"Telephone to a drug-store," demanded Bean after her, but she did not hear.

He continued to die, mercifully unmolested, until the man from Hartford came in to ascertain if his locks had been tampered with.

"Hold to the all good!" urged the man at a moment when it was too poignantly, too openly certain that Bean could hold to very little indeed.

"Uh-hah!" gasped Bean.

"Go into the silence," urged the man kindly.

"You go —" retorted Bean swiftly; but he should not further be shamed by the recording of language which he lived to regret.

The Hartford man said, "Tut-tut-tut!" and went elsewhere than he had been told to go.

There ensued a dreadful time of alternating night and day, with recurrent visions of the flapper, who perfectly knew and said that he had been eating stuff out of the wrong cans.

"'As a man thinketh in his heart, so is he'," affirmed the Hartford person each morning as he shaved.

And a merry party gathered in the adjoining stateroom of afternoons and sang songs of the jolly sailor's life: "My Bonnie Lies Over the Ocean," and "Sailing, Sailing Over the Bounding Main."

On the morning of the fourth day he made the momentous discovery that the image of food was not repulsive to all his better instincts. Carefully he got upon his feet and they amazingly supported him. He dressed with but slight discomfort. He would audaciously experiment upon himself with the actual sight of food. It was the luncheon hour.

Outside the door he met the flapper on one of her daily visits of inspection.

"I perfectly well knew you'd never die," exclaimed the flapper, and laid glad hands upon him.

"Where do they eat?" asked Bean.

"How jolly! We'll eat together," rejoined the flapper. "The funniest thing! They all kept up till half an hour ago. Then it got rougher and rougher and now they're all three laid out. Poor Moms says it's the smell of the rubber matting, and Granny says she had too many of those perfectly whiffy old cigarettes, and Pops says he's plain seasick. Serves 'em rippingly well right — *taggers!*"

She convoyed him to the dining room, where he was welcomed by a waiter who had sorrowfully thought not to come to his notice. He greedily scanned the menu card, while the waiter, of his own initiative, placed some trifles of German delicatessen before them.

"It is a lot rougher," said the flapper. "Isn't it too close for you in here?" She was fixedly regarding on a plate before her a limp, pickled fish with one glazed eye staring aloft.

"Never felt better in my life," declared Bean. "Don't care how this little old steamer teeters now. Got my sea-legs."

"Me, too," said the flapper, but with a curious diminution of spirit. She still hung on the hypnotic eye of the pickled fish.

"Ham and cabbage!" said Bean proudly to the waiter.

The flapper pushed her chair swiftly back.

"Forgot my handkerchief," said she.

"There it is," prompted Bean ineptly.

The flapper placed it to her lips and rose to her feet.

"'S perfe'ly old rubber mattin'," she uttered through the fabric, and started toward the doorway. Bean observed that incoming diners anxiously made way for her. He followed swiftly and overtook the flapper at her door.

"Maybe if you'd try a little —" he began.

"Please go away," pleaded the flapper.

Bean returned to the ham and cabbage.

"Ought to go into the silence," he reflected. "'S all she needs. Fixed me all right."

After his hearty luncheon he ventured on deck. It was undeniably rougher, but he felt no fear. The breeze being cold, he went below for his overcoat.

Watkins of Hartford — or Adams, as he persisted in calling himself — reclined in his berth, his unlocked treasures carelessly scattered about him.

"Hold fast to the all good," counseled Bean revengefully.

"Uh — hah!" said Watkins or Adams, not doing so.

Bean fled. Everybody was getting it. The little old steamer was becoming nothing but a plague-ship.

"'As a man thinketh in his heart, so is he'," he muttered, wondering if the words meant anything.

Then, in the fullness of his returned strength, he was appalled anew by the completeness of his own tragedy. He had become once more insignificant. Forever, now, he must be afraid of policemen and all earthly powers. People in crowds would dent his hat and take his new watches. He must never again carry anything but a dollar watch.

And the Breedes saw through him. He must have confessed everything back at that table when he had felt so inscrutably buoyant. Once in Paris they would have him arrested. They might even have him put in irons before the ship landed.

And back in the steam-heated apartment lay that mutilated head, a sheer fabrication of *papier-mâché*. He wondered if Mrs. Cassidy had swept it out . . . the head that had meant so much to him. There was no hope anymore. If he were still free in Paris he would have one look at that tomb, and then . . . well, he had had his day.

Two days later the little old steamer debarked many passengers in the harbor of Cherbourg, carelessly confiding them to a much littler and much older steamer that transported them to the actual land. Among these were a feebly exploding father, a weak but faithful mother, and the swathed wrecks of the Demon and the flapper.

Then began a five-hour train-ride to the one-time capital of a famous upstart. There was but little talk among the members of the party. Bean kept grimly to himself because the only friendly member slept. He studied her pale, drawn face. She had indeed managed well, but his own downfall had thwarted her. He was a nobody. They were doubtless right in wanting to keep him from her. Yet he would see that tomb, and at the earliest possible moment.

At eleven that night they reached the capital. A dispiriting silence was maintained to the doors of a hotel. The women drooped in chairs. Breede acquainted the reception committee of a Paris hostelry with the party's needs as to chambers.

Thereupon they discovered one of the party to be missing. No one had seen him since entering. They were excited by this, all but the flapper.

"I don't blame him," averred the flapper . . . "Tagging us! You let him alone! I shall perfectly not worry if he doesn't come home all night. Do you understand? And when he does come —"

"Not safe," snapped Breede. "King of Egypt, Napoleon . . . not after money, just principle of thing. Chap's nutty — talk'n' like that!"

"Good *night!*" snapped the flapper in her turn.

XV

*H*e had walked quickly away while porters were collecting the bags. "Keep on the main street," he thought, plunging ahead. He did not change this plan until he discovered himself again at the door of that hotel he meant to leave. It faced a circle, and he had traversed this. He fled down a cross-street and again felt free.

For hours he walked the lighted avenues, or sat moodily on wayside benches, and at length, on a rustic seat screened by shrubbery in a little park, he dozed.

He awoke in the early light, stretched legs and arms luxuriously and again walked. He saw it was five o'clock. He was thrilled now by the morning beauty of the Corsican's city, all grey and green in the flooding sun. And the streets had filled with a voluble traffic that affected him pleasantly. Everyone seemed to speak gaily to everyone. Two cab-drivers exchanged swift incivilities, but in a quite perfunctory way, with evident good-will.

Walking aimlessly as yet — it was too early for tombs — he came again to that hotel on the circle. They were asleep in there. Little they'd worried — glad to be so easily rid of him.

Then he noticed at the circle's center a lofty column wrought in bronze with infinite small detail. Surmounting that column was the figure of the Corsican. An upstart who had prevailed!

He left the circle, lest he be apprehended by the Breedes. Soon he was again in that vast avenue of the park-places where he had slept. And now, far off on this splendid highway, he descried a mighty arch. Sternly grey and beautiful it was. And when, standing under it, he looked aloft to its mighty façade, its grandeur seemed threatening to him. He knew what that arch was — another monument imposed upon the city by the imperial assassin — without royal lineage since the passing of Ram-tah.

"Some class to *that* upstart!" he muttered. And if Napoleon had been no one, was it not probable that Bean had not been even Napoleon. The Countess Casanova had doubtless deceived him, though perhaps unintentionally. She had seemed a kind woman, he thought, but you couldn't tell about her controls.

His mind was being washed in that wondrous sunlight.

He was himself an upstart. No doubt about it. But what of it? Here were columns and arches to commemorate the most egregious of all upstarts. Upstarts were men who believed in themselves.

He retraced his steps from the arch.

Curious thing that scoundrel Watkins had kept saying on the boat. "As a man thinketh in his own heart, so is he." Must mean something. What?

Far down that wide avenue he came to a bridge of striking magnificence, beset with golden sculpture. He supposed it to be one more tribute to the sublime Corsican who had thought in his heart, and *was*.

He had the meaning of those words now.

He, Bunker Bean, had believed himself to be mean, insignificant. And so he had been that. Then he had come to believe himself a king, and straightway had he been kingly. The Corsican, detecting the falsity of some Ram-tah, would have gone on believing in himself nonetheless. It was all that mattered. "As a man thinketh —" If you came down to that, nobody needed a Ram-tah at all.

From the center of the bridge he raised his eyes and there, far off, high above all those grey buildings, was the golden cross that he knew to surmount the tomb. Sharply it glittered against the blue of the sky.

"Be upstart enough," it seemed to say, "and all things are yours. Believe yourself kingly, though your Ram-tah come from Hartford."

He walked vigorously toward that cross. It often eluded him as he puzzled a way through the winding grey-walled streets. More than once he was forced to turn back, to make laborious circuits. But never for long was the cross out of sight.

Constantly as he walked that new truth ran in his mind, molten, luminous. Who knew of Ram-tah's fictive origin, or even of Ram-tah at all? No one but a witty scoundrel calling himself Balthasar.

Bean had become someone through a belief in himself. Ram-tah had been a crude bit of scaffolding, and was well out of the way. The confidence he had helped to build would now endure without his help. Be an upstart. A convinced upstart. Such the world accepts.

Then he issued from the maze of narrow streets and confronted the tomb. Through the open door, even at this early hour, people went and came. The Corsican's magnetism prevailed. And he, Bunker Bean, the lowly, had that same power to magnetize, to charm, to affront the world and yet evoke monuments — if he could only believe it.

He went quickly through the iron gateway, up the long walk and took the imposing stairway in leaps. Then, standing uncovered in that wonderfully lit room, he gazed down at the upstart's mighty urn.

Long he stood under that spell of line and color and magnitude, lost in the spaciousness of it. No Balthasar had cheated here. There lay the mighty and little man who had never lost belief in himself — who had been only a little chastened by an adversity due to the craven world's fear of his prowess.

He was quite unconscious of others beside him who paid tribute there. He thought of those last sad days on that lonely island, the spirit still unbroken. His emotion surged to his eyes, threatening to overwhelm him. He gulped twice and angrily brushed away some surprising tears.

By his side stood a white-faced young Frenchman with a flowing brown beard. He became infected with Bean's emotion. He made no pretence of brushing his tears aside. He frankly wept.

Beyond this man a stout motherly woman, with two children in hand, was flooded by the current. She sobbed comfortably and companionably. The two children widened their eyes at her a moment, then fell to weeping noisily.

Farther around the railing a distinguished looking old gentleman of soldierly bearing, who wore a tiny red ribbon in the lapel of his frock coat, loudly blew his nose and pressed a kerchief of delicate weave to his brimming eyes.

Beyond him a young woman became stricken with grief and was led out by her solicitous husband, who seemed to feel that a tomb was no place for her at that time.

The exit of this couple aroused Bean. He cast a quick glance upon the havoc he had wrought and fled, wiping his eyes.

Halfway down the steps he encountered the alleged Adams of Hartford, who had stopped to open his Badaeker at the right page before entering the tomb.

"A magnificent bit of architecture," said the Hartford man instructively.

"Pretty loud for a tomb," replied Bean judicially. He was not going to let this Watkins, or whatever his name was, know what a fool he had made of himself in there. Then he remembered something.

"Say," he ventured, "how'd you happen to think up that thing you were always getting off to me back there on the boat – about as a man thinketh *is* he?"

"Tut-tut-tut! Really? But that is from the Holy Scriptures, which should always be read in connection with Science and Health."

"I must get it – something *in* that. Funny thing," he added genially, "getting good stuff like that out of Hartford, Connecticut."

He left Watkins or Adams staring after him in some bewilderment, a forgotten finger between the leaves of the Badaeker.

He began once more to lay a course through those puzzling streets. He was going to that hotel. He was going to be an upstart and talk to his own wife.

The tomb had cleared his brain.

"I'm no king," he thought; "never was a king; more likely a guinea-pig. But I'm someone now, all right! I'll show 'em; not afraid of the whole lot put together; face 'em all."

He came out upon the river at last and presently found himself back in that circle of the hotel. He stared a while at the bronze effigy surmounting that vainglorious column. Then he drew a long breath and went into the hotel.

A capable Swiss youth responded to his demand to be shown to his room, seeming to consider it not strange that Americans in Paris should now and then return to their rooms.

At the doorway of a drawing room that looked out upon the column the Swiss suggested coffee — perhaps?

"And fruit and fumed . . . boiled eggs and toast and all that meat and stuff," supplemented Bean firmly.

He tried one of two doors that opened from the drawing room and exposed a bedroom. His, evidently. There was the little old steamer trunk. He discovered a bathroom adjoining and was presently suffering the celestial agonies of a cold bath with no waster to coerce him.

He dressed with indignant muttering, and with occasional glances out at that supreme upstart's memorial. He chose his suit of the most legible checks. He had been a little fearful about it in New York. It was rather advanced, even for one of that Wall Street gang that had netted himself four hundred thousand dollars. Now he donned it intrepidly.

And, with no emotion whatever but a certain grim sureness of himself, he at last adjusted the entirely red cravat. He gloated upon this flagrantly. He hastily culled seven cravats of neutral tint and hurled them contemptuously into a waste-basket. Done with that kind!

He heard a waiter in the drawing room serving his breakfast. He drew on a dark-lined waistcoat of white piqué — like the one worn by the oldest director the day Ram-tah had winked — then the perfectly fitting coat of unmistakable checks, and went out to sit at the table. He was resolving at the moment that he would do everything he had ever been afraid to do. "'S only way show you're not afraid," he muttered. He was wearing a cravat he had always feared to wear, and now he would devour meat things for breakfast, whatever the flapper thought about it.

When he had a little dulled the edge of his hunger, he rang a bell.

"Find m' wife," he commanded the Swiss youth, only to be met with a look of blankness. He was considering if it might do him good to make a row about this — he had always been afraid to make rows — but the other door of the drawing room opened. His wife was found.

"'S all for 's aft'noon," he exploded to the servitor, who seemed not displeased to withdraw from this authoritative presence. Then he engaged a slice of bacon with a ruthless fork.

"Where you *been?*" he demanded of the flapper. Only way to do — go at them hammer and tongs!

The flapper gazed at him from the doorway. She was still pale and there were reddened circles about her eyes. The little old rag of a morning robe she wore added to her pallor and gave her an unaccustomed look of fragility.

"Where you been all the time?" repeated her husband with the arrogance of a confirmed upstart.

The flapper seemed to be on the point of tears, but she came into the room and sat across the table from him. In spite of the blurring moisture in her eyes he could still read the old look of ownership. Time had not impaired it.

"I just perfectly wouldn't let them know I felt bad," she began. "I said I was going to sleep and wouldn't worry one bit if you perfectly never came home all night. And you never did, because I couldn't sleep and watched . . . but I wouldn't let them know it for just perfectly old hundred thousand dollars. And this morning I said I'd had a bully sleep and felt fit and you had a right to go where you wanted to and they could please mind their own affairs, and I laughed so at them when they said they were going for the police —"

"Police, eh? Let 'em bring their old police. They think I'm afraid of police?" He valiantly attacked an egg.

"Of course not, stupid, but they thought you might wander off and get lost, like those people in the newspapers that wake up in Jersey City or some place and can't remember their own names or how it happened, and they wanted the police to just perfectly find you, and I wanted them to, too. I was deathly afraid —"

"I know my own name, all right. I'm little Tempest and Sunshine; that's my name.

"— but I wouldn't let them know I was afraid. And I laughed at them and told them they didn't know you at all and that you'd come home — come home."

He found he could strangely not be an upstart another moment in the presence of that flapper. He was over kneeling beside her, reaching his arms up about her, pressing her cheek down to his. The flapper held him tightly and wept.

"There, there!" he soothed her, smoothing the golden brown hair that spilled about her shoulders. "No one ever going to hurt you while I'm around. You're the just perfectly *dearest*, if you come right down to it. Now, now! 'S all right. Everything all right!"

"It's those perfectly old taggers," exploded the flapper, suddenly recovering her true form, "just furiously tagging."

"'S got to stop right now," declared Bean, rising. "Wipe that egg off your face, and let's get out of here."

"London," she suggested brightly. "Granny has always —"

"No London!" he broke in, visibly returning to the Corsican or upstart manner. "And no Grandma, no Pops, no Moms! You and me — us — understand what I mean? Think I'm going to have my wife sloshing around over there, voting, smashing windows, getting run in and sent to the island for thirty days. No! Not for little old George W. Me!"

"I never wanted to so very much," confessed the flapper with surprising meekness. "You tell where to go, then."

Bean debated. Baseball! Perhaps there would be a game on the home grounds that day. Paris might be playing London or St. Petersburg or Berlin or Venice.

"First we go see a ball game," he said.

The flapper astounded him.

"I don't think they have it over here — baseball," she observed.

No baseball? She must be crazy. He rang the bell.

The capable Swiss entered. In less than ten minutes he was able to convince the amazed American that baseball was positively not played on the continent of Europe. It was monstrous. It put a different aspect upon Europe.

"Makes no difference where we go, then," announced Bean. "Just any little old last year's place. We'll 'lope."

"Ripping," applauded the flapper, with brightening eyes.

"Hurry and dress. I'll get a little old car and we'll beat it before they get back. No time for trunk; take bag."

Down in the office he found they made nothing of producing little old cars for the right people. The car was there even as he was taking the precaution to secure a final assurance from the manager that Paris did not by any chance play London that day.

The two bags were installed in the ready car; then a radiant flapper beside an amateur upstart. The driver desired instructions.

"*Ally, ally!*" directed Bean, waving a vague but potent hand.

"We've done it," rejoiced the flapper. "Serve the perfectly old taggers good and plenty right!"

Bean lifted a final gaze to the laurel-crowned Believer. He knew that Believer's secret now.

"What a stunning tie," exclaimed the flapper. "It just perfectly does something to you."

"'S little old last year's tie," said her husband carelessly.

*A*t six-thirty that evening they were resting on a balcony overlooking the garden of a hotel at Versailles. Back of them in the little parlor a waiter was setting a most companionable small table for two. Such little sounds as he made were thrilling. They liked the hotel much. Its management seemed to have been expecting them ever since the building's erection, and to have reserved precisely that nest for them.

They had been "doing" the palace. A little self-conscious, in their first free solitude, they had agreed that the palace would be instructive. Through interminable galleries they had gone, inspecting portraits of the dead who had made and marred French history . . . led on by a guide whose amiable delusion it was that he spoke English. The flapper had been chiefly exercised in comparing the palace, to its disadvantage, with a certain house to be surrounded on all sides by scenery and embellished with perfectly patent laundry tubs.

The flapper sighed in contentment, now.

"We needn't ever do it again," she said. "How they ever made it in that old barn —"

Bean had occupied himself in thinking it was funny about kings. To have been born a king meant not so much after all. He still dwelt upon it as they sat looking down into the shadowed garden.

"There was that last one," he said musingly. "Born as much a king as any . . . and look what they did to him. Better man than the other two before him . . . they had 'habits' enough, and he was decent. But he couldn't make them believe in him. He couldn't have believed in himself very hard. His picture looks like a man I know in New York named Cassidy . . . always puttering around, dead serious about something that doesn't matter at all. You got to bluff people, and this poor old dub didn't know how . . . so they clipped his head off for it. Two or three times a good bluff would have saved him."

"No bath, no furnace," murmured the flapper. "That perfectly reminds me, soon as we get back —"

"Then," pursued Bean, "along comes Mr. little old George W. Napoleon Bluff and makes them eat out of his hand in about five minutes. Didn't he walk over them, though? And they haven't quit thanking him for it yet. Saw a lot of 'em sniveling over him at that tomb this morning. Think he'd died only yesterday. You know, I don't blame him so much for a lot of things he did — fighting and women and all that. He knew what they'd do to him if he ever for one minute quit bluffing. You know, he was what I call an upstart."

The flapper stole a hand into his and sighed contentedly.

"You've perfectly worked it all out, haven't you?" she said.

"— and if you come right down to it, I'm nothing but 'n upstart myself."

"Oh, splash!" said the flapper, in loving refutation.

"'S all," he persisted; "just 'n upstart. Of course I don't have to be one with you. I wouldn't be afraid to tell you anything in the world; but those others, now; everyone else in the world except you; I'll show 'em who's little old George W. Upstart — old man Upstart himself, that's what!"

"You're a king," declared the flapper in a burst of frankness.

"Eh?" said Bean, a little startled.

"Just a perfectly little old king," persisted the flapper with dreamy certitude. "Never fooled little George W. Me. Knew it the very first second. Went over me just like *that.*"

"Oh, I'm no king; never was a king; rabbit, I guess. Little old perfectly upstart rabbit, that's what!"

"What am I?" asked the flapper pointedly.

"Little old flippant flapper, that's what! But you're my Chubbins just the same; my Chubbins!" and he very softly put his hand to her cheek.

"Monsieur et Madame sont servi," said the waiter. He was in the doorway but discreetly surveyed the evening sky through an already polished wine-glass held well aloft.

*T*he three perfectly taggers meeting their just due, consulted miserably as they gathered about a telephone in Paris the following morning. The Demon had answered the call.

"Says she has it all reasoned out," announced the Demon.

"'S what she said before," grunted Breede. "Tha's nothing new."

"And she says we're snoop-cats and we might as well go back home — now," continued the Demon. "Says she's got the — u-u-m-mm! — says to perfectly quit tagging."

"Nothing can matter now," said the bereaved mother.

"He's talking himself," said the Demon. "Mercy he's got a new voice . . . sounds like another man. He says if we don't beat it out of here by the next boat — he can imagine nothing of less — something or other I can't hear —"

"— consequence," snapped Breede.

"Yes, that's it; and now he's laughing and telling her she's a perfectly flapper."

"Oh, my poor child," murmured the mother.

"Puzzle t' me," said Breede. "I swear I can't make out just how many kinds of a —"

"James!" said his wife sternly, and indicated the presence of several interested foreigners.